DEADLY
LITTLE
SINS

Also by Kara Taylor

Wicked Little Secrets
Prep School Confidential

DEADLY

LITTLE

SINS

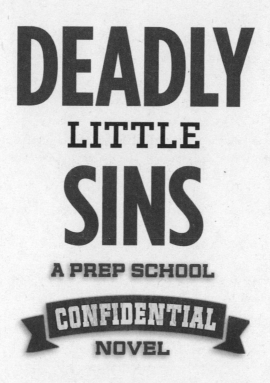

A PREP SCHOOL

CONFIDENTIAL

NOVEL

KARA TAYLOR

THOMAS DUNNE BOOKS

St. Martin's Griffin ❧ New York

THOMAS DUNNE BOOKS.
An imprint of St. Martin's Press.

www.thomasdunnebooks.com
www.stmartins.com

The Library of Congress Cataloging-in-Publication Data
is available upon request.

ISBN 978-1-250-03363-5 (trade paperback)
ISBN 978-1-250-03362-8 (e-book)

First Edition: August 2014

10 9 8 7 6 5 4 3 2 1

For Nene, who showed me that
I'll always have a safe place inside a book.

ACKNOWLEDGMENTS

Thanks to Anne Brewer, Brendan Deneen, Nicole Sohl, and the rest of the team at St. Martin's. Without you guys, I'd probably be playing The Sims right now.

I owe so much to Suzie Townsend, who talks me off ledges, talks up my books, and is overall just a really cool person. The team at New Leaf Literary & Media is pretty cool too—Joanna, Danielle, Jaida, Jackie, and Pouya have every base covered. Especially the ones I don't think of.

Thanks to my family and friends for telling people to buy my books. Thank you Kevin for sharing your desk.

And most of all, thank you, the reader, for sticking with Anne until the end.

Suspicion is the companion of mean souls.

—Thomas Paine, *Common Sense*

DEADLY
LITTLE
SINS

CHAPTER
ONE

The first time I looked death in the face, I blinked and it was gone.

They say your life is supposed to flash before your eyes, but all I remember is the moment after. The adrenaline that filled me, knowing I survived. The weightlessness of having dodged a bullet. Literally.

Watching someone else die was different.

The details are the hardest to forget. The smell of cinnamon and pine furniture polish. The sound of glass breaking in the front door. And worst of all, the way Travis Shepherd's eyes froze as the life left his body.

It's been more than two months since Anthony and I watched Steven Westbrook shoot Shepherd, his former classmate, in the chest. Since then, I've been unofficially expelled from the Wheatley School, grounded for what's quite possibly the rest of my teenage years, and exiled from my friends.

I know that having my phone, computer, and social life taken away is my parents' way of ensuring I have nothing to do all summer but think about the things I've done. If only they knew the whole story—the one that starts with a thirty-year-old photo of a missing student and ends with watching his killer die on the floor of his own foyer—they'd understand that I could never *not* think about what I've done.

I would give anything to be able to close my eyes and not picture the blood blossoming around the hole in Travis Shepherd's chest. If I could, I'd stop it from happening in the first place.

Even though he killed four people, including a five-year-old boy. Even though deep down, I believe that Travis Shepherd deserved to die.

Or maybe that's what I *want* to believe, because if I'd gone to the police instead of Alexis Westbrook that night, Shepherd would be alive.

It was like a horrible move in a game of chess—a move where *bam*, all of your pieces get captured. Shepherd is dead, Steven Westbrook is in jail, and Headmaster Goddard is in hiding. The only person at Wheatley I thought I could trust—Ms. Cross, my favorite teacher—disappeared without a trace.

As for me, I'm the Knight that got kicked back to New York. Right back where I started, but so, so far away from the person I was.

And every day that goes by without word from Ms. C, I can't help but wonder if she was a pawn all along.

I still don't know where I'm going to school in the fall. My parents said, "We'll cross that bridge when we get there," which obviously means no one wants me. There was a time I would have made that work in my favor. Now, I mostly just stay out of their way and hope I don't end up at a school where everyone either has a baby or a probation officer.

I technically haven't been expelled from Wheatley. Yet. My disciplinary hearing has been postponed until July, because of "internal restructuring." Which is a fancy euphemism for the fact that Wheatley, formerly Massachusetts's number-one secondary preparatory school, is up shit's creek.

The administration of the mighty Wheatley School has fallen and now Jacqueline Tierney, aka Dean Snaggletooth, is the last person standing. Maybe she'll wind up running the place. If you ask me, they could use a womanly touch over there, even though Tierney has all the femininity of a jockstrap.

Anyway, none of that matters because the board is almost certain to turn my suspension into an expulsion, which will mark my second expulsion from a school this year.

The official citation in the letter Dean Tierney sent home said I "assaulted another student." I guess they were willing to give me a break for using a Taser on Larry Tretter, the boys' crew team coach and Travis Shepherd's accomplice, since he's currently in jail for conspiracy to commit murder.

The version of the story I gave Tierney and my parents is that I used the Taser on Coach Tretter because he was beating the crap out of Casey, Travis Shepherd's son. Then I took a couple shots of my own at Casey, just for being a Class A douche.

My parents were probably too pissed at me to dig further into what happened. My dad wanted to know why, if I had to kick a boy in the balls, I couldn't wait to do it until we were off-campus. My mom just wanted to know where I got the Taser.

Their reactions probably explain a lot about why I am the way I am.

So my sentence for being not-officially-but-basically-expelled was virtual confinement to our apartment until the hearing. At first it wasn't so bad, because I had a ton of schoolwork to finish. Then I turned in my final exams and realized I had no purpose in life. I was a prisoner in my own home. Except I think I'd prefer actually being in jail, because then I wouldn't have to see my parents every day.

I told my dad this, and he didn't think it was very funny. He decided I needed an attitude adjustment in the form of going to work with him.

His plan to further my misery backfired, though, because I love interning in his law office. I get to research cases and read trial transcripts, and my dad's assistant Leah lets me tag along when she picks up lunch. If we have time, we browse Sephora or the bookstore and I get to feel like a real human being again.

Today is a particularly glorious day, because my father has to be in court at nine A.M. I've been waiting for this moment for weeks.

"Go *straight* to the office," he says as we cross 51st Street outside our apartment. "I'm calling Leah in ten minutes to make sure you're there."

"Dad, chill. I already snuck out to meet my meth dealer last night."

He whirls around and gives me the worst look I've ever seen. "You are not half as funny as you think you are."

Well, that's a little upsetting, because I think I'm hilarious. I lift the hair off the back of my neck and tie it into a loose bun. I'm already planning which layers of clothing I can ditch when I get to the office.

"I mean it, Anne," he says when we're across the street. He lifts his hand up, as if he wants to say something else, but lowers it. "Make sure you're home by five fifteen."

I give him a captain's salute, even though I know it irritates him. I don't know what's wrong with me. It's like I feel if I keep digging my hole, eventually it'll get deep enough that I can disappear.

I catch Leah by the thermostat when I get to the office. Since my dad will be gone all day, we can crank the central air without him bitching about the bill.

And if I play my cards right, I can check my email for the first time in weeks.

Seconds after I set my bag on the extra desk, Leah drops a

stack of collated papers on my desk. "Need you to read up on *State of New York versus Helen Peters*. I flagged the pages."

Crap. This is going to take me at least until lunch. As I flip through the photocopied pages, I watch Leah at her desk. She rolls away from the computer on her chair and starts thumbing through a stack of legal journals.

"I need to make a couple more copies," she says. "Think you can handle the phone if anyone calls?"

"Sure."

"Remember, no personal calls. Your dad *will* find out."

"I know," I say. "He's got this place under *Homeland* levels of surveillance."

Leah flounces out the door. I'm not stupid—she's going down to the lobby to call her boyfriend. First off, we have a perfectly good copy machine in the back room. Second, she didn't even take the journal with her.

It makes me feel a little less lousy about using her computer. When I hear the elevator ping, I slide into her chair and log into my email.

I was able to sneak a few emails to Brent Conroy—my exboyfriend—before my dad figured out I was using my school email for personal business. Disappointment needles me when I see he hasn't replied to my last message. He's in England for the summer, visiting family, so I can only assume he's met a British girl with an adorable gap between her front teeth.

Brent and I broke up under epically bad circumstances. I snooped through his phone so I could follow him and the rest of the crew team into the woods during one of their hazing rituals. And I also may have implied his father was involved in Matt Weaver's murder.

The fact that Anthony, the other guy I was kind-of-sort-of involved with, hasn't responded to any of my emails isn't surprising either. The last time I saw him, we'd just made a promise to each other not to tell anyone what we saw in Travis Shepherd's house. Then I had to leave Wheatley without getting the

chance to say good-bye. He probably thinks I did it on purpose—
almost as if I wanted to leave him, and everything we saw together, behind.

The more I think about it, I don't blame either one of them
for wanting nothing to do with me.

I take a deep breath as I scan my in-box; it catches in my
throat when I spot a message from Muller, Rowan. It's dated two
weeks ago.

Dr. Muller is a physics teacher at the Wheatley School. I
saw him hanging around campus with Ms. Cross a few times
before she disappeared. He was the one who called and told me
I shouldn't bother trying to find Ms. C—I had to hang up before he could tell me why.

All he'd said was that Jessica Cross doesn't really exist.

I open the email.

Anne,

I apologize for the delay. I'd preferred not to say what I had
to tell you through email as long as I was still employed by
Wheatley, but my situation has changed. Is there any chance
you could speak in person when I'm in New York at the
beginning of August? In the meantime, I think you should
check out the following.

Best,
RM

He's pasted two links in the email. I click on the first, which
leads to a LinkedIn profile for a Jessica L. Cross from Cliftonville,
Georgia. According to the page, she has a double BA in English
and classic languages from the University of North Carolina,
Chapel Hill. Her current occupation is listed as "teacher."

And the woman in the black-and-white photo is definitely
Ms. C.

I don't understand—all of this fits with what Ms. Cross told me about herself. I x out of the page and click the second link. The page takes forever to load—I glance at the door to make sure Leah isn't on her way up, but the hall is quiet.

The page—an article from the *Cliftonville Gazette*—finally loads. I have to blink a few times to process what I'm reading.

An obituary for Jessica Leigh Cross, who died eight years ago.

CHAPTER
TWO

I select print from the menu and respond to Dr. Muller's message. Yesterday was the first day of August—he should be in New York by now.

Wajima on 61st, Friday at 1. If you can't make it, call 917-555-9687 and hang up twice. That's my dad's office.

I log out of my email account and delete my tabs from the browser history.

The elevator pings just as the obituary is done printing. I slip it between the journal pages and pretend to be staring out the window aimlessly when Leah comes back inside.

When she's settled back in her desk, I open to the obituary.

Jessica Leigh Cross, beloved daughter, sister, and UNC Chapel Hill graduate, passed away unexpectedly after an illness. She is survived by her parents, Marie and Alan Cross of Cliftonville and sister, Arianne Cross-Duncan of Canton. Jessica is remembered for her

generous and kind nature. In lieu of flowers, donations
may be made to the Acworth Home for Women.

Either Muller is messing with me, or something completely
screwed up is going on here.

For the next couple days, I jump every time the phone rings,
waiting to see if it's a hang-up call. On Wednesday, the phone
rings at a little past ten.

"Dowling and Associates," Leah says. "How can I help
you?"

There's a pause. "He's in court all week," she replies. "What
is the best number to call you back?"

She's quiet, listening to the caller. When her gaze lands on
me and doesn't move, my blood runs cold.

"One moment." Leah is frowning. "I'll connect you to his
cell."

My heart sinks to the pit of my stomach. There are about a
million reasons someone would be calling about me, and none
of them are good. What if the thing I've been so desperately trying to escape has caught up with me? I've been dreading this
phone call ever since Steven Westbrook was arrested.

What if he told the police or his lawyers that Anthony and
I were there that night? Or what if Casey Shepherd figured
out I was involved? What if it's the police calling my father
right now?

Leah presses the transfer button on the phone. "Mr. Dowling, I have Jacqueline Tierney on the line for you."

I think that's almost worse than the police.

I knew this moment was coming, but even though I convinced myself I was okay with it, I'm not. Tierney is going to
expel my ass without losing a minute's sleep over it, and I'll
probably never see most of my friends—April, Kelsey, Cole,
Murali—again.

Leah whispers my name and motions for me to come over to her. She presses a finger to her lips, then points to the phone. And hands it to me.

I could kiss her. I have to hold the phone a few inches away from my face, because I'm breathing so hard I'm sure my dad will hear me. Leah bites her thumbnail.

". . . and Dylan?" my dad asks.

"Away at lacrosse camp," Tierney says. "I never thought I'd miss having a house full of preteen boys."

Dad laughs, and my blood boils. Dean Tierney is calling my dad with the fate of my future in her hands, and they're talking about her damn *kids*? I don't realize I'm making a fist with my free hand until Leah reaches to take the phone away from me. I spin the desk chair away from her.

"—about the delay, I'm sure you can imagine," Tierney is saying. "We're interviewing headmasters, but no one wants to touch this mess with a ten-foot pole."

"Jackie, I asked how *you're* holding up," my dad says, with uncharacteristic gentleness.

There's silence on Tierney's end for a beat. "Quite frankly, I'm sick over the whole thing and would leave this place tomorrow if I could."

I nearly fall out of Leah's chair. This is the same woman who threatened to expel me for suggesting my roommate Isabella's murder was anything but an "unforeseen tragedy." The same woman who threw me out of her office when I told her I knew Matt Weaver assaulted her sister, Vanessa.

"In any case, I'm sorry to keep your family waiting about the hearing," Tierney says.

The hearing. Of course.

Crap.

"We don't make these decisions hastily," she continues. "The last time a student was even expelled from Wheatley was fifteen years ago."

That should make an interesting detail in my college entrance essay. My toes curl in my sandals. I think Tierney has set some sort of record for shutting my father up.

"That's why the board has to vote unanimously to expel a student."

"We understand," my dad says.

And that's when I know there really is no hope left for me. Despite all my dad's huffing and puffing, he knew the fire at St. Bernadette's was an accident. That's why he fought to get me into Wheatley. Because he still believed in me. Believed that I wouldn't screw up again.

"You should know, then, that in light of evidence, the board deliberated for a while about Anne," Tierney says.

"Evidence?"

"Yes. Quite a few of Anne's friends submitted testimony about her character. They believe that Casey Shepherd antagonized her before she assaulted him."

"Well, that does sound like my daughter."

"Regardless, considering the circumstances, there was a board member who felt uncomfortable expelling Anne."

My father is speechless in what I can only hope is some sort of new trend.

"You . . . want her back?" he finally stammers.

"She's not expelled," Tierney says firmly. Message received, Tierney. The feeling is mutual.

"I'm going to need to discuss this with my wife," Dad says. "Obviously I would have reservations about putting her back in that environment."

"*You* have reservations?" It spills out of me in a whisper. I clamp my hand over my mouth and meet Leah's horrified expression.

"Excuse me, Jackie." My father's voice is eerily calm. "I'll have to call you back."

Seconds later, the office phone rings. Leah answers it with a meek "Yes?"

I catch "speak to my daughter." She hands me the phone.

"Are you *trying* to push all of my buttons?" my dad shouts.

"Are you trying to make my life miserable?" I shoot back. "You'd really decide to send me back there without asking me how I feel?"

"Who said I'm sending you back there?"

"That's not the point." My eyes prick, and I don't even know why. "You should at least care how I feel about it. At least ask me."

"Anne," he says, firmly, "we'll discuss this later."

"You mean you'll discuss it with Mom. While I'm locked up in my room." I don't even know why I'm doing this— trying to pick a fight I'll never win. I don't even know why I'm on the verge of tears, or feeling like my lungs are going to collapse.

Maybe it's because the only thing that scares me more than the thought of being kicked out of Wheatley is going back there.

By the time Friday rolls around, there still haven't been any hang-up calls to the office. I know, because I made it a point not to leave my desk at all this week. Not even to pee.

"Are you okay?" Leah asks me around noon. "You seem antsy."

I shrug, not realizing I've been gnawing at my thumbnail until all of the pewter polish on it lifts off. "Just nervous. About school and everything."

It's not a complete lie: My parents still haven't reached an agreement on how to deal with Tierney's invitation to take me back. Every night they close their bedroom door and I hear murmuring.

I shoot a glance at the clock, hoping Dr. Muller got my email about meeting today. I can't help but chew the rest of the polish off my fingers. I really think my father may consider military school or electroshock therapy if he catches me sneaking out for lunch with a man twice my age.

And for what? The last time I got involved in something I shouldn't have gotten involved in, I lost my boyfriend and my parents' trust, and a man died. There's absolutely nothing to gain from trying to find out what's going on with Ms. C.

She was my favorite teacher, and I want more than anything to know she's okay, but if Dr. Muller thinks she's in danger, I'm not the person he should be going to. He can't make the same mistakes I did.

But what is he supposed to tell the police? *Hello, I'd like to report a missing person, and by the way, she's sort of been dead for eight years.* I know better than anyone that it would be a lost cause.

I should at least hear Dr. Muller out.

It doesn't take much to convince Leah we should order Japanese. When I say I could go for a red dragon roll, her eyes glaze over. Sushi is her catnip.

"Call in an order to Matsuki in fifteen minutes," she says. "Ask for extra soy sauce."

I trace an invisible circle on the corner of her desk. "Ugh, their eel sauce gave me such a stomachache last time. Can we do Wajima?"

She looks up from her computer. "But they don't deliver."

"I could pick it up." I shrug, as if I couldn't care less either way. "I mean, I finished reading these case studies, so I'm just sitting around."

Leah contemplates this. Normally letting me leave the office would be an automatic no, but my father is in court all day. It's just us in the office. And if she gets rid of me for half an hour, she can go buck wild and call her boyfriend or do whatever it is she does when the office is empty.

"Okay." She passes me the company credit card. "Just no side excursions."

Am I that obvious? I salute her, making sure I avoid her eyes.

At ten minutes to one, I'm waiting outside Wajima with

our takeout order. I settle in for the wait, but before a minute or two passes, I spot a tall, dark-skinned man at the opposite corner of 52nd and Lexington. I crane my neck to get a better look at him as he waits among a gaggle of tourists to cross the street.

I can count how many times I've seen Dr. Muller on one hand, so I'm not sure it's him. If it is, he buzzed his hair recently. He's wearing khaki shorts and a salmon polo. Not many men can pull off salmon, but Dr. Muller can.

"Anne?" He extends a hand. "I don't believe we've officially met."

I have to swallow away a smattering of butterflies that rises in my stomach. He's totally a perfect specimen, and I don't use that term lightly. "Hi."

His amber eyes move to the bag at my feet.

"I can't stay more than fifteen minutes," I say. "I'm kind of under house arrest."

Dr. Muller massages his chin with his thumb and forefinger. I can't tell if he knows what I did to get suspended. "All right. Shall we go somewhere a little more private?"

We wind up at the sushi bar. Dr. Muller orders a lunch box special and I get a green tea so I have something to do with my hands.

"So," I say, after a moment of uncomfortable silence punctuated by the sushi chefs shouting over each other. "What the hell is going on here?"

Muller smiles with half his mouth. "I wish I could tell you."

"You were dating her, weren't you?"

"We were . . . friendly."

"So, yes."

"Yes." Dr. Muller allows himself a small smile. "You know, she talked about you often."

This catches me by surprise. "Really?"

"You reminded her of herself when she was your age. She

said you're extremely bright. But you don't equate money and brains with the right to be a jerk. Her words." He winks at me. *Stop blushing. Stop blushing.* "Oh."

Muller takes a sip from his tea. "I would have told you all this when she left, but I was still employed by Wheatley at the time. I'd hoped they would hire me permanently, but they found a more experienced candidate."

"So you're not going back there in the fall?"

He shakes his head. "I've completed my PhD at MIT, so my visa is expiring soon. I'm staying in Queens with a friend from university for a few weeks until I return home."

I want to curl up and live inside Dr. Muller's South African accent. He even makes Queens sound actually regal.

"The obituary." I swallow. "I don't understand. Did she fake her own death or something?"

Muller blinks at me. "The obituary . . . that wasn't *our* Jessica. You know that, right?"

I will away my embarrassment. "Yeah, I mean, duh. But the details—it seems like it was the same person."

"I think that's the point. Let me back up a bit." Muller sets his tea down and folds his hands together. "We started spending a bit of time together after I started at Wheatley. Both of us were new to the faculty. But we found we had a lot more than that in common, and, well . . .

"Anyway, I noticed that she was fiercely private. She never wanted to socialize with any of the other teachers, and she didn't like to talk about her past. I didn't think anything of it until early May."

"What happened?"

"I'd invited her to sightsee in Boston a bit with me. We ate at an Indian place, and we were supposed to go to the Isabella Stewart Gardner Museum. I thought we were having a great time; but when we left the restaurant, she was upset. Said we had to go straight home, and she wouldn't say why."

"After that, I started to pick up on other things that

seemed . . . off. She didn't have any photos or personal memen-
tos around her apartment. Never got any mail or phone calls. I
supposed it was because she was new in town, but one night I
noticed she owned a Boston Bruins hockey jersey."

A detail surfaces in my memory: Ms. C had a Bruins pen-
nant hanging in her office.

"She says she's from Georgia, she went to school in North
Carolina . . . yet she's a Boston Bruins fan?" I say.

"I thought it strange, too. I asked her about it, and she got
very defensive. Said it was a friend's. Then she didn't call me
for a few days." Muller traces the rim of his teacup with his
fingertip. "I knew something was off with her, then, but I
didn't want to make her uncomfortable. We all have things in
our pasts we'd like to hide from." Muller hesitates. "But I'll
admit I was curious. I broached the subject with Jess. I didn't
accuse her of anything; I simply said I thought it was unusual.
She was angry with me for insinuating she was hiding something, and said she needed time apart. A few days later, I found
out during a faculty meeting that she'd resigned."

I'm quiet as I digest all of this. Muller must have confronted
Ms. C around the same time I'd asked her to help me find out
what happened to Vanessa Reardon, the girl Matt Weaver assaulted. So Ms. C's disappearance may have had nothing to do
with helping me, like I initially thought, and everything to do
with Muller figuring out that she was hiding something.

"I did some searching around, and found that there really was
a Jessica Cross of Cliftonville," Muller says. "So the woman we
knew was an impostor."

"Like identity theft?" I ask. "How did no one figure it out?"

"It's actually quite easy to assume the identity of a deceased
person," Muller replies. "It's called ghosting. All you need is his
or her social security number. It's even easier if you can obtain
a duplicate of the person's driver's license or birth certificate."

"But Ms. C—why?"

"It's more common than you'd think," Muller says. "There's

any number of reasons why someone would want to disappear and become someone else. Abusive ex-lover, massive amounts of debt, criminal charges—"

"That doesn't sound like her." I realize how dumb the words sound as soon as they leave my mouth. "I mean, it doesn't sound like the person I thought she was."

"It just goes to show you can never really know a person." There's sadness in Muller's voice. He must really care about Ms. C. My stomach clenches as Anthony's face works its way into my mind. I know what it's like to feel connected to someone, only for them to be gone as quickly as they came—to have that intense, staccato burst of feeling, followed by just . . . nothing.

"Do you think she's okay?" I ask.

"I stopped by her cottage," Dr. Muller says. "Everything looked secure. Nothing suspicious."

I let out a breath. "So she's not in trouble or anything."

"Oh, I absolutely think she's in trouble." Dr. Muller's eyes meet mine. "But in danger? I'm not quite sure."

Frustration gnaws at me. "What are we supposed to do?"

"I don't think there's anything we can do," he says. "They call it ghosting for a reason—how are you supposed to find a person who technically doesn't exist?"

Ghosting. The word sends a chill up my spine.

I glance at Dr. Muller's watch. If I don't get back to the office soon, Leah may send out a SWAT team. I thank Dr. Muller for meeting me, even though I have more questions than I showed up with.

"It seems I have the rest of the day to myself," he tells me as we release our handshake. "Any tips for a newbie in New York?"

"Stay far, far away from the people dressed as Elmo in Times Square." I smile at him and turn to leave.

"Anne." He's holding up my takeout bag. I'd almost forgotten it.

"You know," he says, his face thoughtful as he takes me in. "I've had a lot of time to think about her. Jessica. Sometimes the best we can do is stay in place and hope whatever we're running from doesn't catch up with us."

I think of the blood blossoming around the hole in Travis Shepherd's chest. Of the promise Anthony and I made to each other not to tell anyone we were there that night. Of the fear that someone else already knows.

I don't know if Dr. Muller would feel the same way if he knew what I was running from.

CHAPTER
THREE

My dad is supposed to be in court all week, so I know something must be wrong when I get home from the office that afternoon and find him and my mom next to each other on the love seat in the foyer.

"Sit," he says.

My mother throws my dad a look, like *Why do you have to be so abrasive all the time,* as I silently lower myself onto the chaise. Abby, my dachshund, bolts over to me and leaps onto my lap. Her nails catch on the lace overlay of my skirt.

There are creases at the corners of my mother's eyes that I never noticed before. Still, no one believes she's fifty. She and my dad are the same age, but sometimes they get weird looks from people in public who think there's some sort of Alec Baldwin situation going on.

My mother is beautiful, in a classic movie actress way. I got her dark brown eyes, but not her raven hair or high cheekbones. People say my mom looks like my grandma Theresa, who died before I was even a seedling on the Dowling family tree. Every now and then my mom will drop a detail about my grandma into conversation, like how she kept Pomeranians and would randomly lapse into Portuguese.

The sound of our voices is the greatest difference between my mother and me. No matter how hard I try, I'm so loud it's impossible not to know when I'm in the room. My mom sounds like a baby bird.

"How was your day, Annie?" she asks.

"Okay." I don't have the heart to ask her not to call me Annie. Annie is who I used to be—the little girl who practiced her pirouettes on the wood floors of the hallway and got out of trouble by grabbing her dad's leg and yelling, "I love you!"

Annie sounds like guilt, and I can't bear to hear it.

"Honey, we made a couple phone calls this week," she says. "To schools."

My dad puts a hand on her knee and cuts in. Obviously he planned to have my mom start off this conversation, but forgot that it takes her ten minutes to dole out a thirty-second piece of information. "We feel as if the city isn't the best place for you to spend your senior year."

My stomach dips to my feet. He really means that no private school in the city will accept me, and public school won't be an easy adjustment for someone with my reputation. Suddenly, I'm back where I was seven months ago, after I burned the auditorium at St. Bernadette's down and my mother told me they were sending me to . . .

"You can't mean you want me to go back to Wheatley."

My parents look at each other.

"Jackie agreed to remove the suspension from your transcript. Your grades were decent there." My dad ticks off each point on his fingers. He has his defense argument voice on now. "Right now, consistency is your best chance at graduating strong."

"That's not exactly a compelling argument, considering that the vice principal murdered my roommate and tried to kill me, too." I know how painful it is for my parents to hear it, but I don't care. "Have you even been paying attention to the other messed-up shit going on up there?"

Dad doesn't even yell at me for cursing. "Wheatley is over a hundred years old. One bad year doesn't change the fact that it's the best of the best."

My father leans forward, forcing me to make eye contact with him. "You are my only child. You are my life. If I thought there was *any* chance I was putting you in danger, I wouldn't even think about sending you back there."

The worst part is that he means it. For all his huffing and puffing, I've always known it's because he loves me and wants the best for me. He'll always be the man who ran five blocks to scream at a cab driver who almost mowed me down when I was six. He really believes I belong at Wheatley. He doesn't know what I'm running from.

He knows that a former Massachusetts senator walked into a Fortune 500 CEO's home in Cape Cod and killed him for revenge. Everyone knows that now.

But they don't know that I was there; that I'm the reason Steven Westbrook figured out that Travis Shepherd and Larry Tretter killed his wife to cover up their involvement in Matt Weaver's death thirty years ago.

Thirty years. Dr. Muller was right. You can't run from some things forever. The best you can do is hold your breath and hope they never, ever catch up to you.

I finally find my voice. "What choice do I have?"

My parents stand up. My mom puts her arm around me, leading me into the living room. "It's entirely up to you. Registration at RFK High runs through the end of the month. But if you want to go back to Wheatley, we have to let them know by tomorrow."

"And we have something that may make your decision easy," my father says.

That's when I notice that Abby's disappeared. And that Remy Adams is sitting at my dining room table eating a macaron from Ladurée.

She's on her feet as soon as she sees me. There's a huge smile on her face; I can tell that she wants to shriek and hug me in typical Remy fashion, but she's restraining herself in front of my parents. So I shriek and hug her, and we cling to each other and do that weird hopping up and down thing. I don't care how stupid we look—Remy's here and that simple fact makes me happy.

And I believe in that moment that maybe there's enough good waiting for me in Wheatley to block out the bad.

The four of us go out for Persian food. My parents tell me they got Remy's contact info from Dean Tierney: Back before I was even suspended, Remy had requested me for a roommate for this year. Her parents called mine, and arranged for Remy to come spend two weeks with me in New York before we go back to Wheatley together. We have to go back a week before classes start, for something called Senior Week. Most of it will be leading freshman orientation.

When we get home, Remy gives me the nonparent version of how Senior Week is going to go down as we're changing for bed in my room.

"There's only one RA in each dorm for the week, so we can basically do whatever we want when we're not at orientation." She's talking a mile a minute. "The guys already hid a handle of vodka in the locker room during summer drills."

"What?" she says when I don't respond.

"Nothing." I run my fingers through my hair, undoing my fishtail braid. "It's just . . . I might have to sit out all the fun. I'm kind of on thin ice already."

That's actually not true. I *was* on thin ice. But I smashed my foot through the ice, and now I'm treading water, trying not to drown in failure and my parents' disappointment.

Now Remy's the one who's quiet. I watch as she examines the things on my dresser: a glass ballet shoe from my grandmother; a ton of rosebud salve; and Eleanor Pigby, my china pig from a trip to London a few years ago. I'm struck by the familiarity of the way Remy floats around, soaking in the novelty of someone else's room. As if we're in my dorm in Wheatley and I never really left at all.

I flip on the light on my nightstand as Remy and I crawl into bed. My mom's already left a towel and washcloth out for her for tomorrow morning. I have to take inventory of the events of the last few days just to remind myself that this is really happening. I'm going back to Wheatley.

Remy launches into a monologue about everything I missed since May, punctuated by yawns. Kelsey and Cole went to a music festival together the last week of school, but they haven't hung out since because Kelsey went home to Berkshire County for the summer.

"I'm happy," Remy says, with her trying-too-hard smile. "Really."

Cole is Remy's ex. She quickly changes the subject.

Phil, who lives in California, got caught buying weed by his parents while on vacation in Los Cabos and isn't allowed to row crew this year now. And last week, Remy, Cole, and Murali did a 5k run in Boston where people dressed as zombies chased them.

I don't know if she purposely left out Brent. I'm too proud to ask, but Remy rolls from her back onto her side and faces me.

"None of us have heard from him much. Brent," she says.

Just hearing someone else say his name brings back the sensation of falling in my stomach. It's a reminder that for every good memory I have of Brent, there's a shitty one to go along with it, and I'll have to face them all when I see him in seven days.

"I haven't either," I admit. "I just . . . hope he doesn't hate me."

Remy props herself up onto my pillow. "Why would he hate you?"

I search for the appropriate answer. It's tiring, this life I'm leading, where I have to switch between versions of the story based on who knows what. I want to spill everything to Remy, right here. Tell her that I would deserve it if Brent hated me, after I all but accused his father of being involved in Matt Weaver's murder.

"Why wouldn't he hate me?" is what I settle on.

"Is this about . . . Isabella's brother?" Remy's doelike blue eyes probe mine.

I wish it were dark in here so she can't see how my face flushes. Of course Remy remembers the night she basically caught Anthony in my room. "It wasn't like that at all. I swear. *Nothing* happened with Anthony while Brent and I were together. Does he believe me?"

"I don't know what he believes," Remy murmurs. "I mean, I'm sure he *does* believe you. But you know how he is. It's like there's this distance between him and all of us, and it got bigger when you left."

For the first time since I got home, I'm forced to confront the fact that I hurt Brent as badly as he hurt me. Possibly worse.

And Anthony—I don't even know where to begin. It wasn't the first time I hooked up with another guy to get over a nasty breakup. And seriously, it's not like I'm the only girl who has *ever* done that. But the problem is that I hooked up with Anthony first, before Brent and I were together.

Anthony wasn't a remedy for my breakup with Brent; he was a symptom.

I made a huge mess and left it, like a kid who drops a gallon of milk and hides under her parents' bed. But now I have to go clean it up.

"I can't believe I'm going back," I finally say. "I can't believe my parents are *letting* me go back."

"I told them why you hit him." Remy doesn't want to say his name: Casey Shepherd. The guy who bragged to his friends about taking her virginity while he still had a girlfriend. "When they called my parents, I asked to talk to them. I said you were defending me. I wrote a letter to Tierney and told her the same thing before your hearing. I don't know if it helped or anything."

I don't know what to say, so I grab her hand over the covers. She squeezes it, and within minutes, she's asleep.

I turn off the lamp and settle into my new state of being—knowing there's nothing left for me here, and not knowing what's waiting for me up there.

CHAPTER
FOUR

My parents suspend my punishment in honor of Remy's visit. Over the next two weeks, I show her everything New York has to offer. The day before we leave for Wheatley, I take her to The Strand, my favorite bookstore, and we pick up copies of the books on our list for World Lit.

Our train to Boston is early Saturday morning. Before we leave for Penn Station, my dad sets my phone on the table in front of me, right next to my plate of toast.

"I thought about destroying it back in June," he says. "But I didn't want you to lose a piece of your soul."

"Hah! Like a Horcrux." Remy drags her suitcase into the dining room, her hair wet from the shower.

My dad and Remy launch into a debate about the best Harry Potter movie as I eyeball my phone. My social life took a serious blow this summer without it—I basically have no idea what's going on in the outside world. Except, for like, the political unrest in the Ukraine and a landmark gay rights case in the Supreme Court. (I'm allowed to read *The New York Times*.)

But I have no idea what kind of sociopolitical environment

I'm about to walk into at Wheatley. Who's pissed at who? What
are people saying about my suspension? I can't count on Remy
for the gritty details.

All of the calls and texts I missed are still flooding in as
Remy and I get on the train. I start with the most recent
messages and work my way back.

> *Mom says I can come up to Boston for a weekend in*
> *Nov. EEE! xox* (Chelsea)

> *I didn't get to see you all summer* ☹ (needy friend
> Madison)

The reminders that I'm leaving New York aren't helping
with the weight in my stomach, so I return to my text in-box
and scan the messages for any from my Wheatley friends.

An unknown number catches my eye, because it has a Massachusetts area code. I open the message. It's two words—or
rather, a name.

> *Natalie Barnes.*

I've seen this number before. I check my calls to be sure: The
number has called me before. Back in May, and then again a
few weeks ago.

It's Dr. Muller.

I check the date on the text message. Three days ago. I mumble an excuse to Remy about needing to go to the bathroom.

I shoulder my way to a half-filled car at the back of the train
and call Dr. Muller.

Hello! You've reached Rowan. I'm afraid I'm not available
now . . .

I hang up. Who is Natalie Barnes? Is that Ms. C's real name?
Maybe he found her. I allow myself the slightest twinge of

relief as I make my way back to our seats. If Dr. Muller found out who Ms. C really is, maybe she's safe.

Maybe this year will be normal.

Four hours and a twenty-minute cab ride from South Station later, Remy and I are passing through Wheatley. Not Wheatley the school, which looks like Harvard, but Wheatley the town, which looks like something from a Stephen King novel. Our driver ascends the hill leading up to the school, and almost instantly everything looks a little more green and alive.

Once we get on campus, there are signs that say WELCOME SENIORS with red and gold balloons attached. Others direct us to the student center for check-in, where there's a line to get our photos taken for new ID cards. Remy is stressed out because her hair is frizzy from the humidity. "Why can't we keep our old cards?"

A lanky strawberry blond guy in front of us turns around. Dan Crowley. He's grown an inch and buzzed his faux-hawk over the summer.

"We're getting bar codes," he tells us, beaming, because a bar code is exactly the type of thing that would excite Dan. "We get to tap our IDs now instead of swiping them."

Remy frowns. "Why would they change it?"

"Magnetic stripes are so outdated. Bar codes are the way of the future," Dan says. "I bet by next year everyone will be using their phones to get in and out of the dorms."

Remy smiles politely, obviously wishing he would stop talking. Dan turns to me.

"So how was your summer?"

"I was grounded," I say. "You?"

Half-listening about the fancy software design camp he attended, I glance up and down the line. Brent is nowhere in sight. Neither are any of our other friends. Kelsey and April are already in Amherst, our dorm building—Remy texted them as soon as we got to Massachusetts. I offer a limp smile for the photographer and wait with Remy while our new IDs are printed.

The back of my T-shirt is soaked with sweat by the time we trek over to Amherst with all of our bags in tow. I desperately want to shower after we drop our crap off in the room—an exact replica of mine from last year—but April and Kelsey have already met up with Cole and Murali in the refectory, and Remy doesn't want to be left out, I guess.

Remy and I are starving. She wants a grilled cheese, but after I say I'm getting a salad, she wants a salad. I have to battle nerves as we pick our way around the tables in search of the group. A girl in Ray-Ban frames sitting by the window waves to us. I have to blink to convince myself it's Kelsey—her signature long blond hair is cut into a chic chin-length bob.

She hops up from the table to meet Remy with a hug. She then gives me a squeeze. "I can't believe you're really here!"

"Me neither." I force a smile, because over her shoulder, Cole Redmond has caught my eye. In tow are our friends Murali and April, plus two other guys I've met briefly at parties and through class: Diego Almeida and Graham Drummond.

There's a flurry of greetings. Murali envelops me in a bear hug so strong that my feet leave the ground. Cole offers me a thin smile as we all try to fit at the four-person table.

Six months ago, Cole would have hugged me, too. That was before I hurt his best friend and said something shitty about Cole's mom's affair with Senator Westbrook.

I'm thankful for all the overlapping conversations, because the heat is off me and my suspension. Also, someone else brings up the question I've been itching to ask.

"Where's Conroy?" Graham asks.

Cole peels the label off his water bottle. "His flight doesn't get in until late."

I feel a small prick of disappointment, followed by relief. I have until tomorrow to figure out what I'm going to say to Brent.

You had all summer to figure out what you're going to say.

I tap Diego on the shoulder. "You were in my Latin class last year, right?"

"I think so." He knows so. And that's not being arrogant or anything. I shot the vice principal in the leg. That's bound to get a girl noticed.

The unofficial story that spread after Dr. Harrow was arrested was that he tried to kill me because he thought Isabella told me she was sleeping with him. The real story is that Isabella didn't tell me anything, and I found out on my own. With help from Brent and Anthony.

They're among the few people who know the truth. But I don't want to think about that right now.

"So what's the deal with Ms. C?" I ask Diego.

"She quit." He shrugs with one shoulder. "The other language teachers divided up her classes. We got Fisch."

"I know. He gave me a B minus on my final."

"That sucks." Diego's face freezes. "Not the B minus. I mean, that Fisch gave it to you. He's not even a Latin teacher."

"It's okay. I know it sucks." By Wheatley's standards, at least. "Do you know why Ms. C quit?"

There's that one-shoulder shrug again. "No one said. But she probably found out she wasn't being hired back this year and got pissed."

"How do you know? That she wasn't being hired back."

"Ninety percent of first-year teachers or something don't get hired back. Not even that Muller guy, and everyone loved him, too."

Two well-liked teachers let go at the end of a scandal-ridden year for Wheatley. Is it a coincidence, or am I missing something?

There's a loud bang behind me, and the sound of glass shattering. A small shout escapes my throat.

So much blood.

I whip around to the source of the noise: Dan Crowley

standing over a shattered glass. Someone starts a slow clap. Dan flushes to his ears.

But everyone at my table is staring at me. I look down; I'm gripping the edge of the table so tightly my knuckles turn white.

I mumble an excuse about forgetting dressing for my salad and get up. But I've really lost my appetite.

Remy doesn't bring up the scene during lunch on the way back to the dorm. But once we settle into our room and start unpacking, I catch her sneaking glances at me. Definitely wondering what the hell happened back there.

"Oh, look what I got for us." She holds up a clear plastic storage container, showing off the removable divider trays a little too enthusiastically. "For all of our nail polish!"

"Cool," I say. "I actually didn't think to pack mine. . . ."

"That's okay!" Remy sounds like Minnie Mouse—if Minnie had been hitting the pipe. I hang up the last of my Wheatley blazers and sit on the edge of my bed.

"Hey, I didn't mean to freak you guys out at lunch," I say. "I'm just exhausted and kind of jittery about being back, I guess."

The worry leaves Remy's eyes. "Totally understand. We can unpack later, and take a nap before dinner if you want."

"That's a fabulous idea."

Remy shuts the light off and climbs into her bed. "I'm sure you'll feel better once you rest up."

"Mm-hmm." I roll on my side and let the sound of her chattering lull me to sleep. I guess I am exhausted, after all.

Or maybe I'm getting so used to my lies that I'm starting to believe them.

I wind up sleeping until eight. Remy is up and unpacking. I yawn and drag myself to my computer, which is just about the only thing I've unpacked. And I google Natalie Barnes.

There are so many results that I narrow my search terms to "Natalie Barnes + Massachusetts." There are two Natalie Barneses living in the area: a fifty-something-year-old doctor and a stay-at-home mom who is really into knitting and *Downton Abbey*, according to her blog.

All I can discern from my other searches is that there are 104 Natalie Barneses living in the United States. One website offers me the mug shot of a Natalie Barnes who was arrested nine years ago for the bargain price of $14.99.

I eye the credit card that's linked to my parents' account. It's for emergencies only, and while this qualifies as an emergency in my mind, I doubt my parents will be happy to see me buying mug shots on their tab.

In my dresser is a velvet pouch filled with all of my cash savings—birthday money from over the years, a fifty spot here and there from guilty grandparents I never see. I have a couple hundred, easily, but there's no way around using the credit card unless I pay someone to do it for me. Which may wind up being more trouble than it's worth.

Besides, Ms. C isn't the mug-shot type. She was slightly dorky and really into her job. I can't picture her doing anything that could get her *arrested*.

I click out of the screen. It's probably another Natalie Barnes. I *hope* it's another Natalie Barnes.

The next morning before the assembly, Remy and I meet up with Kelsey and April, who are in even fouler moods because they were accidentally placed in a triple on the first floor with a junior.

Cole and the guys saved seats for us in the last row of the lower level of Blackman Hall. The orientation itinerary describes the assembly as "Senior Welcome Ceremony: Led by Dean Jacqueline Tierney."

Wonderful. Just the person I want to see on my first day back.

But I guess it's better than the alternative: ex-headmaster Benjamin Goddard.

A lot of people at Wheatley had to answer for their crimes last year, but Goddard was not one of them. In fact, the opposite happened. Goddard stepped down and the media portrayed him as a martyr: the *great man* who took the fall for the corruption that had managed to poison his beloved school.

Goddard knew another student was stalking Isabella before she died and fired an administrator for trying to protect her. Goddard had a "don't ask, don't tell" policy when it came to the famed crew team's dangerous hazing rituals.

And now he gets to spend the rest of his days cloistered in some million-dollar waterfront property that his severance pay from Wheatley is no doubt financing.

I realize I'm clenching my fist as I sit down next to Murali. I let it go as Remy sits next to me. Cole is on the other side of Murali, talking to Graham.

"I heard the new vice principal is this guy who ran a public school in Roxbury for like, twenty years," Remy says to me and to Kelsey, who's on the other side of her. Murali and April are both glued to their phones, not listening; April's playing Candy Crush Saga and Murali is on his Associated Press news app. He told me last year that he wants to go to Northwestern for journalism, but his parents practically have his medical school picked out already.

"Roxbury?" Kelsey's nose twitches. "That's really different from Wheatley."

"Maybe that's the point," Remy says, her voice quiet.

I don't say it, but she's on to something. Why else would a tier one prep school hire a vice principal from the inner city unless they were trying to send a message: Wheatley is done with scandal. Wheatley means business.

Professor Matthews, my history teacher from last year, walks down the center aisle and sits in the empty end seat next to April. He tells us he volunteered to help out with Senior Week and nudges April to put her phone away.

Tierney has taken the stage. She doesn't need a microphone; there are only fifty kids in the senior class. Fifty teenage bodies in the auditorium.

Well, forty-nine. Brent still isn't here.

"Welcome back, everyone," Tierney says. "You all look well rested."

A few polite chuckles. Remy whispers at Murali, who's still on his phone, "Matthews is gonna yell at you."

"Shut up for a second," Murali hisses back. Remy blinks at him, shocked. Murali is not the type of guy to tell a girl to shut up.

"What's wrong?" I whisper to him, at the same time as I see the headline of the news story he's reading on his phone.

Dorchester home invasion victim identified as MIT graduate

Murali scrolls down, revealing a picture of Dr. Muller.

CHAPTER
FIVE

"What?" It spills out of me, loudly enough for Matthews to turn his head. Cole looks over Murali's shoulder, at the screen of his phone.

"Holy shit," he says.

"Gentlemen," Matthews hisses.

My pulse races. Murali slips his phone into his pocket, frowning. Matthews seems mollified. I pinch the inside of my wrist, hard. There's no way this is real life. There's no way Dr. Muller is dead. I just saw him two weeks ago.

He texted me three days ago.

But of course, I can't tell anyone that.

When Matthews isn't looking, I get out my phone. I search "Rowan Muller" and click on the first news article. It's dated yesterday.

The family of Rowan Muller, PhD, arrived at the
South African Embassy in Boston, Massachusetts,
this evening to identify their son's body. Muller, 29,

*missed his flight from Boston's Logan Airport to Cape
Town last Monday. Police visited his apartment in
Dorchester and found Muller dead of a single gunshot
wound.*

"What's it say?" Cole leans over Murali.

"Mr. Redmond and Miss Dowling." Matthews whispers so
loudly that people in the row in front of us turn around. Fucking
Cole. I put my phone away and try to focus on Tierney. My cheeks
heat when I see that she's paused, and staring straight at my row.

"This week, I implore your help in setting an excellent ex-
ample for the incoming freshman class. In light of recent
events, Wheatley's reputation has suffered. But not its morale."
She clears her throat. "That's why you may notice several
changes around campus this year."

Yeah, I think. *Like a disturbing trend involving teachers
going missing.*

As soon as we get back to the dorm, I turn on the local news.
April and Kelsey crowd into our room, since they didn't hook
up their television yet. On screen, police officers tape off the
area outside an apartment complex.

"This is so horrible," Kelsey says. "I didn't have him, but
everyone says he was the nicest—"

I don't have it in me to tell her to shut up, so I raise the
volume on the television to the maximum.

*". . . an apparent home invasion gone wrong. Several per-
sonal items were stolen from Muller's home, including a laptop
and the victim's phone."*

A photo of Dr. Muller with his family in South Africa
flashes across the screen. Remy, Kelsey, and April are still talking. I resist the urge to choke them all. *Shut up. You don't know
what this means.*

"Anyone with information is asked to call 1-800-555-TIPS."

And then the anchor is onto the construction delays in the Back Bay.

"So horrible," Kelsey repeats. The girls shake their heads reverently.

"That's why they call it Deathchester, I guess."

Remy jabs April in the ribs.

I can't take much more of this. I grab my cell phone and find a quiet nook in the hallway on the floor above us. I call the number from the new spot and get an automated message assuring me that my call will remain anonymous. I swallow away the sour taste in my mouth.

A bored voice cuts off the hold music. "Mass Crime stoppers."

"I think . . . I think I have information about a murder case," I say. "Rowan Muller. I saw him, two-ish weeks ago, and he told me—"

"Hold on, hold on," the man says, as if I should know how this works. "I'll transfer you to the officer assigned to the case."

A click. More elevator music accompanied by a recording about how together, we can stop crime. My eyelids are drooping before a woman picks up the phone.

"Officer Gonnelly."

I try to launch into my story, but she cuts me off with a stream of generic questions. How long did I know Dr. Muller? When did I last see him? Did anything seem suspicious when I last saw him?

"That's what I'm trying to tell you," I say. "He was looking for his girlfriend. They were both teachers at the Wheatley School. She disappeared last May."

A pause. "So Rowan Muller was dating another teacher. Can anyone confirm this?"

I pull my knees up to my chest. "I don't know—they didn't tell anyone, I don't think. They were both new, and wouldn't want to get in trouble—"

"Got it." Officer Gonnelly is gruff. No doubt, if I were there

in person, she'd be the type of cop who wouldn't stop scrib-
bling notes long enough to look me in the eye. "Does this girlfriend have a name?"

This girlfriend. Like I'm making it up. Officer Gonnelly is
definitely not going to like my response. "That's the problem.
She went by Jessica Cross at the school, but Dr. Muller said
that wasn't her real name. She stole the identity of some woman
who died years ago."

Another loaded pause. I picture Gonnelly waving over her
partner, covering the mouthpiece of the phone and whispering,
Come listen to this crap. "So Mr. Muller was seeing another
teacher. Can anyone else confirm the stolen identity story?"

"No, but he texted me before he went missing. He gave
me the name Natalie Barnes. Just look up Jessica Cross from
Cliftonville, Georgia, and get Ms. Cross's personnel file from
Wheatley—"

"Thanks, honey. We'll look into it."

My toes curl. Once someone drops a *honey* bomb on you, it's
pretty much a given they're not going to take anything you say
seriously.

"Wait," I say. "I know it sounds crazy, but I swear I'm not
making it up."

"We'll call you if anything comes of your tip. What's the
best number to reach you at?"

I clench my jaw and give her my cell.

If the BPD won't find Natalie Barnes, then I will.

By lunchtime, we all have an email from Dean Tierney in our
in-boxes.

Faculty, staff, and students,

I regret to inform you that Dr. Rowan Muller, a former
teacher at Wheatley, has died in tragic circumstances.

Although Dr. Muller was not with us for very long, he was well liked among faculty and students. Anyone wishing to pay their respects may note that Muller's colleagues at Massachusetts Institute of Technology are holding a small memorial service this Thursday at ten in the morning.

"Do you think they'll let us out of orientation if we want to go?" Murali's upper lip quivers for a millisecond. He catches me staring at him and turns his head.

"I doubt it." Cole spears the hard-boiled egg on top of his spinach salad. For some reason, it only reminds me that Brent still isn't here. Brent is the only one who would listen to me about Dr. Muller—that this isn't some random murder.

And then I realize that I'm thinking of the old Brent—the one who helped me find Isabella's killer. The new Brent is the one who called me crazy for even thinking I could find Matt Weaver—and then pulling farther away from me when I did.

We all start our walk to the quad, where we're breaking into groups of four to start "orientation leader training." (Read: Get a stupid T-shirt and do trust falls.) It's a picturesque late summer day—it's early enough that it's balmy, even though it'll be hot as Satan's balls by the afternoon. The flowers lining the walkways are in full bloom, and the whole scene looks like it was torn out of a brochure for the Ivy Leagues. The occasional shout and high-pitched giggle from the quad punctuate the calm.

It's eerie as hell. After Isabella was murdered, the quiet was different. It was a loaded silence—as if everyone was afraid to talk. Now that a teacher we barely knew has been killed, it's as if the quiet stems from the fact that we have nothing to say.

Sucks the physics teacher got shot in the head. Wonder if they'll have potato salad at the welcome barbecue?

Campus is swarming with families, their attention focused on freshmen who look mortified to be breathing the same air as their parents. A woman in a pantsuit holding a map in front of her face steps sideways into me on the quad path. She doesn't apologize. I almost spit a snotty remark at her—then I see the girl standing to the side of her.

"Mama." Her deep brown eyes are wide. Her mother ignores her and loudly wonders where the freshman dorms are.

"I'm so sorry," the girl says to me. She's pretty, with bronze skin and a thick black braid that reaches almost down to her waist. I soften a bit.

"It's okay." I smile at her. She flushes. "If you're looking for the dorms, just pick a path and go straight."

There's chaos on the quad; apparently our first task for the day is picking up orientation leader T-shirts before we meet up with our groups. I wait for small shirts with April and Kelsey as Remy trots off to the extra-small line. Someone taps my shoulder, and I turn around to face Brent. He's wearing half a smile, and a Black Keys concert T-shirt with his aviator sunglasses hanging from the collar.

"Brent!" Kelsey and April shriek. He gives them both a one-armed hug. Steps back instead of reaching for me. With his thumb, he scratches the outermost point of his eyebrow. It's his nervous tic.

I wonder what mine is. Whether I'm doing it right now, and if Brent notices.

"Hey, ladies."

April and Kels start asking him a million questions about England, but they all fall short of my ears. I know it's selfish to want him to myself right now. Brent was their friend first, and now that I'm not his girlfriend, I'd better get used to being just one of the girls.

We take a collective step forward as the group in front of us moves away, shirts in hand. Brent's voice is in my ear.

"You're back."

"I am," I say.

"You could have texted me or something." His voice is light. Not accusing. And he doesn't seem all that surprised to see me. Remy must have told him already.

"I had my phone taken away," I say. "But I'll be sure to tell you next time I'm expelled then sent back here against my will."

Brent lowers his voice. "This isn't easy for me either."

"What? Seeing me?"

His lips part, but nothing comes out.

We don't talk as we get our T-shirts and break away to find our groups. The sad thing is, I'm not even offended that he basically admitted he was dreading seeing me.

I wish the worst thing that could have happened this week was realizing I would have to eat breakfast, lunch, and dinner with my ex-boyfriend. Dr. Muller's murder eclipses all of my BS problems.

His murder is a reminder that what happened last year isn't over.

I make my way to the table marked GROUP 10. The other three members are already there—Peter Wu, a sullen kid who carries a briefcase to class; Peepers, a boy with enormous glasses who looks like a future serial killer, but who happens to be really nice; and Jill Wexler, future Yale Division I volleyball player who is not very nice at all. At least not to me.

"Hi guys," I say, settling into a free spot on the bench next to Peepers. He beams at me—he's wearing a nametag that says ARTIE. Jill is writing out hers with a Sharpie, drawing a little heart over the *i* in her name.

The rest grunt hello. I look around at the other groups—everyone but me seems to have gotten a chatty bunch. Remy is with April, Dan Crowley, and Cole, and they're all laughing at something together.

I find Brent at a table with Lizzie Hansen, creepy Lee Andersen, and Zach Walton. At least someone got a worse group than I did.

But I don't really mind—it'll make it easier to break away from them this week and figure out what the hell is going on around here.

CHAPTER
SIX

When orientation breaks for the day, I call Anthony again, even though I have a feeling he won't pick up. Again.

Hey, it's me. Leave a message.

I don't leave a message this time. Instead, I call Dennis, Anthony's friend who works at the Wheatley Police Department, and ask if I can stop by. His shift starts at four—if I leave now, I can get there as he's arriving and still be back in time for dinner at six.

"Hey," Dennis calls to me from outside the front entrance of the police department. Dennis is built, with a close-shaved head and blue eyes. He looks like he should be in a box-office flop about a band of Navy Seals. Really, really good-looking Navy Seals.

Dennis snuffs out a cigarette with his heel, and just like that, he's instantly less good-looking. I don't like guys who smoke. "Is everything okay?" he asks.

"I want to report a missing person."

"Has it been more than forty-eight hours?"

"Try eight years."

His gaze probes mine. "Is this related to another missing persons case? One that was recently solved?"

"I don't know," I say. "But I need your help."

"Officially, or unofficially?"

I hesitate. "Unofficially."

"I've got a lot of eyes on me now," he says. "I can't chase another one of your hunches."

"When I tell you what's going on, you'll see why no one will believe me. And last time I checked, one of my hunches got you Matt Weaver's body."

Dennis's mouth forms a line. "Why don't we talk inside?"

I follow him past the reception area to a desk cordoned off by filing cabinets. Dennis pulls out a chair and settles into the seat across from me.

"You have a cubicle." My gaze lands on his nameplate: DE-TECTIVE DENNIS DICHIARA. "You're a detective now?"

He nods and leans back, pressing his fingertips together in front of his face. I hadn't noticed that he's wearing a jacket and tie instead of his plainclothes uniform. "As of last month." He hesitates. "Your tip, about the lake house—it helped me tie a couple things back to Shepherd and Tretter. Higher-ups were impressed. So thanks."

"So you kind of owe me then, right?" I lean forward in my seat. "And I mean, I don't think your boss would be *happy* that you withheld information about your sources. And you gave me a Taser."

"Jesus, Anne." He sighs, massaging his temples. "Okay. What's going on?"

I start with the moment I went to say good-bye to Ms. C and learned she left. I tell him about my meeting with Dr. Muller, and his last text message to me before he was murdered.

"Hold up," Dennis says. "The home invasion in Dorchester?"

"Yeah. I called the tip hotline, and this woman totally blew me off, like I was some dumb kid telling stories."

"I don't think it's personal." Dennis spins back and forth,

making small semicircles with his chair. "Boston Police have a lead on that case already."

"I thought they didn't have any suspects?"

"They don't, technically," Dennis says. "But the MO—the way what's-his-name was killed—matches an unsolved double homicide in Brockton. All three vics were tied up, robbed, and shot execution style."

I dig my nails into my kneecap. I don't like the way Dennis is talking about Dr. Muller. As if now that he's a detective, he can start talking about murder victims like they're not people. Just bodies to be sliced open and searched for answers.

"BPD's looking for a serial home invader," Dennis continues. "You gotta realize that this looks like a random thing. Dorchester's crime rate is so high, we call the place Deathchester."

"So I've heard." My neck gets hot. There's not enough air in this station. "You have to realize that it doesn't look random to me. I'm telling you, there's someone else in danger."

"Anne, I hate to say it, but it sounds like the only danger your teacher's in is getting busted for fraud."

"You don't know her. Ms. C wouldn't have . . . *changed* her identity in the first place if she wasn't in trouble," I say. Dennis's lips part and I know I'm losing him. My blood pressure ratchets up. "So she disappears, and three months later, the guy she was dating winds up dead? Come on. I can't be the only one who sees a connection."

He sighs, and I know I've got him. "The murder isn't in my jurisdiction, and Boston isn't going to appreciate some rookie from the suburbs calling and telling them how to run their investigation. But I'll dig up whatever I can on this Natalie Barnes."

I nearly stand up and hug him. "Thank you. Thank you."

"Yeah, sure. But you should probably let me handle this," Dennis says. "I'm kind of surprised to see you back here. How did that happen?"

I open my mouth, but opt for a shrug instead. Because I'm

still trying to figure out the answer to that question myself. As I get up to leave, I can't help but turn around.

"Have you heard from Anthony lately?" I ask.

Dennis leans back, puts his hands behind his head. "Probably . . . July. Before he got fired from Alex's."

"He got fired?"

"Sorry, just assumed you knew." Dennis looks at me funny. "When was the last time *you* heard from him?"

"A while." I hope my cheeks aren't as red hot as they feel. "Do you know if he's okay? Or where he's working now? I'm kind of worried about him."

"My mom saw him busing tables at Fiorello's," Dennis says. "Italian place around the corner from here."

I thank Dennis and try not to flip any tables over on my way out.

Fiorello's is a five-minute walk from the Wheatley School. And I'd thought he was MIA.

Against my better judgment, I'm going to see Anthony. Ever since the news of Muller's murder, I'm numb and all I want is to feel something. Even if it's the sting of rejection.

The staff at Fiorello's is setting up for their dinner shift. It's the type of place with cushioned booths leaking stuffing. Vintage family photos on the wall. Whatever's cooking in the kitchen smells excellent.

I ask the host if Anthony is working tonight. "Out back," he says. "Want me to get him?"

"It's okay." This conversation is best had outside anyway. I head around the back of the building, following the noise of a Dumpster slamming shut. Anthony turns around before I can announce my presence.

He just sort of stares at me for a bit. He's in jeans, a white T-shirt, and a black apron. His hair is longish again, tied in a man-bun at the nape of his neck, exposing his tattoo. It's a black, elongated star with eight points. I'd always thought it was some intricate design ripped from a heavy metal band's album cover.

Last year, I finally asked him what it is.

Polaris, he said. The North Star.

I'm staring. "Hi."

"Hey." He shifts his feet, watching me almost as if he doesn't recognize me. But something in the way his shoulders have tensed tells me that yes, he recognizes me. Whether or not he's happy to see me is another story.

We just kind of look at each other for a bit. I wonder how he sees me; how *I've* changed since May.

"I called you," I say. "A couple times."

"I know," he says.

Anger ripples through me. "And you have no reaction to that."

"I don't know how you want me to react." Anthony rubs his chin. He's letting his sideburns grow out, and the lower part of his face is covered in black stubble. "You pretty much Dear Johned me."

"I told you I had my phone taken away," I say. "I couldn't call you all summer."

"I'm talking about before that." His eyes flash. My chest constricts.

I never said good-bye to Anthony. In the car home, I sent him a text.

Going home. I'm probably not coming back. I'm sorry.

"Things are different now," I say. "I'm back . . ."

A laugh escapes his nostrils. "You really think this could work? Anne, I couldn't even take you to the prom without everyone recognizing me as the guy who got arrested for killing his sister."

"You didn't kill her."

"Yeah, well." Anthony sighs, runs a hand through his hair to get it away from his forehead. "A lot of people think I could have if I'd had the chance, you know?"

"No," I say. "I don't. I'm not saying we should . . . date, or anything, but I like hanging out with you. I don't believe the things you think about yourself. I've seen how you really are."

He watches me, as if waiting to see if there's more.

"I like you," I say.

"Do you like me, or the person you think I could be with a little work?"

I feel like I've been slapped. "That's not it. . . ."

"I like you, too, Anne," he says. "But I'm trying to put everything behind me."

"Is this about what happened at Shepherd's?"

Anthony clenches his fists. "Would you keep it down? I thought we said never to talk about that."

The backs of my eyes prick. Blood. So much blood. "You're really going to sit there and tell me you don't think about that night?" I pause. "Why did you get fired from the mechanic shop?"

Anthony's eyes flash. "Who told you that?"

Crap. "Dennis."

"Anne, what the hell are you talking to him for?"

"It's got nothing to do with you," I say.

"I don't care what it's got to do with. Dennis could put us at the scene of that night, if he really wanted to." For the first time since I've known him, I see real fear in Anthony's eyes. I've seen him fight off an intruder in my dorm room, run at a man with a gun holding nothing but a baseball bat, but now—now is the first time I'm seeing him scared.

He takes a step toward me "We broke into a guy's house. We could go to *jail* if they prove it. Don't you get that?"

"Of course I do. Don't talk to me like I'm an idiot."

Anthony wipes his hands down his face. "I don't know what you're doing hanging around Dennis for, but I can't be a part of it. We've already seen too much, and whatever else you're trying to do, you can't drag me down with you."

I'm speechless. *Anthony* is the one who wanted to pursue the Matt Weaver thing. He wanted to go into Shepherd's house that night and get into his safe. He helped me uncover the truth, and now he wants to bury it and pretend it was my idea all along.

"I didn't ask you to follow me into the house," I say. "I didn't ask you to help me. You *wanted* to."

His eyes flash. "You're right. If only I knew then it wasn't fucking worth it."

Something in me snaps. I slap him in the face.

CHAPTER
SEVEN

My ex-boyfriend is barely speaking to me because I accused his father of being involved in a murder, and I just slapped the other guy I was involved with in the face.

Romance. Clearly, I'm doing it right.

There was a time when Brent and Anthony were assets. Like when Brent helped me distract Sebastian to get crucial information about Isabella from his computer. Or the time Anthony helped me dig up a box of evidence from Matt Weaver's neighbor's yard.

Now, they're both liabilities. Distractions I can't afford. One teacher at Wheatley is dead, and another is next if I don't find a way to unravel the truth first.

If she's not already dead to begin with.

The next morning, we meet up with our groups in the quad after breakfast. Today, we've doubled in size. Three freshmen boys huddle together, avoiding eye contact with Peter Wu and Arthur Colgate, the other seniors in my group. Arthur goes by Artie, even though people call him Peepers behind his back.

The freshmen boys are all bronzed, as if they're fresh off a

Nantucket sailboat. I look inside my packet—their names are Bingham, Banks, and Oliver. They all probably own purebred golden retrievers and monogrammed sheets their mothers ordered from Williams-Sonoma.

Barbara, an excitable woman who's in charge of student services and orientation, clears her throat until there's quiet and tells us she has an exciting activity planned for us today. Jill is standing as far away from the guys as possible, her eyes glued to her phone. She looks up and gives me a wave. According to the packet, we're missing someone named Farrah Nassir.

"Um, is this Group Ten?"

I turn to see the girl from yesterday—the one whose mother bodychecked me. She reddens and smiles sheepishly.

"Hey, yeah," I say. "You're Farrah, right? I'm Anne."

"Sorry I'm late," she says. "Kind of hard to find it here from the dorm."

I look around at the other freshmen girls. Most of them seem to be paired off, tugging at the ends of their hair together, whispering to each other. No doubt Farrah's roommate left her to fend for herself.

When Barbara makes her way to our group, she takes attendance and hands me a manila envelope. Apparently I'm pack leader. She also gives me a digital camera and tells everyone to hand over their phones.

"Uh, why?" one of the boys asks through his nose. I want to elbow him in it.

"Well, because you could use them to cheat during the scavenger hunt," Barbara says brightly.

I groan inwardly. Jill looks similarly miffed about having to traipse around campus in ninety-degree weather doing an activity better suited for a ten-year-old's birthday party.

We hand over our phones—and in Peter's case, his mini tablet—and take a look at the list of stuff we need to find. The scavenger hunt is a poorly disguised "get to know your peers!" exercise: The first item is "the youngest group member's memento from home." Bonus points if it has the name of the person's hometown on it.

We're in luck: Farrah, who is from Baltimore, has an Orioles hat. But after two hours, we're only on item five on our list. It would be so much faster if we could divide and conquer, but Barbara already thought of that by giving us only one camera. We sit on the bench outside the refectory to regroup after reading the fifth item: a photo of the teacher at Wheatley who was nominated for a Nobel Prize.

"Anyone know the answer?" I survey the group. I'm met with blank stares.

"How are we supposed to figure that out without our phones?" Banks tosses a pebble at a squirrel, scaring him away.

"Before we had iPhones, there were these things called computers," I say.

Jill snorts.

"Yeah, well, we get disqualified if we use our laptops," Banks says.

"The library," Artie says. "The computer lab might be open."

"If not, we could go through old yearbooks." Peter shrugs. "It's gotta be mentioned in the teacher's bio, right?"

We plod off to the library, a scattered pack, with Banks and company at the back, muttering about how lame this is. The library computer lab is locked and dark, so we ascend to the second floor where all of the old yearbooks are kept.

"This place is mad creepy," Banks says, eyeing the low ceilings and creaky oak floors. It's the first thing he's said today that I agree with. I shepherd everyone to the last row on the right, where the yearbooks are kept.

"We should break up into pairs," I say. "We can cover more ground that way."

I catch Banks muttering something that sounds like *Who*

made you Queen bitch? I stare him down. "You can be my partner."

Bingham and Oliver laugh as I drag Banks to the next row, where the yearbooks from 1990 until now are stashed with the various volumes of *A History of the Wheatley School*. On the other side of the stacks, Jill removes a yearbook. She catches my eye through the hole where the book was. And she smiles. I return it as Banks plops on the floor with a yearbook.

I grab the yearbook for 2001 and sit across from Banks. I flip through several pages of photo collages at the front of the book, pausing when I see a picture of Professor Robinson, my art history teacher from last year.

I smile, because Robinson has slightly more hair and better teeth than he does now. He's at the center of a group of about ten students. A pug-nosed brunette is holding up a sign that reads ART CLUB.

I do a double take—not because of the brunette. The girl next to her.

What's that called, when your brain is so fixated on one thing that it starts telling your eyes to see things that aren't really there? I think that's happening to me right now.

Because there's no way the girl is really *her*.

Ms. Cross.

I flip to the student portraits so fast I nearly give myself a paper cut. I scan the freshman class for the name Natalie Barnes. Nothing. Same for the upper grade levels.

I turn back to the art club photo. The girl has a round face, in that freshman-with-baby-fat way. Her blond hair is cut short, with thick, American Girl doll–like bangs.

It's so hard to remember the details of someone's face when you haven't seen them in months. But I squeeze my eyes shut and picture Ms. C. She has long hair the color of copper, and gray eyes that squint when she smiles. She's girl-next-door adorable yet pretty enough to be an actress in a Kate Mara–type way.

I cover the bangs of the girl in the picture so I can peruse every one of her facial features. Slightly long canine teeth. Round, gray eyes, and the slightest dimple in her chin.

It's not my brain convincing me to see something that's not there. I've found Ms. Cross.

CHAPTER
EIGHT

"Boom," one of the boys says from the other side of the stacks. I think it's Bingham. "Found him. Professor David Scheckel. Chemistry, 1998."

Crap. I can't leave the library yet—not when I've finally had a breakthrough.

"Give me that." I jerk my head toward the 2002 yearbook in Banks's hands. He shrugs and rejoins his friends.

"So I guess we go make a copy of his portrait," Jill says.

"I'll meet you guys downstairs," I say. When they're gone, I reexamine the picture. Ms. C is wearing a woven leather bracelet that's identical to the one the girl next to her is wearing.

They could have made them together in art class, but none of the other girls in the photo is wearing one. It's more likely that the girls are friends, and bought the bracelets together somewhere.

I flip to the student portraits in Banks's yearbook: no Natalie Barnes. But I notice something strange—a whole page of pictures of kids I don't recognize from the 2001 yearbook.

Somehow, I doubt that Wheatley gained ten students in a year.

I return to the 2001 yearbook and flip to the class portraits, more deliberately this time. Just as I suspected, there's an entire page of students missing, as if someone tore it out carefully. From the looks of it, it's students A-B.

Which would include Natalie Barnes.

I sit back against the stacks, the cold metal of the shelf jabbing into my spine. Someone tore out the page. But who? The most logical conclusion is that Ms. C did it. If she really is Natalie Barnes, a former student, she would have had to clean up her bread crumbs to be Jessica Cross without getting caught.

I don't know for sure if Ms. C's real name is Natalie Barnes, but I at least know how I can find out.

It doesn't take me long to identify the girl standing next to Ms. C in the art club photo: Caroline Cormier-Frey, Class of '05. Massachusetts State Junior Equestrian champion. Science Olympiad finalist. Harvard Class of '09.

In every one of her photos, she's glaring as if it would physically pain her to smile.

This should be fun.

During lunch, I google Caroline to see what she's up to now. Apparently she works at the Massachusetts Republican Assembly in Weston, Massachusetts. Even more fun.

There's no contact information for Caroline on the MRA's website. But I know where I can find out where she was living thirteen years ago. The tunnel system beneath the schools leads to the basement, where all of the school's old records are kept, including student files.

I plan to head straight for the tunnels after orientation breaks for the day, but I need my laundry basket so I don't raise any suspicions about going into the basement empty-handed. But as it turns out, Brent is sitting outside my room, his back against the door.

"April let me in, but Remy's not here," he says.

"I'm sure she's on the quad with everyone else."

"I didn't come here to see Remy."

I lower myself until I'm sitting cross-legged next to him. I'd invite him in, but my clothes are all over my bed. Besides, I don't need people spreading rumors about me leading Brent into my room.

"What's up?" I ask.

"I've been here less than forty-eight hours. My mom's called four times to make sure I have all my meds, Cole talked about Princeton until two in the morning, and Remy already has my whole weekend planned out." He turns to me and tilts his head against the wall. "Be my friend again? I'm starting to think you're the only normal person here."

I hope not, since I'm the one who spent her morning at the police station trying to convince a detective that a missing woman using a stolen identity is the key to solving a murder. "That's not true."

"Well, my kind of normal," he says.

I breathe him in—the familiar scent of his grapefruit-smelling Ralph Lauren cologne. He only wears it because his sister gave it to him as a Christmas gift.

It takes me a couple seconds to settle on what I want to say. There's a lot I wish I could say, but these moments never last as long as they do in my head. "I'm sorry I didn't tell you I was coming back."

He attempts a smile, but it doesn't reach his eyes. "I wouldn't be bursting to see me either, after the way I treated you."

"Yeah, well, I wasn't girlfriend of the year, either." I bump my shoulder into his. He gives a hollow laugh, and I wish he'd smile because I miss the way it looks on him: a little crooked and self-conscious. It balances out how cookie-cutter cute the rest of him is.

I look away from him, realizing I'm staring.

"You okay?" he asks.

"Yeah, just anxious, I guess," I lie. "I have a ton of ass-kissing to do to fix up my transcript. Definitely not getting into Princeton, that's for sure."

"I don't think the Ivy League is for you anyway." He pokes my side. "You like . . . *fun* too much."

I poke him back. "Okay, Mr. Straight and Narrow, where are you applying?"

He shrugs. "No idea. My mom's been hassling me to look at Notre Dame. My dad thinks I can do better."

"I asked what *you* wanted."

"I'm not . . . really sure yet."

His words come out slow. Deliberate. Brent hates talking about himself, as if he'll somehow say the wrong thing and mess up how he wants you to see him. He's the guy who shamelessly admits to nonessential things, like having a One Direction song on his iTunes and getting his first boner at a performance of *The Nutcracker*. He'll talk to anyone who will listen about some TV show he discovered on Netflix or the new *Game of Thrones* book, but ask him what he wants to be when he grows up and you've crossed a line.

I used to be drawn to that about him; Brent was this nut I'd do anything to crack. And I thought I did, when he opened up about his diabetes and we started dating and I learned about how screwed up his family is. Now it's a reminder of why we broke up: Brent puts up walls when he gets mad. Brent looks for reasons not to trust people.

Brent didn't believe me. If the situation were reversed, I probably wouldn't have believed him. I'd *never* believe that my own father was involved in a murder, or covering one up.

I should have understood why he wanted me to let the Matt Weaver thing go. But I couldn't, so I lied to him and went behind his back.

I want to believe that things could be different this time. That he'd believe me if I told him what was going on with Ms. C.

But wanting something isn't enough to make it happen.

———

Once I get rid of Brent, I grab a laundry basket from my room and head for the Amherst basement. I push the bookcase that conceals the tunnel entrance, but it doesn't budge. I catch my breath—I can't really be *that* out of shape from sitting in my apartment all summer. (It is *not* easy to do Pilates in an eight-by-eight-foot bedroom, but I managed.)

I plant my feet close together to anchor myself and push again. The bookcase isn't going anywhere.

It's bolted to the wall.

I run my fingers behind the half an inch of space between the bookcase and the wall, searching for the rough wood of the door.

Instead I find smooth drywall.

Wheatley finally closed off the tunnel entrances.

CHAPTER
NINE

Someone at this school is one step ahead of me. If I can't get into the tunnels, I need a Plan B to get Caroline Cormier-Frey's information—and anything else I can dredge up on Natalie Barnes.

Anything she didn't get to first.

After the morning orientation activities, I ditch lunch and head for the Student and Alumni Services building.

The receptionist is on the phone. Even though there's a waiting area outside with a couch and an armchair outside the office, I hang out in front of his desk.

He covers the receiver. "Can I help you?"

"There's something wrong with my schedule."

"You have to file a report through the student portal to make an appointment with your advisor," he says.

"I already did that. I never got a response."

His mouth forms a line. "Could you wait outside until I'm done here?"

"Sure." In fact, I was counting on it. I sit on the couch and glance over at the door. I can't see the receptionist, which means he can't see me. But I can hear him on the phone.

With a quick sweep of the hall to make sure no one's coming, I head for the water cooler. I grab a paper cup and pull back the lever for cold water. Then I keep pulling until the lever snaps off and the water spills out onto the floor.

I head back into the office and tap on the receptionist's desk until he looks up. The jerk isn't even on the phone anymore. "I think the water cooler is broken."

He looks over and sees the water spilling all over the carpet. He leaps up and rushes out of the office. I run around to the other side of the desk.

"Come on, come on," I whisper as I scan the icons on the computer's desktop. Bingo: There's one labeled ALUMNI DIRECTORY.

I type in "Natalie Barnes" and hit Search.

It says, "No results found."

Does that mean she didn't graduate? I gnaw my lip. I don't have time to speculate. I try "Caroline Cormier-Frey" and poke my head around the desk. The receptionist is gone; probably getting paper towels. The cursor spins as the system runs the search. One result loads as footsteps sound outside the office. I take a picture of the screen with my phone.

"Did you do this?" The receptionist holds up the detached lever.

I muster up my best *who, me?* look. "It was an accident."

The receptionist shakes his head and lifts up a ruined magazine from a basket on the floor. The entire waiting area carpet is soaking wet. I do feel kind of bad about that. Shame to waste a perfectly good *Vogue*.

"Maybe I should come back later?"

"That would probably be best," he snaps, before heading back into the office.

As I head down the hall, I pull up the photo I took of the screen.

Caroline Marie Cormier-Frey, born February 8, 1987. Class of 2005. Current address: 65 Sugar Maple Lane, Weston, Massachusetts.

I've almost ditched the building when a very tall woman in tweed sidesteps me.

"Anne," Dean Tierney says. "I've been meaning to speak with you."

I settle into the red leather chair across from her desk. The last time I was in here, Tierney threw me out. I may have accused her of not caring that Lee Andersen was stalking Isabella, which is pretty messed up considering that Tierney's own sister was Vanessa Reardon—the girl who woke up in Matt Weaver's bed after a party and didn't remember getting there.

So the bright spot is that it would be hard for this meeting to get worse than that.

"We need to talk about getting you back on track." Tierney already has my file pulled. The woman doesn't beat around the bush; I'll give her that. "Your situation isn't ideal, but some of your teachers from last year have agreed to boost your grades half a mark if you do an extra credit assignment of their choosing."

I'm stunned. "Why would they do that?"

"There are people at this school who believe in you." Tierney gives me a hard look that lets me know she's not one of them. She passes me a stack of papers, divided by different-colored paper clips. "These are the assignments. I'd suggest you start them now, before classes begin and you find yourself overwhelmed."

My stomach sinks as I flip through the assignments. A book report, an article review . . . I'm never going to finish all these when I have to spend all day at orientation. I'm barely going to be able to find the time to track down Caroline Cormier-Frey as it is.

"I'll try," I say.

"Try isn't good enough." Tierney's voice is sharp. "Someone took a leap of faith for you. Don't pull the rug out from under them."

I eye the extra-credit assignments, trying to see the point in all of this. Best-case scenario, I can pull my GPA up to a 3.0. *If* I get all A's this semester. In prep school world, a 3.0 may as well be a 2.0. There's no way I'd get into my first choice college if I even had one.

I screwed up at St. Bernadette's. All the SAT prep classes I blew off didn't matter as much before I burned part of the auditorium down, but now every bad mistake I ever made is coming back to haunt me. Every skipped class. Every extracurricular I lost interest in.

I'm a trust fund fuck-up, and doing my homework and going to class on time like a good girl isn't going to make me a Wheatley kid.

I have a chance to do something that matters here. I can find Dr. Muller's killer, and I can get answers to what happened to Natalie. The truth is what matters—not the lie I'd be telling myself by trying to be the person my parents expected me to be.

"Don't let yourself down, Anne," Tierney says. She shuffles the files on her desk. I watch her hesitate and motion to cover a file on her desk with mine.

But she's not fast enough—I catch the label on the file.

Natalie Barnes. Expelled.

CHAPTER
TEN

Tierney knows that Ms. C is really Natalie Barnes. Is that why she had to leave? Tierney busted her as a fraud and she slipped away in the night before anyone else could find out?

And I've got to find out what the folder on Tierney's desk means before she figures out that I know the truth about Ms. C, too.

Unfortunately, we have to be ready by seven on Friday morning for an excursion to the Wheatley annex. According to the packet, it's a plot of land a fifteen-minute bus ride away dedicated to "team and leadership building activities." Remy says we'll basically be going zip-lining and picnicking.

Her group and mine are assigned to the same bus, so we head to the front gate together. It looks like all of our group members are there. I do a mental head count.

"Where's Farrah?" As soon as I ask, I see her by the curb on a cell phone, talking hurriedly in another language.

"The terrorist has been on the phone for the last ten minutes," Banks says around a yawn. "I bet the school is about to blow up."

I'm on him, the collar of his T-shirt in my grip before anyone can stop me.

"Anne." Brent pushes Bingham and Oliver aside. "Put him
down."

"You heard what he said."

"He's an asshole. But he's not worth getting expelled over."

Banks smiles at me. The little shit weasel actually *smiles*. I
stalk off, hoping my blood pressure will go down. Brent follows me.

"I would not be pulling crap like that if I were you," he says.

"He shouldn't get away with saying those things."

"I know. But he will, because he's an entitled little twat,
and his father is on the school board. He could make your life
very miserable."

"I'm not afraid of a stupid school board," I say, even though
I know I sound like a whining little kid who wants to watch an
R-rated movie instead of going to bed.

"Maybe you should be, since they're the ones who let you
come back." Brent's eyes are pleading now. "Don't leave. You
just got here."

I sigh and follow him back to the group. Banks is wearing a
self-satisfied smirk, until Brent grabs him by his collar. Banks's
feet dangle off the ground.

"Make another comment like that, you'll be shitting the
rubber from my shoes for a week," he says, his voice pleasant.

Brent drops Banks, whose cheeks are flaming red. I scowl at
Brent. "Why are *you* allowed to do that?"

"I believe what you meant is 'thank you.' Come on, the buses
are here."

The annex is an hour outside of Wheatley. The space between
buildings gets wider the farther north we go, and eventually
there's nothing around but trees. It seems like autumn comes
earlier in Massachusetts—some of the leaves are already

tinged with red and gold. I think of everything about my favorite season—getting hot cider from the Union Square farmers' market, picking out a Halloween costume for Abby—and have to swallow away a lump in my throat.

I was expecting the annex to be a plot of dirt, but this is the Wheatley School, so I should have known better. We're greeted by an enormous sign with gold lettering welcoming us to the Wheatley annex, founded in 2005 by Headmaster Benjamin Goddard.

In small letters at the bottom are the words THE WILLIAM H. GODDARD SANCTUARY.

"This place isn't that old," I say aloud.

"It took years to build. And millions of dollars." Artie's voice comes from behind me. "It was Goddard's legacy project."

"This sign says there were two Goddards."

"One wasn't headmaster. William Goddard was Benjamin Goddard's father. He was a student at Wheatley a long time ago." Artie shrugs.

I look into his face. I have to do a double take—he's not wearing his glasses.

"New look?" I say.

"Nah. Contacts. My mom will kill me if I break another pair of glasses."

There's snickering to our left. I look over to see the three dipshits gathered together. Bingham is making a rabbit face—probably imitating Artie's slightly large front teeth. I scowl at him, and the boys turn away.

"Anyway, I figure there's a decent chance of glasses breakage," Artie says, ignoring them. "Since we had to sign that waiver and everything."

"Waiver?"

"That paper with our emergency contact forms. The one that says we're not allowed to sue the school if we break anything today. Your parents had to sign."

Lovely.

We follow the RA assigned to us—Kyle, who works on the guys' floor in Amherst—over a footbridge. A brook babbles underneath. That's when a gigantic structure made out of trees comes into focus. Three trunks converge to make a pyramid, with knotted ropes extending from the top point to the ground.

"Do we have to climb that?" Farrah asks behind me.

"Later," Artie says. "Our group's first obstacle is *that*."

He points to two trees, each about fifty feet high. They're connected by a log, which I assume we have to walk across. Below, the ground slopes downward in a steep bank covered with rocks and ferns. The tree overhead rustles; an acorn falls. We never hear it drop.

Farrah makes a panicked noise next to me. "I hate heights."

I squeeze her hand.

"Listen up." Kyle emerges from the shed, holding a harness and a helmet. Next to the shed is a log cabin. It says OUTHOUSE, but I'm sure there's a bathroom attendant and potpourri inside.

Kyle demonstrates, on Jill, how to adjust our harnesses. We'll be tethered to a rope, which our partner will belay as we walk across the log. A few people groan at the term *partners*.

I turn to Farrah, but Banks is already next to her. He gives her a wolfish smile and extends a hand. She shakes it with one hand and tugs at the end of her braid with another. Artie and Peter have already teamed up, as have the other two boys. I'm stuck with Jill.

I avoid her eyes as Kyle leads us over to the trees. Bingham and Oliver, who volunteered to go first, start climbing the boards nailed to the trees.

"I thought he hated me," Farrah whispers, tilting her head toward Banks.

"He's a jerk. He's not worth your time."

"I don't know . . . he seems nice." Farrah shrugs, pink seeping into her facial coloring.

Something protective—and vicious—stirs in me. "Look,

you need to be careful who you trust here. Don't be so naïve. These kids—they're not out to make friends."

Farrah blinks at me, stunned. We stand in silence until it's her turn. Banks makes an "after you" gesture and spots her as she climbs the tree. I can see her foot shake as she feels around for the steps on the way up.

All the color has drained from her face when she reaches the top.

"Good, Farrah," Kyle says. "Now hold onto your rope while he hooks you in."

Farrah spreads her arms out and puts one foot in front of the other like she's supposed to. Beyond the trees, I can hear the other groups cheering their members on. I cup my hands around my mouth and shout a word of encouragement up at her. Farrah doesn't look down—she'd lose her balance—but her expression sets, and she stands up a little straighter.

And that's when Banks lets out a sneeze. A very loud, fake sneeze.

Farrah whips her head around, startled. Her foot slips, and Jill gasps next to me.

My own gasp turns into a scream as she tumbles off the log, even though I know Banks has got the other end of her rope.

But the impact is too much. The rope flies out of Banks's hands, and Farrah crashes to the ground.

"I'm okay," she snaps as everyone crowds around her. Then she bursts into tears.

"What hurts?" Kyle demands, hovering over her. She points to her ankle.

"Everyone out of the way," Kyle barks. "Jill, head to the lodge and have Barbara call an ambulance."

Banks shimmies down the tree, landing on his feet with a thud. His eyes are wide as he watches Farrah, holding her ankle and sobbing. I want to slam him against the tree, but Brent's voice is in my head.

"You did that on purpose," I yell in Banks's face.

"Anne." Kyle's voice is sharp. He's still bent over Farrah. "Let me handle this."

"You saw him do it! He pretended to sneeze to screw her up."

"*Anne.* Get away from him." Kyle turns to Banks. "Go to the lodge. Now."

Banks's face falls. I allow myself to breathe. For once, maybe someone at this school is going to get what they deserve.

When he moves past me, he slows down just long enough to mutter two words in my ear.

"Prove it."

CHAPTER
ELEVEN

Farrah has a sprained ankle. Banks isn't in trouble. I'm seething, which probably means it's a bad idea to pay a visit to Caroline Cormier-Frey.

But I do it anyway.

The only way to Weston is to head into South Station and change to the commuter rail. When I'm on the train, I slip on my Wheatley blazer, convert my ponytail to a high bun, and reapply my rosebud lip salve.

I wriggle past the throng of commuters getting off the train at Weston. My phone says 65 Sugar Maple Lane is ten minutes away by car, so technically I could walk. But a bored-looking cab driver at the station waves me over.

I have him stop a block away from Caroline Cormier-Frey's house. "Could you wait right here? It'll probably be about twenty minutes."

"Mm-hmm." He's already turning his radio to the Red Sox game.

Sugar Maple Lane looks like a snapshot from a real estate brochure about a neighborhood no one can afford to live in. All of the houses are two or three stories, with white columns and nineteenth-century masonry. In between them, I catch glimpses of a lake.

I almost turn around when I see the elaborate brick-and-ivy mailbox with a gold-plated number 65. People with ivy wrapped around their mailboxes don't let just anyone into their homes. If Caroline Cormier-Frey detects even the faintest scent of bullshit, this won't work.

A security camera trains on me as I ascend the driveway. I focus on tugging my blazer down so I don't look straight at it. Best not to have a record of me being here.

I ring the bell and step back as a dog begins to bark inside. I expect a housekeeper or something to come running. Instead, a woman I assume is Caroline Cormier-Frey answers the door. She's wearing a baby blue sleeveless blouse and khakis, and her chin-length brown hair is perfectly blown out. Her face is wide and round, the corners of her mouth lilting downward as if she's on a horse tranquilizer.

"Yes?" Her eyes move to my Wheatley blazer, something like contempt flashing in them.

"I'm looking for Miss Cormier-Frey."

Caroline eyeballs me. "Why?"

"I'm a student at the Wheatley School, and I was wondering if you had a moment to hear about the Alumni-Student Liaison."

Caroline stiffens, her hand moving to the door handle. "I already received information about that in the mail."

"Listen," I lower my voice. "I have to do this to be a member. Please—I'll only take five minutes of your time."

Caroline's gaze moves to the staircase. On the second story, someone yells at the dog. *Calm down, calm down.* "What did you say your name was?"

I didn't. "It's Elizabeth."

Caroline opens the door for me and turns down the hall. I assume she wants me to follow, so I trail after her.

"Why would you want to be a member of that awful club?" she asks, without turning around.

"College applications." I follow her into a spacious living room off the foyer. She takes a seat on a cream-colored couch next to a fireplace the height of my closet. I sit opposite her in an armchair.

"So," I say, folding my hands in my lap. Something about Caroline's hard stare makes me feel like I could pee myself. "When did you graduate from Wheatley?"

"Two thousand five," she says. "Isn't that on file?"

"Just making small talk," I mumble. "Sorry."

I realize what it is that freaks me out about Caroline: She doesn't blink. Not once.

"My family has donated quite a bit of money to the school over the years," she says. "I'm not quite sure what else I could contribute without attending one of those dreadful events. You know, where the board members try to ingratiate themselves with wealthy alumni by shoving their noses in their asses like untrained poodles."

"Um, well . . ." I try not to fixate on the fact that she still hasn't blinked.

"Are you a poodle?" Caroline says. A nervous laugh escapes my lips, but when her stony expression doesn't change, I realize she was serious.

"No," I say. "I'm not here to ask you for money. I had a question about another graduate who's joining the liaison. I believe you and she were friends."

Caroline's lips form a line in a way that makes me think this chick wasn't exactly rolling in friends in high school. Not exactly a shocker, if so.

"Oh really," she says. "And who is that?"

"Natalie Barnes," I say. "What can you tell me about her?"

Caroline leans across the coffee table separating us, as if she's about to tell me a secret. "You have thirty seconds to get out of my house before I call the police."

I grip the armrests of my chair. "So you did know Natalie?"

Caroline gets up. I leap out of the chair as she advances on me. "Natalie Barnes is a lying, conniving little psychopath, and I haven't seen her in over ten years."

"I'm not trying to cause trouble," I say, backing up. The backs of my heels meet the wall. "Natalie is missing, and I just want to find her."

"So you came to *me*? Is this a sick joke?" Caroline's eyes flash. "I didn't *touch* Natalie. Get. Out. Of my house."

"I don't know what you're talking about. That's why I came—"

"GET OUT OF MY HOUSE!"

The dog resumes barking its head off. I bolt for the door as a pug with a horrendous overbite barrels down the stairs, followed by a tall brunette yelling after it.

"You've got to be freaking kidding me," the brunette says as my feet hit the porch steps.

I whip my head around. You've got to be freaking kidding me is right.

The brunette is Alexis Westbrook.

CHAPTER
TWELVE

"What are you doing here?" I demand.

Alexis's nostrils flare. "In what possible scenario could you possibly be the one with the right to ask that question? I *live* here."

"What—why?"

"How did you find me here?" she demands. "No one was supposed to find me here."

"Are you . . . related to *Caroline*?"

"No," Alexis snarls. "Her mother is my stepmother's sister. Amanda Cormier-Frey."

Crap. I should have known that if something sketchy was going on at Wheatley, the Westbrook family would be involved somehow. I glance around the Cormiers' expansive property, looking for an escape route. Alexis mistakes it for admiration.

"Mary Ellen brought us here to avoid the reporters back home," she says. "She calls it *rustic*."

Poor Alexis, having to downgrade from a multimillion-dollar brownstone to a house worth a humble seven figures.

"You're uncharacteristically quiet," Alexis snaps. "Why are you here?"

"It doesn't matter. I was leaving."

"Oh, no you're not." She steps in front of me.

"I am. Now get out of my way before your cousin calls the cops on me."

"*Step*cousin," Alexis says. "And I'm not done talking to you. Is this about what happened with my father?"

I freeze. "No. But I'd go back and stop your dad from going to Shepherd's house if I could."

Alexis's eyes flash. "I'm glad Shepherd is dead."

"So then we don't have a lot left to talk about." I try to get around her, but she blocks my path.

"What are you mixed up in now?" she asks. "If Caroline is involved, I know it can't be good."

I glance at the house. For once, I agree with her—Caroline actually makes Alexis look normal.

"It's nothing," I say.

"You can't BS me," Alexis says. "I'm not one of those half-baked guys you lead around. I know you're onto something."

"You don't know anything." I force my way past her.

For Natalie's sake, I hope that Caroline has absolutely nothing to do with her disappearance. Because I know too well what happens when someone gets caught in the Westbrook family's crossfire.

So my visit to the Cormier-Frey house did not go well.

Even if it weren't for Caroline's ridiculous reaction to Natalie's name, I definitely can't go back. Not as long as Alexis is there.

There's a long list of people I would rather deal with than Alexis Westbrook. All of my ex-boyfriends. A drug cartel. My dad.

But Caroline's words linger in my head. *I didn't touch Natalie.*

I never said she did.

I find myself on the chocolate chip pancake line the first morning of classes. Now that all the grades are moved in, the dining hall is back to feeling the way it did last year—like the main level of the 34th Street Macy's in December.

The four freshman girls in front of me laugh in unison. Freshmen travel in packs, with these nervous faces like they're afraid of missing something if they're not always with their roommate and the girls across the hall.

We inch up the line, and I see what the girls are laughing at. Or rather, *whom*. Banks Sherwood.

"So you didn't have to do any of those stupid games?" one of the girls is saying.

"Nope. They even had Wi-Fi in the annex lodge," he says.

"Ugh, lucky," two of the girls say at the same time.

Banks looks up, almost as if he feels me shooting daggers at him.

"Hi Anne," he says sweetly.

"Hi, Banks. Are you always such a smug little shit when you send a girl to the hospital?"

I've wiped the smile off his face. The girls nudge each other, inching up the line and avoiding my eyes.

"It was a joke." Banks's voice is even, but the tips of his ears are red. I can tell by his expression that he was raised never to let a girl embarrass him. And even though I'm older than him, I'm still a girl.

"Farrah's on crutches," I say. "Some joke."

Banks looks at me, lets out a laugh, and turns back to the freshman girls, as if I'm some crazy bitch who isn't worth his time. When the girls accept their pancakes and walk away, he mutters something to me.

"You were the dead girl's roommate. You got a thing for dumpy brown chicks?"

Maybe it's because three weeks ago, I had lunch with a man who's now dead, or maybe it's because Banks is an asshole, but I lose it. I grab his wrist.

"Why don't you call Farrah that to her face, you little motherfu—"

"I wouldn't complete that thought, young lady."

I drop Banks's wrist and whip around. A man is behind us. He extends a hand to me.

"I'm Mr. Buckley. Your new vice principal."

Sitting in John Buckley's office is really putting a damper on my morning. Especially since it's Dr. Harrow's old office. Obviously someone thought a new Pottery Barn couch and executive desk would mask the fact that a murderer used to work out of this office, but I'm not fooled.

"So." Mr. Buckley leans back in his chair. He looks like he could be one of my friends' fathers. So—innocuous enough. "What did that young man do to draw your wrath?"

"He's a racist and entitled brat, and I had to spend the entire week with him."

Mr. Buckley nods, smiling.

"Is there any way you could . . . not tell Dean Tierney about this?" I ask.

"I'm amenable to that," Buckley says. "To be quite honest, I'm still getting a hang of this prep school thing. I was principal of a public school in the inner city for ten years, but this is a whole new ball game."

"So I'm not in trouble?"

"We'll call it a warning," he says. "Sorry for taking you out of breakfast, but I wanted to send a message to your audience."

"And what about Banks?"

Buckley presses his fingers together. "How about you fill

out a conflict report with what he said, and I'll hang onto it in case he does it again?"

"That sounds fair," I say, but Buckley is already rifling through his desk drawers. It's a mess—folders askew, pens and Post-its strewn everywhere. He slides a drawer shut and sits back.

"The dean's secretary has the forms. Excuse me a minute."

He slips out the door, and I'm alone. Buckley's ID card stares up at me from the desk.

Only someone who's been huffing paint would actually consider stealing a teacher's ID—especially someone in my situation. But Tierney has Natalie Barnes's file on her desk. If I can just get into the building after hours and get my hands on it, I can prove that the school knew Ms. C was a fake, and that they're covering something up.

I need the ID card.

But I'm not going to steal it.

Instead, I take out my phone and snap a photo of the ID, making sure the bar code is in full focus. I put my phone away just as Buckley enters his office, clutching a paper triumphantly.

"Here you go," he says. "Bring it back to me whenever. Unless you have a change of heart."

I thank him and shove the conflict report in my bag when I'm outside his office. I'm not going to fill it out, and it's not because I've had a change of heart. I just have better things to do with my time than waste it on someone like Banks Sherwood.

And one of those things is finding out if Dan Crowley was right about bar codes being the way of the future.

Mr. Buckley didn't think to write me a pass, so I'm the last one to arrive to my first class: AP American Government.

"Don't sit," a thin-lipped woman barks when the hour strikes and we all move to choose seats. "I have my own chart."

I groan inwardly and glance at my schedule. This is Professor Kazmarkis. I looked her up online this morning, to see if

I could find any helpful information on that RateMyTeacher site. The only review consisted of a sad face.

Kazmarkis sits everyone at the tables of two in alphabetical order.

"Brent Conroy." She taps the back of a seat in the first row. Brent smiles at me with half his mouth as he slides into the chair. I didn't know we had this class together.

Kazmarkis looks down at her chart. A quick inventory of last names in the room tells me what's coming. "Anne Dowling."

Kazmarkis eyes me, her probing stare lingering on me a second longer than the other names she's called. I tell myself it's because she doesn't recognize me from around campus, and not because the mere mention of my name has put me on her radar.

"Next to Mr. Conroy."

A couple people titter behind us, enjoying the schadenfreude of me sitting next to my ex. Kazmarkis tells them to be quiet.

Brent whispers in my ear. "Made a new friend at breakfast?"

"He let me off with a warning."

Brent smiles. Kazmarkis shoots us a dirty look. I write a note in the corner of my notebook, tear it off, and pass it to Brent.

Do you know anyone who went to Muller's memorial service?

Brent's eyebrows knit together. He holds my gaze. I know what he wants to say—am I seriously going to start digging into a home invasion now? I tap my pen on the paper to get his attention. He slides it away from me and scribbles a note back.

The whole science dept. probably. Also Matthews and Robinson.

Robinson. My art history teacher from last year.

My statistics teacher holds us an extra five minutes because he forgot to hand out textbooks at the beginning of the hour, so I have to run over to the humanities building at the end of the day. I'm hoping to catch Professor Robinson before he leaves.

I knock on his doorframe, relieved to see him hunched over his desk, packing up his briefcase.

"Anne. Hello, dear." He smiles at me. "Glad to see you back. There's been a dearth of sassy little quips in your absence."

I slip inside the room. "Hi, Professor. How are you?"

That's when I notice the extra sag to the skin under his eyes. "I've been better. It's been quite a sad week."

I sit in an empty desk. "Dr. Muller?"

Robinson nods. "Such a brilliant lad. So kind."

Robinson doesn't know this, but I saw him and Dr. Muller together when I followed Coach Tretter into the staff-parking garage. Dr. Muller was driving Robinson home after he'd had a few too many glasses of champagne at a faculty presentation.

"I went to the memorial at MIT last week." Robinson takes his reading glasses off and slips them into his jacket pocket. "You expect to eulogize your friends when you're my age, but, well. Not like that."

"Professor . . . did you happen to see Ms. Cross at the memorial?"

Robinson frowns. "I'm sorry?"

"Ms. Cross. Professor Upton's replacement."

"Oh." Robinson blinks. "You know, I can't say I would have recognized her if she was there. I don't think I ever spoke to her."

That can't be right. When I asked Ms. C for help finding out what happened between Matt Weaver and Vanessa Reardon, she knew to lead me to Professor Robinson, who Vanessa confided in. Unless Robinson is telling the truth, and Ms. C found out another way.

Like through old records in the tunnels.

"Professor," I say. "Did you have a student named Natalie Barnes? About thirteen years ago."

"The name sounds familiar," Robinson says. "I don't believe I had her in class, but she may have been in one of my clubs."

"Blond, possibly friends with Caroline Cormier-Frey?"

"Oh, yes, Natalie!" Robinson taps his temple. "This old thing surprises me every so often. Yes, Natalie was in Art Club for a year. Very quiet girl. Can't say I remember much about her, I'm afraid."

A portrait of Natalie Barnes is forming in my brain. Quiet, unassuming. Didn't leave much of an impression.

Almost as if even thirteen years ago, she was preparing to disappear.

CHAPTER
THIRTEEN

Chicken fajitas are on the menu tonight, and it's a good thing, because I'm going to need that extra protein in order to stay up late and break into the administration building.

Although technically, I'm not breaking in, because I have a key.

I feel bad about using Mr. Buckley's ID for illicit purposes, because he actually seems like a cool dude.

But so did Dr. Muller. And Ms. C. If someone doesn't get to the bottom of what's going on around here, cool teachers have a pretty poor prognosis for sticking around. And staying alive.

I can't fall asleep, because my alarm will inevitably wake Remy up. So I lay in bed and read for World Lit. At around one thirty, I put on my jacket and most comfortable shoes.

I have to sneak out of a window in the first floor lounge to avoid the RA at the front desk. To avoid the security camera in front of the administration building, I head for the back door.

The security guards don't watch the video feed from the cameras on campus. They're only there in case something happens, so they can go back and rewind the feed.

In any event, I don't want to be on it.

I have my phone ready with the photo of Mr. Buckley's ID. I zoom in on the bar code. *Please, please work.*

I tap my phone screen to the sensor pad outside the door. The light remains red. Shit. I zoom in so the bar code takes up the whole screen and try again.

The sensor pad beeps. The light turns green.

I make a mental note never to doubt Dan Crowley again.

I head for the second floor, where Tierney's, Buckley's, and Goddard's offices are.

Well, Goddard's old office.

I tap my phone screen to the sensor pad on Tierney's door. The light stays red.

Damn it. I should have figured the bar code would only allow Buckley access to the campus buildings and his office. What the hell am I supposed to do now?

Well, I'm here, so I may as well see if there are any files related to Dr. Muller or Ms. Cross in Buckley's office. I think I remember hearing last year that the vice principal is in charge of employee personnel. Since Dr. Harrow was arrested, Tierney took over his duties. Which means she would have hired both Ms. C and Dr. Muller.

Once I'm inside Buckley's office, I turn on my flashlight. I can't risk putting his office light on and having someone see from the outside.

It doesn't take long to find the filing cabinet marked EM-PLOYEE PERSONNEL FILES. I flip to the divider labeled *C*.

CROSS, JESSICA.

It's a thin file. The first page is a cover letter. I do a double take at the date—it's from two years ago. That can't be right; Ms. C got Upton's job last February. I read the letter.

Dear Ms. Watts:

I am interested in the open teaching position at the Wheatley School. I believe that I am the ideal candidate for the role of English teacher.

English teacher? I scan the rest of the letter, coming to a rest at the bottom of the page. It's signed Jessica L. Cross.

There's another cover letter behind it. It's nearly identical to the first, but dated last February.

Dear Ms. Tierney:

I am interested in the open teaching position at the Wheatley School. I believe that I am the ideal candidate for the role of Latin teacher.

I think back to Ms. Cross's class; I didn't think it was weird at the time that she never really spoke in Latin. She made *us* speak the words, and she gave us assignments, and she graded them—but did she really even know the language?

Attached to the cover letter is a completed teaching application and a resume. The educational background Ms. C— Natalie—has listed looks like it was lifted right from the real Jessica Cross's obituary. Cliftonville High School, advanced honors diploma. A bachelor's in comparative languages from UNC Chapel Hill.

Under work and internship experience, she's listed a seafood restaurant in North Carolina. Apparently she was there from 2007 to 2009—when the real Jessica Cross was already dead.

I scan the half a dozen jobs Natalie has listed—a tutoring center in Boston, a page at the Cambridge Library, babysitting. I wonder how much of this is made up.

I boot up Mr. Buckley's copier and put the resume facedown on the tray. The machine spits out a fresh copy for me.

And that's when I hear a door slam down the hall.

A whimper catches in my throat. *Crap. CRAP.* How the hell did someone see me? I triple-checked that I was alone on the walk here, and that I avoided the security cameras on my way inside the building.

I glance out the windowpane on Buckley's door. A dark figure—medium height, definitely a man—walks down the hall. I turn off my light and hide behind the couch. A beam of light passes over the windowpane. Then it's gone.

I stand up, wincing at the cracking in my knees, even though there's no way my friend out there could have heard it. I peek out the glass—the man is at the end of the hall.

Outside Goddard's office.

He shines his light inside, his back to me.

He's looking for something inside of Goddard's office. Looking for me?

I stuff the copy of Ms. C's files back in my bag and press my ear to the door. *Go inside. Go inside Goddard's office.*

I hear the faint beep of the keypad, then the sound of Goddard's door opening. He's in.

Then I make a run for it.

Buckley's door slams behind me. No doubt the man heard it, but I have a decent head start. I'm at the end of the hall when the beam of his flashlight comes up behind me.

Don't look. Don't let him see your face.

He takes off running behind me.

CHAPTER
FOURTEEN

I take the stairs two at a time, nearly falling on my face at the bottom. The man is far behind—at the top of the stairs, judging from the position of his light. *Older. Possibly out of shape.*

Goddard? It can't be.

I do a 180 at the bottom of the stairs and run out the back door. Instead of cutting across the quad, I dart behind the classroom buildings, taking the long way back to Amherst.

When I get to the open lounge window, I let myself double over, gasping for breath. I lost him.

Or he stayed behind.

What I was able to observe about the man in the admin building, in order of increasing relevance:

1. He was somewhat bulky and slow.
2. He passed over Tierney's office and went right for

Goddard's, which he seemed particularly interested in—
why?

3. He must have had a key to get into the building.

Is he a teacher? Administrator? He was too tall to be Mr.
Buckley. Too . . . male to be Tierney. But how else could he
have gotten in, without a key?

And more importantly—*how did he know I was there*?

There's a chance the man left or entered through the front
door of the building, which means he would have been caught
on the security camera.

It's a place to start.

There's only one person capable of hacking into the campus
security feed. He's playing ultimate Frisbee on the quad during lunch. I grab a chicken Caesar wrap and eat it on the bench,
waiting for the game to break.

"Anne!"

I turn around to see Farrah coming toward me, wobbling on
her crutches. I groan inwardly, because her timing couldn't be
any worse. But I haven't seen her since the last day of orientation, when she got hurt at the annex, so I'm relieved to see her
smiling.

"Hey." I grab her bag from her shoulder so she can sit. "How
are you holding up?"

"Fine, I guess. It's a little hard to get around." She's panting.
I keep one eye on Dan, who dives for the Frisbee Zach Walton
throws him.

"You know you can come find me if you need anything,
right?" I say. "Even if it's to punch Banks in the nuts."

Farrah smiles.

When the game breaks, I turn to Farrah. "I'll be right back.
I have to talk to this guy, quick."

"It's okay," Farrah says. "I just wanted to say hi. And
thanks. For being so nice to me."

I motion to help her up, but she says she's fine, and waves a crutch in the air. "It's my last day that I really need these things anyway."

My chest is heavy as I leave her. How pathetic is it that she actually has to thank me for being nice to her?

When Dan Crowley heads for the sidelines to chug his Gatorade, I call his name. He wipes his brow and trots over to me.

"Yo."

"Yo," I say. "Got a question."

"I figured."

I raise an eyebrow at him.

"When do you ever find me to discuss current events?" He sips his Gatorade. There's a red ring around his lips.

"Point taken. So. The security cameras outside each building."

"What about 'em?"

"They're on a wireless server, right?"

"Mm-hmm." Dan glances back at the Frisbee game.

"I need to get on it so I can see a video," I say.

Dan's brow creases. "How far back?"

"Last night."

"Yeah, it'll be on the server still."

"So . . . can you get me on?"

Dan shifts onto his other foot. Sticks a hand in his back pocket. "I don't know. I've never tried."

"Do you think it would be hard?" I ask.

"I mean, it would probably be really easy to bypass the password for the remote log-in page, but I don't know if I should."

"Why not? You always do that stuff."

Dad's face turns pink. "That's the problem. Know that camera I installed in the Aldridge common room to see who was stealing my food from the fridge?"

I nod. Dan shared his footage with me to show me how he caught a crew team hazing ritual on tape.

"Well, after you got suspended or whatever, one of the RAs found my camera and reported me to Tierney," Dan says. "She called it a serious invasion of my peers' privacy. Which is such bullshit, when you consider that the NSA reads our emails and listens in on—"

"So you can't hack the feed for me," I say.

Dan shakes his head. "Sorry. You know I would, but I'm kind of on probation. Hey, aren't you, too?"

Someone taps my shoulder at dinner, almost making me drop my tray.

"Sorry," Farrah says.

"It's okay." I will every muscle in my body to unclench. Lately, I can't deal with people sneaking up on me, but I'm not about to tell Farrah off.

"Can I talk to you about something?" She has a curious look on her face. I look at my table; Remy keeps glancing over at us, like she's waiting for me to run off and ditch everyone again.

"Now's kind of a bad time," I tell Farrah.

"It's about what you asked that boy earlier," she says. "That punk kid."

I'm waffling between annoyance that she eavesdropped and amusement that she called Dan Crowley *that punk kid.*

"You listened to us?"

"I didn't mean to, but he's kind of loud." Farrah isn't being too discreet herself. I tap her shoulder and motion for her to follow me behind the soda machine.

"About what you heard—"

"I don't want to tell on you." Farrah holds her hands up. "I want to help you."

Her face is so sweet, so earnest, I can't even laugh at her. *Farrah . . . a hacker?*

"You think you can get on the security feed?"

"I don't know." She's smiling, almost as if I'm not in on the joke. "But I got onto Banks's iCampus account and requested he get switched from water polo to modern dance. . . ."

Now Farrah's wearing a full-blown grin. I can't help but match it.

"Farrah. You're *badass.*"

She flushes, but doesn't say anything.

"You'd really do that for me?" I whisper.

Farrah nods. "When I get back to my dorm I'll check the model of the security camera and try to access the remote log-in site. I'll let you know if it works."

We trade phone numbers, and I can barely contain my anticipation as I bounce over to my table. If I can identify the man who was in the administration building last night, I may have a real lead.

As soon as I sit down, I get a text message. I ignore it, because Remy is insisting I play Apocalypse with everyone. It's this game Murali invented where we pretend we have to buckle down for the end of the world on campus and we can only pick two other survivors to help us.

"Peter Wu," Kelsey says. "He's one of the smartest, so obviously."

"Why would you pick someone so boring?" Cole asks.

"Who cares about boring?" Remy says. "It's the *apocalypse.*"

Brent snorts. "What Phil left in the toilet this morning has more personality than Peter Wu."

"Come on, man," Phil mutters as Remy squeals *ew.*

Brent shrugs and drinks his chocolate milk. "Shoulda flushed."

I catch his gaze as Remy mutters *I hate boys.* Brent smiles and looks down into his milk.

"Your turn, Anne," Kelsey says.

My phone buzzes again. "One sec."

Meet me in the alumni garden.

NOW.

When I see who it is, I realize I have no choice in the matter.

I make up a panicked excuse about forgetting to email an extra-credit assignment to Professor Matthews and ditch the dining hall.

When I get to the alumni garden, Alexis is sitting on a bench. I stay standing. "What are you doing here?"

"Discussing our mutual enemy," she says. "Hopefully."

I sit, tentatively. "Caroline?"

Alexis's shoulders stiffen. "Caroline Cormier-Frey is the worst person I have ever met."

Pretty high praise coming from Bitchface herself. But Alexis hasn't tried to get me expelled, arrested, or otherwise ruin my life in months, so I decide to hear her out. "What'd Caroline do to you?"

"She's hated me since I was a kid. Totally out of her mind jealous of my father. Hers died when she was eleven. Ferry crash." Alexis's voice is devoid of sympathy. "Caroline's mother, Amanda—my stepmom's sister—slammed the city with a wrongful death lawsuit before his body was even cold. She hired a *professional photographer* to make sure Caroline's sad little face was all over the news. They became filthy rich and stopped speaking to my family. Until they burned the settlement money out and my father won his election."

Alexis's expression darkens. "Caroline's grown up to become an even worse version of Amanda. If my stepmom goes to jail for trying to cover up what my dad did—" Alexis's voice cracks. She breathes in, composes herself. "Then Amanda will be appointed my little brother's guardian. I can't let that happen. Not when Caroline already has her eye on his trust fund. I can't let him *live* there, knowing what she's really like."

"What do you mean?" I ask.

Alexis exhales. "Amanda had the family therapist move into the guest house the summer before Caroline went to

Wheatley. This was after Caroline pushed her friend off her bike in the street. While a car was coming."

"She tried to *kill* her friend? When she was *thirteen*?"

"Caroline claims she didn't see the car coming," Alexis says. "They diagnosed her with anger and ODD. Then her sophomore year, she attacked her roommate."

Alexis looks at me, the ghost of a smug smile on her lips. I know that face: It's her *I-have-something-you-want* face. "If I remember correctly, her roommate's name was Natalie."

"Are you just saying that because you heard me ask Caroline about someone named Natalie the other day?"

Alexis snorts. "I have better things to do than invent stories for your amusement. Caroline flipped out at this Natalie girl and drew blood, and it got her sent back to therapy."

Something about the way Alexis says the words *drew blood* makes my stomach churn. "What did Natalie do to get on Caroline's bad side?"

"Caroline only has one side," Alexis mutters. "Trust me, it wouldn't take much."

I level with Alexis. "Let's say all of this is true. Why tell me?" I pause. "What do you want from me?"

Alexis tosses her hair over her shoulder and readjusts her signature black velvet headband. Unease settles over me: Alexis clearly isn't going to tell me to stay the hell away from her family, like she did the last time she sought me out.

"The same thing you want," she finally says. "Answers. Caroline has been acting more bizarre than usual lately. Lots of hushed phone calls. Accusing me of things, like going in her room. I even caught her lying about being at an equestrian outing. Something is going on."

I run my hands over my sweater sleeves, wishing I had a jacket. "How long is *lately*?"

"I don't know. A few months. Maybe more?" Alexis shrugs.

Or around the time that Natalie reappeared in Wheatley— then disappeared again.

"Who is this Natalie person?" Alexis asks, invading my thoughts. "I checked Caroline's yearbook, and there was no Natalie in her graduating class. Did she just . . . disappear?"

"Basically," I murmur, drumming my fingertips on my knee. "Caroline could be involved. Or she might know something. I haven't figured it out yet."

"Well, if you're going to get to Caroline, you'll need my help," Alexis says.

"I need to get into the tunnels. And you can't help me with that. They're closed off."

"Not so fast." Alexis presses the pad of her index finger over her lips, thinking. "It's a long shot, though."

I give her a sideways glance.

"There's a rumor—myth, or whatever—that there are three secret entrances around campus," Alexis says.

"Where?" I ask.

"Did you not hear the 'secret' part? All I know is that one might be in the library."

"That's not much to go on," I say. "The library is huge."

"I know."

We look at each other, then down at our hands. It feels weird—agreeing with each other.

"Start with Renee Linden, nee Jones. She was Caroline's RA," Alexis says. "She still works here, as head of student housing."

"What's she going to tell me?" I ask.

Alexis rolls her eyes. "Why Caroline went off on Natalie. The people who work here have more secrets than the rooms in your precious tunnels."

Alexis motions to get up.

"Wait," I say. "How do I know I can trust you?"

Alexis cocks her head at me. "Because we want the same thing."

I'm not exactly sure that's true. But sometimes a deal with the devil is better than no deal at all.

aside at dinner parties. *Your mom sure loves her Chardonnay, huh?* Stacy will talk shit about anyone as long as she can sniff out someone who's willing to participate.

I'm getting a very similar vibe from Renee Linden.

"Yeah." I throw in a nervous laugh. "Isabella was . . . well, I'm sure you've heard."

Renee's eyes glint greedily. "It's always the ones you don't expect, right?"

I want to reach across and shake her, ask her what type of sixteen-year-old, exactly, she would *expect* to be statutorily raped and murdered by a teacher. But I clutch my armrests and give her a grim smile. "That's kind of why I'm here," I say. "I have a college interview with a Wheatley alum, but I kinda want to cancel because she just seems . . . I don't know, weird? And I heard you were her RA, so I figured you may know her well."

"Oh yeah, I was an RA for two years." Renee beams. "Who is she?"

"Caroline Cormier-Frey."

"Oh, do I *know* her." Renee has completely forgotten about the line of students outside her office. "Caroline. Huh. Wow."

I lower my voice. "I heard she *attacked* her roommate."

"Uh-huh." Renee's voice tells me this isn't the first time she's told this story. "Looked like a cat pounced on poor Natalie's face. When girls fight, they can be *vicious*."

I don't say it, but I've had the urge to drag my fingernails down another girl's face. Caroline's own cousin, no less. Maybe that makes me vicious, too.

"Why would Caroline hurt her friend?" I ask. "They *were* friends, right?"

"Natalie was her only friend. That was the problem."

"Oh. So Caroline was a stage five clinger?"

"Something like that. Caroline had a lot of trouble fitting in, and Natalie eventually found her own group. Caroline probably couldn't take the rejection. Poor thing hasn't had an easy life."

CHAPTER
FIFTEEN

There's a line the length of a football field outside Renee Linden's office. All freshmen—some near tears, some complaining to the person behind them about how their roommate is the *worst*. Renee Linden must find their problems exhausting, because when it's my turn, she calls out "Next!" in a harried voice.

Renee Linden is tiny. Tiny enough to shop in the juniors section. Her desk is a shrine to her children; I count three of them as I take a seat across from her.

She looks at me and forces a smile—it's not unkind, but she obviously wants to get rid of me quickly.

"I don't know you," she says. "How come?"

"I'm new," I say. "Or I was last year. I'm Anne Dowling."

Renee's eyebrows lift a bit. "I do know you. I placed you in a room with Isabella Fernandez. Some year *you* must have had, huh?"

I don't miss the way Renee has leaned forward in her chair. I can practically smell the curiosity coming off of her. She reminds me of my mom's friend Stacy, who always pulls me

I wonder what qualifies as a difficult life for a Wheatley alum. Purebred stallion never placed at the Massachusetts derby? Then I remember that Alexis said Caroline's father died, and I feel like an awful person. "Sounds sad."

"It really is." Renee makes a sympathetic face. "The reason Caroline went after Natalie in the first place is because Nat requested a room change."

And now any kinship I felt with Caroline Cormier-Frey is lost. I mean, I had the urge to attack Alexis because she started a rumor that I'd killed my own roommate. But drawing blood over wanting to move out?

I'd hate to think what Caroline's capable of if someone *really* screwed her.

"Hey, Ms. Linden," I say, before I get up. She holds up a hand. "Call me Renee."

"Okay. I was kind of hoping to talk to Natalie, but I don't know what happened to her. Does she have family in the area or anything?"

"I know she had a brother," Renee says. "Liam? Lucas? I can't remember. Why do you want to talk to Natalie, anyway? Can't you just change your interview?"

I smile. "I don't think I can, actually."

In history, I whisper to Brent.

"Have you heard about a secret room in the library?" It comes out a little louder than I meant it to, because Kazmarkis snipes from across the room about the importance of being quiet while she finishes handing out today's outline.

"Everyone's heard about the mythical library room," Brent says. "It doesn't exist."

I bite the inside of my cheek as Kazmarkis strides back up to the front of the classroom. I have to balance the suspicion that Alexis may have been screwing with me about the library room with my irritation at the fact that we already have an essay due on Friday. Also, that Brent thinks I need clarification that a myth is something that isn't real.

He pulls my notebook toward him and writes in the inside flap.

What's this all about?

His forehead creases as he adds something.

Dr. Muller?

No, I write back.
Bullshit.
I slide his pen from his fingers and cross it out.

At the end of the painfully long hour, someone says my name. He's so quiet I barely hear it over the shuffling of papers and the zipping of laptop cases. I stand up and see Artie getting up from the table next to us, to Brent's left.

He passes a Post-it note to me. He's written *Shakespeare sonnet 40.*

"Find the book," he says, before slipping in with the line of people leaving the classroom.

I leave dinner a few minutes early to head to the library. The tables and study carrels in the main stacks are empty, save for a few overachievers. Starting tomorrow, the place will probably be mobbed.

I search for "Shakespeare" using the online catalogue. There are several hits, but only one looks like a complete volume of his sonnets. I write down the call number on the back of Artie's Post-it and do a few aimless laps around the stacks before enlisting the librarian's help.

"Excuse me," I ask. "But where can I find this book?"

She squints, reading the call number. "That's in the poetry room."

She points to a door at the back of the main stacks. I deflate a little. Is this the room Artie thought I was talking about?

"Thanks." I slip the Post-it in my pocket and head for the room. It's small—or cozy, if you're being polite—with a gas fireplace and a leather couch. There's a Scrabble box on the coffee table and a floor-to-ceiling rotunda-style bookcase. There's no overhead light—just a faint glow afforded by the sconces on the walls.

I trace my finger along the shelf toward the bottom, past Schuyler, Shelley, before I land on *Shakespeare's Complete Works: Sonnets.* I thumb through to forty and read it to myself, lingering on the last two lines.

Lascivious grace, in whom all ill well shows,
Kill me with spites yet we must not be foes.

Is this a clue or something? A riddle buried in some obscure Shakespearean sonnet? I don't have time for this crap. I'm about to close the book when the light catches the page, revealing a series of scratches in the white space at the bottom.

I run my fingers over it. Something is written here.

I hold my phone over the page for more light, but it's hard to tell if the scratches are letters or numbers. I fumble in my bag for a pencil. Once I find one, I place the Post-it note over the markings and shade the area with my pencil. Chelsea and I used this technique to trade notes in middle school.

I hold the Post-it note up to the light to study the impression.

UP – 3
RIGHT – 8

My gaze drops to where the book of sonnets was. I hold that place with one hand, and count in my head. The book up three spaces and eight to the right is a Norton anthology of poetry. It's a beast of a thing; I have to use both hands to dislodge it.

I'm about to give up, leave, and ask Artie why he led me on a poetry wild goose chase when I notice some sort of metal fixture at the back of the shelf, behind where the Norton anthology was. I reach and feel around the area.

It's a latch. I pull on it, not expecting the loud click that sounds. Like a lock being unbolted.

The right side of the rotunda creaks ever so slightly, opening to reveal a room behind the wall.

The hair on the back of my neck pricks. The door is about my height; I duck through it and gently close it behind me The room is wall-to-wall bookshelves. Priceless first editions.

The light from the room only reaches the first few steps, so I have to use the glow from my phone to guide me. The familiar smell of lime and damp air meets me at the bottom.

I've never been this far down the tunnels. I visualize the layout of the campus in my head—the library is on the southwest corner, on the opposite end from the dorms, and the secret tunnel to the Wheatley quarry. I head east, toward the center of campus where the tunnels converge.

As a precaution, I turn off my phone light and use the wall as my guide until I sense the floor sloping upward.

Lexington Hall was one of the oldest buildings on campus until it burned down in the fifties. But the basement was unscathed, and now the rooms house all of the archived student records. I know, because I've gone through them before.

I pause, shining my light down the hall.

Something isn't right: All of the room doors are open.

And the ground is littered with paper. Torn up, yellowed paper. Some are damp, the ink bleeding away from the rainwater that seeped up through the concrete.

I swallow away the lump in my throat and pick up a folder by my feet, the contents strewn god knows where. It's empty. A piece of beige paper with bleeding ink is stuck to it.

It's a handwritten page. A very poorly handwritten page. I hold my light up to it, but it's hopeless. Only two lines are legible.

My arm is still broke from the jail and I can't sleep without the headaches starting. If they make me go there again I don't think I'm coming back.

My stomach sours. I drop the note—journal entry?—and decide I need to get what I came for and get out: Caroline's file. And any others that mention Natalie Barnes.

I gasp when I look inside the room where the student records are kept. The door is unlocked; the filing cabinets are on their sides. Folders are strewn everywhere—torn records.

Someone turned this place inside out. Did they find what they were looking for?

And more importantly—what the hell was it?

CHAPTER
SIXTEEN

When I get back to my room, I can't shake the image of the mess in the tunnels. Someone was down there, looking for something.

I put all of my energy into finding Natalie Barnes's brother. Renee gave me an important clue—I google every male's name that starts with *L* plus the last name *Barnes* in the greater Massachusetts area.

I get a hit: Lucas Barnes, from Warwick, Rhode Island. Went to Pomona College in California and is now living in Boston, where he runs his own social media company called Net Space.

Warwick isn't that far from Boston. And kids from all over go to the Wheatley School—Phil is from California, I'm from New York. I think one of the dude bros—either Bingham or Oliver—is even from Rhode Island.

There's an address for Net Space.

After class, I head for the Back Bay area of Boston. I study the note from the tunnels on the train. After studying it for most of the ride, I can make out part of another sentence.

Want to run away but (something something) get beat like (something).

I can also discern a name: Charlie. I feel uneasy; is this a journal entry from someone who went to Wheatley years ago? If so, why is whoever wrote it talking about broken arms and beatings?

The conductor announces that we're at Fenway. I pocket the journal entry, doubtful that it's connected to Ms. C or Dr. Muller, but disturbed nonetheless.

Lucas Barnes's address is about a five-minute walk from the Fenway T stop. I follow the sign upstairs to a sleek, ultra-modern office space. It's clear whoever designed this place was going for "Zuckerberg."

A receptionist looks up at me as if I must be lost. "Can I help you?"

"Does Lucas Barnes work here?" I ask.

She smiles, as if I'm adorably stupid. "Of course he does. He founded Net Space."

I don't care enough to pretend I know what Net Space is. "Would I be able to speak to him?"

The receptionist glances at the enormous screen of her Mac-Book Pro and frowns. "He's booked until the end of the day. Maybe if you told me what this is about?"

"His sister."

She cocks her head at me. I can tell this is the first this woman has heard about Lucas Barnes having a sister.

"He'll be taking lunch in about fifteen minutes," she says. "You could wait for him, and see if he's free to chat."

I look up when I hear murmuring; the receptionist is looking at me while she says something in the ear of a tall, lanky man in square-framed glasses. He's wearing skinny jeans and a plaid shirt. He's kind of hipster-cute. But not in an ironic way. More like he probably had this look all of his life and one day it became cool.

He takes me in, polite confusion registering on his face.

"Hi," I say. "You don't know me, but I was wondering if I could ask you a few questions. I go to the Wheatley School."

Recognition flits across his face. I'm sure he's going to tell me to get the hell out, until he smiles and hooks his thumbs through the belt loops of his jeans. "Sure. I'm pretty hungry though, so would you mind if we do it over lunch?"

"Not at all. Thanks, Mr. Barnes."

He laughs. "Call me Luke. Mr. Barnes reminds me of my dad."

Luke holds the door for me as we leave the office. "I'm sorry, I didn't get your name," he says.

"It's Anne." I follow him into a pizza place next door. He tells the cashier his name and takes out his wallet to pay for the spinach calzone they had waiting for him.

"Want anything?" he asks.

I shake my head. I'm thrown slightly off balance by how familiar this feels. Ms. C was the same way—always checking to see if there was anything she could do for you.

Not was. Is. I can't start thinking of her in the past tense.

We find a table as Luke prattles on about how this place makes the best pizza in Boston. I don't say that that's like being the cleanest pig in the pen. He takes a bite of his calzone and makes an apologetic gesture while he chews. "You look a little young to want a job at Net Space."

"I don't want a job. Actually, I don't know what Net Space is."

Luke smiles. "We're a social media platform. Kind of like Foursquare. You can check into places on your phone and interact with people who are checked in."

"Like, to meet people?"

"You'd be surprised how hard that is to do in the city," he says. "So, you don't want to work at Net Space."

"I wanted to ask you about Natalie."

Luke takes a pull from his soda. "Natalie. My sister."

"Yeah."

"Huh." Luke contemplates this. "I haven't seen Natalie in ten years." There's no trace of emotion in his voice.

"She was my teacher," I say, slowly. "At the Wheatley School. For a few months."

"That's impossible. She didn't go to college. Last we heard, she'd been arrested. Plus, she was expelled from Wheatley in the ninth grade."

"Tenth," I correct him. He sets his calzone down.

"Why are you looking for her?"

"We were sort of close." I shrug. "She just up and left, and then I found out that she was using a fake identity. Have you heard the name Jessica Cross before?"

Luke shakes his head. "You're sure it was Natalie?"

"I'm positive. She left in May, and no one's seen or heard from her."

"Well, that does sound like Natalie."

"What do you mean?"

Luke leans back in his chair and sighs. "Look, the thing you have to understand about my sister is that she was really screwed up. Ever since she was a baby. Always freaking out if my parents were a minute late getting home. Super clingy, always crying about something."

"You said 'my' parents."

"Natalie was adopted. An overseas thing, when I was little. It was all really sketchy . . . the lawyer said she was from the Ukraine, but they could never come up with a birth certificate. The psychiatrists said lots of kids in those situations have social problems. But Nat's issues got worse when she went away to school."

"You didn't go to Wheatley?" I ask.

"Nope. I went to Catholic school. Nat's social worker said the structure of boarding school would be good for her. She was a smart kid, always reading above her age group and stuff like that."

"So what happened?" I ask. "Why did they expel her?"

"She snuck out and got caught off campus with some older guy," Luke says.

"Do you remember his name?"

Luke shakes his head. "I'd know if I heard it—the guy was a big druggie. Parents were loaded, obviously. He actually got onto the Olympic snowboard team a few years ago. Got kicked off when he failed a drug test."

"What happened to her after that?"

"I . . . well," Luke says. "Being expelled from Wheatley is a huge deal, apparently, and she had to go back to public school. It was brutal there for her. When she stared cutting herself . . . my parents sent her to this program for teens. Then she ran away from it."

Luke polishes off the rest of his calzone as if he'd just told me a story about a great-uncle who smoked three packs a day, and not his own sister's downward spiral. Luke notices me watching him and wipes his mouth.

"I know I sound a little . . . harsh when I talk about Nat," he says. "But she put us through a lot of crap. We all tried to help her, but she just didn't care. My parents spent all this money on rehab, and tutors to get her through high school. Then she'd turn around and steal whatever she could pawn for more pills and run away. My parents finally cut all ties with her when we heard she was living with a dealer."

Luke looks up and frowns when he sees my expression. "I loved my sister, but she's a train wreck. There was nothing we could do to help her. I haven't even seen her in years."

I don't know what to say; not because I don't believe Luke, but because I'm having trouble reconciling the version of Ms. C I have in my head with the version of Natalie he's given me.

He's her brother. *You were her student for a few months.*

Is the answer as simple as Natalie trying to escape her past? Did she feel like becoming Jessica Cross was the only way to leave behind the person she was?

I think of Dr. Muller, bound and gagged on the floor of his apartment.

The simple explanation doesn't cut it for me. Not when the only other person who knows Ms. Cross's secret is dead.

"When did you last hear from her?" I ask Luke.

"Probably nine, ten years ago. She called my mom from Georgia when she was released from jail. Said they were turning her over to some halfway house for women. My dad had just died, and my mom wanted to go get her, bring her home. But Natalie said she couldn't come back."

"Why?"

"She probably realized she used up most of her chances."

I hesitate. "She's different. I saw her every day, for two months. She wasn't on drugs. She was happy. She had a boyfriend."

Luke smiles, but it doesn't reach his eyes. "I'll believe it when I see it." He wraps up the rest of his sandwich and leans forward in his chair. "I've got to get back to work. Here's my card, in case you hear from her."

I drop Luke Barnes's card into my bag. "Thanks. Should I give you my email address, in case she contacts you?"

Luke gives me a wry smile. "If I know my sister, that's not going to happen. Trust me."

"Thanks again for your time."

I leave the pizza place. I'm ready to cross the street when a car speeds by, startling me back onto the sidewalk.

"Asshole," I mutter.

That's when I notice the restaurant across the street. CURRY HOUSE is lit up in red neon. Something pings in my brain.

Dr. Muller had said he and Ms. C ate at an Indian restaurant on their date.

I pull up a map on my phone and search how far the Isabella Stewart Gardner museum is from here.

It's three blocks away.

They were *here*.

Luke may be telling the truth about not seeing Natalie, but I'm almost certain that Natalie saw him.

CHAPTER
SEVENTEEN

Ms. C—Natalie—was here with Dr. Muller, about five months ago. It may as well have been an entire lifetime ago.

The fact that she got nervous about running into her estranged brother tells me nothing new. After all, if Luke walked up to her and said her name, she would have had a ton of explaining to do to Dr. Muller, her new boyfriend who knew her as Jessica.

Natalie not wanting to see Luke doesn't tell me anything about who, or what, she was running from, and even more important, why she came back—but I'm here.

They were here.

And that fact alone gives me hope that she's still out there. Possibly even alive.

I send Alexis a text when I'm on the train.

Need a name . . . Wheatley guy Caroline's age.
Olympic snowboarder?

She replies almost immediately.

Spencer Vandenberg. Caroline DEFINITELY wouldn't have been friends w/ him.

I respond:

He was with Natalie the night that got her expelled. Need to talk to him.

I watch the little ellipsis at the bottom of the screen that says Alexis is typing. It goes away. After about a minute, she responds.

I can make that happen. Brookline Country Club. Sunday at noon.

When I get back to the dorms, I google "halfway houses in Acworth, Georgia." I call the closest one to the women's penitentiary where I assume Natalie would have been sent after her arrest.

"Acworth Home for Women."

"Hi. Um. I'm looking for my sister. I think she may have stayed with you guys before."

"We don't give out information about former patients," the woman snips.

"Please. I'm really worried about her. She might be in trouble, and you were the last ones to have seen her."

"Try the National Center for Missing Adults," she says.

"Look, I just need to know when she was last with you guys. Her name is Natalie Barnes."

"I'm sorry, but I can't help you." The woman hangs up on me. I almost throw my phone across the room. No one can help me, from the looks of it.

There are a couple of hours until dinnertime, and Remy has been texting me nonstop to meet her, April, and Kelsey on the quad. The quad is where everyone hangs out when the weather is nice. Today is picturesque—the rare type of warm fall afternoon you'd sooner see on a CW show set at a college.

I swap my blazer for a cardigan and grab my bag. As I'm reaching for my phone, I get another text.

But it's not from Remy; I don't recognize the number. Or the area code, for that matter.

ADMIN BUILDING BASEMENT. ROOM 105.

The only rooms in the Administration Building basement are in the tunnels.

Who are you? I text back.

Maybe there's someone who can help me after all.

There's still no response from the number when I reach the library steps. Cole and Murali emerge from the front doors, waving when they see me.

"You're not going to the quad?" Murali asks.

"Just have to print something for class quick," I say. "I'll see you guys there."

They don't question why I need to do this on a Friday afternoon. I slip inside the library, doing a lap around the stacks instead of heading straight for the poetry room. I don't know who could be watching me—including the person who texted me.

I hide behind a bookshelf and text the number again.

Really . . . who are you?

I poke my head around the shelf and scan the study area. No one sitting at the tables takes out their phone. I don't hear a text message alert or a vibrating sound.

I nearly talk myself into heading back toward the quad. Someone could be down there, waiting for me in Room 105. Someone with whom I may not particularly want to be trapped underground.

I come up with a plan: I'll keep my flashlight off and feel my way around, so if someone is down there, they won't see me coming. That way I'll have a head start if it's someone I don't want to see. I triple-check my purse to make sure I have my pepper spray and my metal nail file. I hate to consider the possibility that I'll need the file for something other than picking a lock, but, quite frankly, if it comes to it, I'll stab a bitch.

I don't need Anthony or Brent to follow me down this time. I've got my own back.

There's a wiry freshman or sophomore boy on the couch in the poetry room, reading Camus's *The Stranger*. His hair is swept to the side.

"Hey," I say. "Did anyone . . . come through here?"

The boy blinks at me and goes back to reading. "No."

"Are you sure?"

"Yes." He doesn't look up at me this time. I roll my eyes, because I've read *The Stranger*, and it's not *that* absorbing. Or this kid is just a pretentious little shit who thinks I'm not worth his time.

In any case, I can't open the secret passage right in front of him, so I need him out of this room. Stat. I plop down next to him on the couch, even though there are several open seats. He gives me the side eye.

I grin. "Gorgeous day, huh?"

"Yup."

"So are you reading that for a class?"

He turns the page. "No."

I have to hand it to him—he has a high tolerance for annoyance. I fish around my bag for headphones and queue up the most annoying song in my iTunes. I stick the headphones in my ears and blast the volume so anyone within a ten-foot radius can hear the music.

The boy makes a disgusted face and gets up, stuffing *The Stranger* into his messenger bag. Then I'm alone.

I find the hidden latch on the poetry bookshelf and slip through the door. I descend the staircase, leaving the light from the library room behind. I don't want to risk using my flashlight, so I have to feel around with my foot to find the next step until I get to the bottom.

Right, left, straight ahead. I practically have the layout of the tunnels memorized by now. I use the wall to guide me, taking the path a step at a time. It's silent down here, save for the occasional *plink* of water hitting stone.

I'm holding my breath by the time I'm beneath the administration building. I don't see light emanating from any of the rooms. I relax a bit and let myself shine the light from my phone on the doors until I find 105.

It's cracked open. I grab the knob with one hand, standing behind the door as I pull it open. "Who's there?" I whisper.

Silence. One hand hovering over my canister of pepper spray, I shine my phone light into the room. It's empty.

I reach for my flashlight to get a better look at the contents of the room as I step inside. It's empty, except for a rusted metal folding chair and a water-stained cardboard box.

As I let go of the door, it slams shut behind me. My heart leaps into my throat. I turn around and shine my flashlight over the door. There's no knob from the inside.

Panic corners me. I slam my palm against the door. "Is someone out there?"

I press my ear to the door, expecting to hear footsteps. Nothing. I'm alone down here. I shine my light around the room. There's a rubber doorstop at my feet. I must have kicked it out of the way when I opened the door.

I check my phone, even though I know I'm too far underground to get any service. All that's on the screen is a "Message

Delivery Failed" notification, for the text I sent to the mystery number earlier.

Calm down, calm down. They sent you down here for a reason. I tear open the cardboard box and force myself to look inside, fearing this may be a *Se7en* type situation and Natalie Barnes's body is inside.

But there's nothing except ancient-looking math textbooks.

And a note scribbled on computer paper: one that was definitely torn from outside room 105's door.

DO NOT SHUT DOOR!!! LOCKS FROM THE INSIDE

All of the air leaves my lungs. Whoever texted me *did* send me to this room for a reason.

Because they want me to die down here.

CHAPTER
EIGHTEEN

I bang on the door until the skin on my knuckles is raw. It's useless: No one can hear me. No one saw me come down here. I made sure of that.

I ignored every single instinct I had, and now I'm trapped.

How long will it be before anyone notices I'm missing? Probably not until check-in tonight. And even then, no one will think to look for me down here. The tunnels are sealed off: They're the last place anyone will think to look. If Dean Tierney or any of the other teachers even know about the secret entrance.

Tierney. For all I know, she could be the one who sent me down here in the first place. She knows something about Ms. C—she had Natalie Barnes's file on her desk. If she's involved, or trying to cover something up, what better way to shut me up than to stage my unfortunate demise?

It could be days before anyone finds me down here.

"Help!" I scream until my lungs are sore, beating my fists against the door. "HELP!"

I stand back, one shoulder out, ready to charge at the door.

Then I crumble to the ground, near tears. There's no way I'm breaking that door down. My breathing quickens: I think I'm having a panic attack.

I walked right into a trap. But who set it? If not Tierney, it's someone else who's familiar with the tunnels. Who knows about this room and the broken door.

Someone who went to Wheatley—like Caroline Cormier-Frey.

Or Alexis.

Or, more likely, someone with easy access to campus and the tunnels. Like the man in the administration building the other night.

The scent of mildew and dust in the room crowds out my thoughts. I've never been claustrophobic—I mean, hello, I live in Manhattan—but reality is quickly sinking in.

I stand and pick up the folding chair, forcing it closed. And I charge at the door.

Anne!

I drop the chair. Someone called my name. A guy. I beat my fist against the door. "In here!"

"Anne?" There it is again. I'm not hearing things. A cry of relief bubbles in my throat. I bang both fists on the door until someone yanks it open, and I nearly fall forward into the hall.

Cole grabs my arms to steady me. I jerk away from him. "What are you doing?"

"How about a thank you?" Cole opens the door, inspecting the area where the knob should be on the inside. "What are you doing down here?"

I search his face, but it's too dark to gauge his expression. "Did you follow me?"

I sense him shift where he's standing. "Yeah," he says. "I wanted to talk to you, but you never came out of the poetry room. You left a book out. That's when I saw the latch in the shelf."

"You *followed* me."

"You're lucky I did!"

I inhale through my nose. Out through my mouth. I'm not sure being down here with Cole is any better than being trapped in that room. "Let's just get out of here."

He doesn't argue; instead, he shines his phone light ahead of him and leads the way. When the ground begins to slope upward, the bricks unevenly spaced, he extends an arm to me. Because even though we're not on the best of terms, Cole is a gentleman.

"Thanks." I lay my hand on his forearm tentatively. "You said you wanted to talk to me. That's why you came down here."

Cole hesitates. "I just . . . wanted to say sorry. For making things weird."

He's also a terrible liar.

"What is this really about?" Worry and suspicion surround me like unwelcome friends. Even though we've had our issues, I've never explicitly thought that I can't trust Cole. He's always the levelheaded, thoughtful one, reining Murali and Brent in when they're doing something on the wrong side of stupid.

But something feels off about him being down here. When I catch him glancing down the tunnel that leads to Aldridge and beyond, I know exactly why he's really here.

"You knew I was coming down here," I say. "That's why you followed me. To figure out how to get back in the tunnels."

"What are you talking about?"

I stop in my tracks, halting us both. "I'm not dumb, Cole. I know that you guys—the crew team—you use the tunnels for the Drop."

The muscles in his forearm tense when I say the words. *The Drop.* The dangerous initiation prank the crew team members play on the new recruits. Blindfolding them and making them jump off a quarry into freezing cold water, tied to what they believe are cinder blocks.

If the guys can't get into the tunnels, their secret path to the quarry is cut off.

"I'm sorry," Cole says. I jerk my hand away from his arm and walk ahead of him.

"You could have just asked me how to get down here."

"And what, you would have told me?" Cole snorts, catching up with me in two strides. He's the tallest guy in school—nearly six feet. Lean, yet muscular. He's also probably the best looking, but we're kind of past that.

"Anne, you have to admit that you've been acting super sketchy," he says. "I mean, one minute you're asking me where to find Casey Shepherd, and the next day, everyone's saying that his dad and Coach Tretter killed Matt Weaver."

It's been a while since anyone's said Matt Weaver's name to me. It sounds all wrong coming out of Cole's mouth—as if my two lives are colliding. In one, almost everyone believes the "official" story from last year. In the other, I'm just biding my time until the real story comes out. Because if I've learned anything from what happened with Matt Weaver, it's that the truth can't stay buried forever.

"I didn't have anything to do with that," I tell Cole. We're at the bottom of the stairs that lead up to the library room now. He's quiet until we get to the top. Until we've reached the light, and I can see his face clearly.

He doesn't believe me. But I definitely don't expect the words that come out of his mouth next. "You must think we're the biggest assholes in the world."

"What do you mean?"

"The stuff . . . we do to the younger guys," Cole says. "We didn't come up with it, but we do it anyway. You probably think we're the scum of the earth."

And if he knew the secrets I'm keeping, he'd think even worse of me. "It's fine."

Cole runs a hand through his hair. "Just don't hold it against Brent, okay? I know he's messed up over everything that happened."

"It's fine," I say. "I don't hold it against any of you."

Cole smiles, his face relaxing. But I'm not thinking of Brent—or Cole—as we step into the poetry room, shutting the secret door behind us.

I'm thinking of Room 105—and tracking down the son of a bitch who sent me there.

Cole and I arriving at the quad together raises a few eyebrows: namely, Kelsey's and Remy's. An unpleasant feeling passes through me, like my stomach is trying to swallow itself. I have no idea what's going on between Cole and Kelsey—if they're together or not and I've violated some sort of girl code.

I'm becoming a fringe member of this group, and I have no one to blame but myself.

Remy's the one to say something. "Where were you guys?"

"Had to print the reading for Knight's class," Cole says. "I used my paper quota for the week. Anne lent me some."

Murali shoots Cole a questioning look, and I have to wonder if he was in on the plan the whole time: Follow Anne. Find the tunnels.

Kelsey passes around a pack of gum, seemingly satisfied with Cole's explanation. Remy shoots me a probing glance, and just like that, I'm back in Casey Shepherd's kitchen during the spring formal after-party. I remember the look Remy gave me when she walked in on Cole and me. Saw me drunkenly leaning on his shoulder.

I don't have time for this crap. The conversation shifts to after-dinner plans, and I take out my phone. When no one's looking at me, I dial the number from earlier and discreetly press the phone to my ear.

The number you have dialed is not valid.

Remy shakes me awake. My heartbeat thunders in my ears. *Fire. Intruder.* I jolt upright.

"You were freaking out." Remy looks wide awake. Her alarm clock says it's three A.M. I wonder how long she's been up. "Like, tossing and turning. And whimpering."

I put a hand to my chest, willing myself to calm down. In my dream, I was in the basement of Amherst, where the tunnel entrance used to be. And someone locked the door at the top of the stairs, trapping me down there.

I squeeze my eyes shut, trying to remember the person's face, even though it means nothing.

"Anne? You okay?"

"Yeah. Just a nightmare. Sorry I woke you."

Remy gets up from the edge of my bed, and I nearly reach out. Beg her to stay next to me. "Hey—Rem?"

"What's up?" she asks around a yawn.

"I don't know. I'm just kind of too freaked out to sleep." I pull my comforter up to my chin.

Remy crawls into bed next to me. "Scoot."

I shift so I'm pressed against the wall. "Sorry I'm being such a baby."

"You're not." She yawns again. "I . . . get them too sometimes."

My throat is dry, my voice raspy. "Is it because of everything that happened last year?"

I know I'm testing dangerous waters, but Remy is my best friend here. And I want to talk to someone about everything that happened—not my parents or any of the worthless psychiatrists they sent me to. Definitely not Anthony, even though he wouldn't listen anyway.

"I don't know." Remy pulls her knees to her chest. "I try not to think about it. I mean, I just can't, you know?"

"What do you mean?"

Remy's porcelain skin is radiant in the bit of moonlight sneaking through the blinds. "I . . . I've slept over at his *house* before. Mr. Westbrook's. I never thought he—I just don't like to think about it."

Her voice has changed. And I know then that I'll never be able to confide in Remy. How would our friendship change if she knew I was there? If she knew I was still in contact with Alexis?

"Me neither," I lie.

I feign a yawn and roll onto my side. As I'm pretending to doze off, Remy climbs out of my bed and returns to hers.

CHAPTER
NINETEEN

I'm not thrilled about being forced to ask for Dennis's help again—especially not after last time, where I got the vibe that he wasn't taking me seriously.

But I'd say that what happened with Room 105, and the text message, has escalated this situation to very serious.

Remy and Brent have a Student Government Association meeting after breakfast, so I'm able to sneak away and head downtown.

Dennis is smoking a cigarette outside the police station. He stubs it out when he sees me, swatting the air in front of him to clear the smoke.

"Anne. Hey."

"Hey. Do you have a few minutes?"

Dennis scratches behind his ear. He seems uncomfortable—maybe embarrassed I caught him smoking again. "I'm actually headed out for a bit. Coffee break."

"Mind if I tag along?" I hesitate. "Something came up, and I don't really know who else to go to."

He doesn't question why I can't tell Tierney, or an adult I trust at the school. I don't have an adult I trust at that place.

"Sure," he says. "Let's talk while we walk."

The Dunkin' Donuts is two blocks from the precinct. I tell Dennis what happened yesterday afternoon, and how a Google search of the phone number didn't turn up anything.

"Texts are near impossible to trace. If the number isn't attached to a valid account or business, you won't find anything with reverse lookup," Dennis says. My face must fall, because he softens a bit. "Here, let me see the message."

I open the text and hand him my phone. Dennis mouths the number to himself as he enters it into his own phone and dials. He frowns, getting the same invalid number message I did.

"I don't even think that's a valid area code." He hits end call. "Seems like the person is hiding behind a burner."

"A burner?"

"There are apps to disguise your phone number," Dennis says. "Generates a fake number that expires within hours or minutes of using it."

My stomach sinks. "So there's no way of tracking the person down."

"It's not impossible."

But it may as well be. Or at least that's what I'm gathering from his tone.

"Anne, if someone's harassing you, you've got to file a police report," Dennis says. "There's only so much I can do to help you. Off the books, at least."

My head feels heavy. You'd need an ancient scroll to list the people who would want to lock me in a room and never see me come out.

It's possible that the Room 105 trap has nothing to do with me digging into what happened to Dr. Muller and Natalie Barnes.

Dennis pauses outside the Dunkin' Donuts, clearly signaling that he wants to go in alone. And I see why when I look through the door.

Anthony, waiting on the other side.

"Shit," I mutter.

Dennis casts an apologetic glance my way as Anthony looks up. Confusion registers on his face when he sees me. Then something else: annoyance.

"I didn't know you were meeting someone," I tell Dennis. "I'll—I guess I'll talk to you some other time."

"Hey—Anne—wait. I called Ant to check up on him. I didn't know—"

My eyes feel prickly as I turn to get the hell out of there.

"Wait."

But it's not Dennis who called after me. Anthony jogs to catch up with me, bringing the faint scent of motor oil and Big Red gum with him.

"I had no idea you were meeting up with Dennis today," I say. I can't bring myself to look at his face. "I wasn't, like, purposely trying to make things awkward."

"You think I care about awkward? Anne, hold up. You told him you were *worried* about me?"

I stop. I face him, even though I'm terrified I'll cry if I look him in the eye. "Yes, and now I look like a freaking idiot because obviously you're fine, and it's really only me you don't want to see."

He opens his mouth, as if he's going to disagree, then closes it. "I told you to stay away from Dennis."

"I'm sorry. I wasn't aware I had to obey your commands."

Anthony tilts his head back, makes a frustrated noise. "You know I don't mean it like that. You *have* to stay away from Dennis, or we'll both wind up in deep shit."

"Is that why you're staying away from me? You're afraid of getting in trouble?" I don't know where this is coming from. Probably from the part of me that isn't content with how our last conversation ended. Even though slapping him in the face felt good at the time. "A few months ago, you told me you're falling for me, then last week, you said all that horrible shit."

Anthony takes a step toward me so no one can hear him. "I almost took a bullet for you. What more do you want?"

I don't know. That's the honest answer. This summer, I would have said that I wanted to be with him. To pick up where we left off. To see if that spark between us—the crazy hot kisses, that inexplicable pull—could possibly translate into something real.

But I don't know what's real anymore. And that whatever it was—the thing that drew me to Anthony like a moth to the light—is gone.

CHAPTER
TWENTY

The first thing of mine that Ms. C ever graded was a response paper to Cicero's argument before Caesar. I completely BS'ed my way through it, because I figured I was already screwed with a bunch of subpar grades from when Professor Upton taught the class.

Ms. C handed it back to me with a note on the back: *Anne, this is thoughtful, thorough, and smart. Well done!*

At first I thought she was screwing with me. But she wore me down with her exhaustingly nice personality and refusal to accept anything from me that wasn't my best. She was funny, too, in that self-deprecating way nice people use to let you know that their niceness isn't just an act.

Too bad it was after all.

And even though I have no one to blame but myself for it, I feel similarly duped by Anthony. I should have recognized his passion for aggression, his bravery as the inability to walk away from a fight.

I should have realized that I was ignoring Anthony's worst qualities because they mirrored my own.

But Ms. C is different. I want to believe that the woman I knew was the real Natalie Barnes—not the mysterious train wreck that her brother described.

She believed in me. She was the only teacher at this school who didn't view me as some sort of screw-up. I don't know if it was real or not, but it doesn't matter.

Someone out there knows what happened to her and Dr. Muller, and I'm going to find them.

After going for a jog with Remy on Sunday morning, I shower and leave to meet Alexis at the Brookline Country Club.

If I keep running around the greater Boston area like this, I'm going to spend all of my allowance for the semester on Charlie cards and train tickets. Maybe I should get a job. That would really make my dad crap himself.

I get lost looking for the country club, so it's about twenty after twelve by the time I get there. There's a black Escalade parked by the curb. I tap on the driver's window.

Alexis scowls when she rolls the window down. "You're late."

"That's quite an astute observation." I'm feeling pissy. "Just a tip—if you're trying to avoid being recognized, you might want to get rid of the WESTBROOK FOR SENATE bumper sticker."

"Get in," Alexis snaps.

I swallow as I round the other side and open the door. I can't believe I'm getting into a car with Alexis Westbrook. I'm still not convinced this scenario won't end with my body being dumped in a wetland somewhere.

My gaze wanders to Alexis's cup holder. Her phone, in a pink and green Kate Spade case, rests inside it. My fingers itch to scroll through it, see if Alexis is the one who sent me to Room 105.

But why would she help me if she was just going to turn around and try to get rid of me? As much as I'd rather believe she's lying to me, I can tell that Alexis's hatred for Caroline is real.

And I know Alexis well enough by now to be sure of one thing: She only fakes niceness. Her hatred is always real.

"Are you sure Spencer's going to be here?" I ask as she flashes an ID card to get us through the security gate.

"Yes. And he'll be here every day until his trust fund runs dry and he has to find a real job."

I trail after her once we're in the lot. "Real job? He works here?"

"Not exactly." Alexis eyes me, like I'm a child who needs everything explained to her. "Spencer Vandenberg is the biggest dealer for Massachusetts one-percenters. He ran Wheatley's most infamous prescription drug ring."

"Drug ring?" I'm not naïve—I went to a prep school in New York City. Kids stole Xanax and Oxycontin from their parents and sold them all the time. But since I've been at Wheatley, I haven't heard a peep about drugs other than weed.

In any case, an actual drug ring is serious shit. If Natalie had gotten mixed up with a dealer—a dealer with a ton of money, no less—we could have a real lead.

I follow Alexis up the steps to the clubhouse. A sprawling golf course, tennis courts, and an Olympic-sized pool loom in the background.

"Hello, Miss Westbrook." An attendant flashes Alexis a wary smile as he eyes her member card. "I see you have a guest. We'll need to photocopy her ID so we have it on file."

I pass him my Wheatley ID and he disappears into the back. Alexis gives me the side eye.

"You knew you were coming to a country club. Did you have to dress like a Kardashian?"

I keep my mouth shut, but if she says something like that again, I swear I'll punch her in the boobs. I'm wearing camel-colored jeans and a slouchy cream cardigan over a black tank top. I was *going* for Kate Moss. Alexis can suck it.

The attendant gives me back my ID and tells us to enjoy our day. Alexis doesn't thank him as she yanks me toward the restaurant area, which has a 180 view of the golf course with floor-to-ceiling windows.

She drags me to the bar, where a girl in a white blouse pounces on us. "What can I get for you, ladies?"

I eye the drink special for the day: a vodka Collins. I wonder if she'll card me. Alexis gives me the stink eye as if to say *Don't even think about it.*

"Two lemonades," Alexis says. She leans in to whisper in my ear. "To our right."

I glance over my shoulder, at an elderly couple trying to crack open a lobster.

"Not them." Alexis nods a few degrees left. A good-looking guy is sitting by himself, nose in his iPhone. He has ear-length honey-colored hair and a killer tan. He looks like one of those guys who makes a living out of accusing people he went to college with of stealing his ideas.

The guy lifts his gaze. When he sees Alexis, a sly grin spreads across his face. Alexis grabs her drink and nudges me to follow her.

"Well, well, well. Look who's here." Spencer leans back in his chair, folding his arms across his chest. "Who's your friend?"

"Anne, this is Spencer," Alexis sniffs. "Spencer interned in my father's office. Until he got fired."

Spencer's jaw sets. "Still in hiding?"

"Still unemployed?" Alex smiles at him, but her eyes shoot daggers.

Spencer laughs. "I just got back from a board tour of the Alps. Would you ladies like to join me?" He's already pulled out two chairs for us. Alexis sits, and I follow her lead. Almost instantly, a waitress appears.

"A bottle of that sparkling rosé for the table." Spencer grins at her.

The waitress nods, without a second glance at Alexis or me to ask for our IDs.

"And a Waldorf salad," Alexis adds.

"So," Spencer says when the waitress is gone, "how did I get so lucky? I hope you're not trying to get me arrested or anything."

"Don't be disgusting. This isn't a social call." Alexis picks up her fork and examines it. She waves the waitress back over. "Excuse me? This is dirty."

"People like you are the reason the terrorists hate us," I hiss at Alexis.

Spencer laughs. Alexis glares at him. "Tell us about Natalie Barnes."

"Whoa." Spencer sits forward. "What are you guys asking about Natalie for?"

"You tell us. Why'd she get expelled for being off campus with you, while you only got a slap on the wrist?"

"Oh, Lex." Spencer takes a sip from his water. "I think you know the answer to that. I was a champion."

"Some champion. Remind me again, what'd the Olympic drug committee find in your system?" Alexis demands. "Adderall?"

Spencer's smile fades. I want to shake Alexis; first rule of interrogating someone is to make sure they don't get hostile.

"We just want to know what happened between you and Natalie," I cut in. "That's all."

"Look, I barely remember her," Spencer says. "We hooked up a couple times. I didn't talk to her at all after she got kicked out."

I lower my voice. "I know you were with her. The night she was caught off campus."

Spencer covers his mouth with the back of his hand. A classic move when someone is trying to maintain a poker face. "You have to understand, I was kind of a dick back then."

"Oh, we understand completely," Alexis says.

"Whatever. Do you want to hear what happened or not?" Spencer looks at his Rolex. "I've got a meeting in a few."

"Please continue," I say, shooting Alexis a look. She stabs

her salad that's materialized before her, keeping one eye on Spencer.

"Okay, so before construction started at the annex, it was kind of a thing to sneak on the land to hang out." Spencer mimes smoking a joint. "That night, I was meeting . . . a friend. Natalie wanted to tag along. I made her go ahead while I waited by the car."

"For your *friend*," Alexis cuts in. She and I share a look. No doubt that Spencer was selling drugs to this friend of his.

"Yeah. So, I finish up and go to find Natalie, and I hear footsteps. Running. She screams, then some guy yells at her 'Get back here, what are you doing here,' and then I saw the cop car parked at the overlook," Spencer says. "Someone must have seen us trespassing and called them. So I took off for my car."

"You didn't wait for her?" I ask. "Great boyfriend."

"It didn't make a difference anyway," Spencer says. "I got busted sneaking back into my dorm. Goddard expelled Natalie the next morning. He was *pissed*. I heard he called every headmaster and dean he knew and told them what she did." Spencer looks thoughtful for a minute. "Never got my Sox jersey back from her."

I stare at him. "So you definitely haven't seen Natalie since?"

"Nah. We didn't keep in touch." He shrugs, returning my stare.

"How about my cousin?" Alexis cuts in. "Caroline Cormier-Frey. Do you remember her? She was Natalie's roommate."

Spencer laughs. "I can't remember what I had for breakfast, Lexie."

Alexis grabs my wrist under the table. *L-I-E* she spells out with her finger.

"Good talk," Spencer says, standing up. "I really do have somewhere to be, though." He nods to Alexis. "Give my regards to your pops."

Alexis's expression is murderous as Spencer slips out the door, onto the golf course.

"How do you know he was lying?" I say.

"Because," Alexis says. "Caroline interned in my father's office after college. She and Spencer would have worked there around the same time."

"Maybe he just didn't notice her."

Alexis raises an eyebrow. "It's hard not to notice someone who calls a meeting over the copy paper tray being left empty. The other interns called her Caro-whine."

Sounds familiar. When she still went to Wheatley, Alexis once left me a sticky note for daring to have a coffee maker in my dorm room.

"I need you to do something," I tell Alexis. "If you're comfortable snooping through Caroline's phone, that is."

Alexis smirks at me. "Do you realize who you're talking to?"

CHAPTER
TWENTY-ONE

While I'm waiting for Alexis to get the chance to comb through Caroline's phone in search of a burner app—or any incriminating text messages—I gather more intel on Spencer Vandenberg.

There's a lot of information about him, since he was in the public eye leading up to the Winter Olympics eight years ago. But there's nothing that suggests a connection to the Barnes family, or even that Spencer is anything more than your standard drug-peddling yuppie scumbag.

U.S. Olympic Team Cuts Competitive
Snowboarder Who Failed Drug Test

The Olympic Committee announced Tuesday morning that FIS World Championship silver medalist Spencer Vandenberg, 22, would not be competing in the Torino games. The announcement follows last week's headline that Vandenberg, an alum of the Wheatley School, tested positive for trace amounts of a banned substance during an International Olympic Committee drug test.

Neither Vandenberg nor the coach of the men's snowboard team could be reached for comment.

There's a picture of Spencer, posing with a banner for Mountain Crush energy drink. I'm going to venture a guess that he lost that sponsorship.

So Spencer got off with a slap on the wrist because he was an Olympic hopeful, only to throw his chances at a medal down the toilet. Meanwhile, Natalie gets expelled, her life takes turn after turn for the worse—and somehow, years later, she returns to the scene of the crime.

Did she blame Spencer for everything that happened to her? Was making her way back to Wheatley the first step in a plot for payback?

Something keeps bugging me about Spencer's story. He said Natalie was screaming and running from a man. I've been busted being somewhere I wasn't supposed to be before. Many times. You always run, but you never scream. Crying and pleading for forgiveness is the best way to handle a cop.

You don't scream unless you have a reason to.

Maybe Natalie didn't scream because she saw a police officer. Maybe she saw something else—something she wasn't supposed to see. Spencer had just conducted a drug deal at the annex; what if someone other than the cops were waiting in the woods and Natalie had gotten caught in the crossfire, so to speak? Even slimy, low-level high school drug dealers have enemies.

Possibly, enemies so powerful that Natalie had to take drastic measures to evade them. But if Wheatley really was the scene of the crime, why would she return?

Unless her only option was to hide in plain sight.

By Friday, I still haven't heard from Alexis and I'm almost fresh out of leads. So I start digging into Ms. C's personnel file. She was good at pretending to be Jessica Cross, but she must have slipped up to someone in the past eight years—given someone a reason to doubt her real identity.

One thing sticks out to me on the resume—Ms. C worked at the Cambridge Public Library for three years before taking the job at Wheatley. Cambridge is nearby—maybe tomorrow I can stop by. On Sunday, Remy is dragging me to a BC-Notre Dame football game, and Monday is Columbus Day, which means the library will be closed.

After class, I meet up with Kelsey for a trip to the campus grocery and convenience store. Murali's birthday is tomorrow, and I agreed to help her bake him a cake. The store doesn't have his favorite—Funfetti—so we buy a box of vanilla mix and three packages of M&Ms.

"They won't melt in the oven, right?" She pushes her glasses up her noise as we pay and leave.

"If they do, it'll be delicious." I'm now aware of how empty my stomach is. I had to skip lunch today to finish my homework that was due in my afternoon classes. I was up late last night, combing news articles for mentions of developments in Dr. Muller's case.

Something Dennis said to me the first time we met up doesn't fit with my theory that Dr. Muller's murder is connected to Ms. C's disappearance. According to him, the police in Dorchester are looking for a serial home invader, whose MO matches a cold case in another town called Brockton.

I google "Brockton + homicide" and get a hit. Ryan and Tyler Becker, two brothers in their twenties, were shot execution style in their apartment, in what looked like a robbery gone wrong. They were both tied up—the killer stole money and some valuables.

And, according to people who knew the Becker brothers, a lot of weed. The police found "drug paraphernalia" in the apartment but no actual drugs. The standing theory is that Ryan and Tyler were killed by either a burglar who was surprised to find them home, or a rival dealer.

Spencer's wolfish grin works its way into my mind.

Spencer could have known about Room 105. But I only talked to him for the first time last weekend, *after* I got the text message. Unless someone tipped him off and gave him my number.

When Kelsey and I get to the lounge, Remy and April are at the wide circle table, surrounded by textbooks, highlighters, and index cards. Their college-credit human anatomy class already has them spiraling into a panic.

"It's a Friday. Why are you doing this to yourselves?" I ask, checking the oven temperature.

"It's the only college-level science class that fit into my schedule," Remy says over the top of her pencil. She's chewed half the eraser away.

"It'll look good on my med school apps." April drains her soda from the dining hall loudly. "I want to be an aesthetician. They're the highest-paid doctors."

Remy stares at April. "Anesthesiologist. You want to be an anesthesiologist. Aestheticians work in spas. They give *facials*."

I snort. Kelsey rolls her eyes. April just shrugs as Remy grips her pencil. I have to turn around to hide my smile; it drives Remy *batshit* that April acts like a lost toddler in a mall yet has a higher class ranking than she does.

I'm stirring the M&Ms into the cake batter when Kelsey groans.

"The oven is broken."

Remy looks up. "It just takes a while to heat."

"Thanks. Because I haven't lived here for over a year." Kelsey rolls her eyes.

Now April looks up. Rem's mouth hangs open; I wonder if I should do something to diffuse the tension. Like spill the rest of the M&MS on the floor.

Kelsey blinks, as if she's fending off tears. She slams the oven door shut. "It's not heating at all."

"I'll call the guys," I say. "They can get rid of Murali for a little while, and we can use their oven."

I find Brent in my contacts, forgetting that I still have him on speed dial until I see the lightning bolt next to his number. My throat feels tight. Next to me, the redness is fading from Kelsey's face.

"Sorry," she mumbles in Remy's direction, pulling her hair into a messy bun. "PMS."

Brent picks up on the third ring. "Yo."

"Yo. Is Murali around?"

"Taking his afternoon siesta, I think," Brent says. "Why?"

I explain the situation. He promises that even the surviving members of Led Zeppelin reuniting and rocking out next to his bed won't wake Murali up, and Kelsey and I trudge over to Aldridge with a pan of raw cake mix.

"So," I start.

"I know I'm a bitch, and it's not her fault, but what am I supposed to think when Cole and I had an amazing time at formal and at the concert, then he and Remy spend all week together during orientation and he gives me his *I-don't-know-if-I'm-ready-for-a-relationship* speech?" Kelsey sucks in a breath. I'm afraid she'll pass out if she doesn't slow down. "He's not over her. I'm just *sick* of not being good enough."

"But we don't have to talk about it," she amends, even though I haven't said anything. "Remy is your best friend. I'll get over him."

I'm thrown a bit by how easily she called Remy my best friend. For the past five years, Chelsea has been my best friend. But now that I'm hearing it out loud, I realize how true it is.

Remy's my best friend now—the one who fills up my text in-box while she's in class, even though we live together. She's the one I went to when everything went down with Brent last year. She's the person I'd punch a shitbag guy in the face for—and I have.

It only makes the fact that I went behind her back with Alexis—her ex-best friend—even worse.

Brent meets us downstairs. He waits with his hands in his

pockets, removing one to wave when he sees us. I'm careful to balance the cake pan as we step into the elevator. Brent fishes an M&M off the top of the batter and eats it.

"You're an animal," I say. "I hope you washed your hands."

"Yup. Right after I picked my nose." He wiggles an eyebrow.

"Gross," Kelsey says. The elevator dings. We get off at his floor and he lets us into the dorm, where Cole and Phil are playing PlayStation 3 in the living room. Kelsey instantly tenses next to me when she sees him.

"I'll wait for the cake to bake if you want to head back," I whisper to her.

And that's how I wind up alone with Brent at the guys' kitchen table.

"Did anything happen between Cole and Remy during orientation?" I ask him. Even though the living room is attached to the kitchen, the other guys can't hear us from there because the volume is too loud on the television. I shoot a glance at Murali's bedroom door. Brent wasn't kidding about his sleeping.

"He wouldn't tell me if it did," Brent says. "He knows I'd be pissed if he treated Kels like that."

"Like . . . nothing even happened between them," I find myself saying out loud. "Is that how I made you feel?"

Brent shrugs. Unscrews the cap of the water bottle he's been carrying around. "No. Not really."

"Good," I say. "Because I never wanted to. Make you feel like that."

He smiles, his eyes falling to the cap in his hands. He turns it over and over. I'd kill to know what he's thinking right now.

My phone buzzes on the table next to me. Probably Kelsey, or Rem wanting to know why Kelsey is mad at her. I leave my phone faceup and swipe to open the message.

From: 819-001-3702
No cops or I kill her.

CHAPTER
TWENTY-TWO

"I . . . need the bathroom," I mumble. My legs tangle with the chair as I push myself up. I sink to the floor, reaching for my phone. It slips through my fingers and lands by Brent's feet.

I motion to snatch it away, but Brent looks down and sees the message.

I grab my phone and stumble to the bathroom. I'm not going to throw up—not really—but I feel clammy and nauseous, and I just want to lie on the cold tile until my head stops spinning. Brent follows me in.

"Anne, what the hell is—"

"It's a stupid prank." My voice is trembling. "Someone is screwing with me."

"Who is *her*?" He sits on the floor next to me.

"No one," I say. "Brent, let it go. Please."

His mouth forms a line. "Did something happen this summer in New York?"

"No."

Brent hands me his water bottle. I sip it, allowing the blood to flow back to my face.

"Is this about Ms. Cross?"

I snap my head to face him. "Why would you ask that?"

"Every email you sent me after you left mentioned her, asking if she was back," he says. "People are saying—there's rumors—she and Dr. Muller were hooking up."

I sip the water, silently.

"What's going on?" he asks again. His hand is on my knee.

I block him out, go back to both times I went to see Dennis. I wasn't careful enough. What if someone was following me? They could have been behind me on the sidewalk the whole time, listening to me tell Dennis about the Room 105 text.

The nausea returns; Anthony is the only person who knows for sure that I went to see Dennis.

I have no clue what's going on. And I don't think I can stand to find out.

Brent isn't happy I blew him off, and Kelsey isn't happy she has to go pick up the cake. I text her as I'm running back to Amherst. Remy is still in the lounge with April, so I duck into our empty room.

I call the number that texted me. Get the same invalid number message.

I fire off a text message, even though I know it won't go through.

who the hell are you and what did you do with her

I sit on my bed, curling onto my side. I can't freak out. I can't lose it. Not when there's a chance Ms. C is still alive.

I can't turn my back when I might be the only one who knows she's in danger.

If they haven't killed her yet, too.

I put the thought out of my head. My phone begins to buzz,

and bile shoots up into my throat. I swallow it away; it's only Brent calling. I hit ignore.

I want to pull the covers over my head and hide—pretend I'm not in so deep that hiding is still a possibility. But it's not; Caroline knows who I am now. So does Spencer.

And the man in the administration building.

Someone knows I'm trying to figure out what happened to Dr. Muller and Natalie. And I have to hold fast to the hope that they're threatening me because they think I'm getting close to the truth.

No cops? Fine. I never really needed them anyway.

The next morning I call Fiona Riley—Ms. C's reference at the Cambridge Public Library—and ask if she remembers an employee named Jessica Cross from two years ago.

"Of course!" Fiona Riley sounds way happier than anyone in a library on a Tuesday morning has the right to be. "Is Jess being considered for a new job?"

"Not exactly." I twist a fold of my skirt between my fingers. "Could I ask you a couple questions about her, though?"

"Sure, sure," Fiona says. "Why don't you stop by the library? I'm here until six."

I cringe. I was hoping to ask her now, over the phone. People like to criticize my generation for not doing things face-to-face, but maybe there's a reason we don't like to. It's a pain in the ass.

"Okay," I say. "I'll see you then."

It's not hard to find Fiona Riley. Everyone at the circulation desk knows who she is. They point me to the children's section.

I step around a toddler smacking a naked Barbie against the floor while her mother sits aside, texting. When I get to the desk, a youngish woman with her hair tied back in a scarf looks up at me.

"Hi," I say. "Are you Ms. Riley?"

The woman shakes her head and points at a tiny woman pushing a cart along the stacks. Fiona Riley blinks at me from behind red cat-eye glasses as I introduce myself.

"I called earlier—about Jessica Cross."

"Oh!" She beams at me. "Sure, sure. Jess is such a sweet girl."

I follow her down the aisle as she replaces picture books. I point to the one in her hand. "*Owl Moon*. That was one of my favorites."

"Still is one of mine." Fiona winks at me.

"Did Jessica work in the children's section, too?" I ask.

"Oh, no. When she was here, we were both on the main level," Fiona says. "I was her supervisor."

Fiona's hand lingers on the spine of *Owl Moon*. "Do you know her?" There's the slightest trace of suspicion in her voice. Or maybe it's just curiosity, and my mind has been trained to always expect suspicion.

"She was my Latin teacher," I say.

"Oh wow, good for her. Teaching was her dream."

"She quit, really suddenly. We were close. I never got to say good-bye. And I don't know how to find her."

Fiona's lower lip juts out slightly. "That's too bad. Come to think of it, I haven't seen her in a few months either."

"When was the last time you saw her?"

"Must've been March. She stopped in to say hi while she was doing research."

"Do you mind me asking what she was doing research on?"

"That old school." Fiona waves her hand dismissively. "Jess loved old things. Old languages, old buildings. Always looking them up, studying them when she wasn't working. Poor thing didn't have any friends or family."

But she did have family. Her brother is a fifteen-minute train ride away.

"Did she say what happened to her family?" I ask. "I think she mentioned a brother to me."

Fiona's tongue pokes out and searches her upper lip. She frowns. "Told me her parents died when she was really young. Said she was an only child."

"And no friends," I repeat. "She never mentioned spending time with anyone outside of work?"

"Jess spent all her time studying and saving to get a master's degree. Was so disappointed when she didn't get that English teacher job at Wheatley." Fiona looks around, and lowers her voice to a near whisper. "Everyone knows those charter and prep schools hire teachers with no experience and pay them dirt."

"You said the *old school*," I say. "She was doing research on Wheatley?"

"Oh, no, not Wheatley," Fiona says. "Plymouth. The reform school they tore down years ago."

CHAPTER
TWENTY-THREE

As if this situation wasn't bizarre enough, I now have another strange piece of the puzzle: Natalie's odd obsession with an old reform school.

What I know about Plymouth: It was a boarding school for boys that were in some sort of trouble with the law. Kind of like an old-fashioned juvie. And, according to Artie, the school used to stand where the Wheatley annex is now.

I have to put my research on hold, because Sunday is the football game. Remy picked Murali, Brent, and me to go with her, and I haven't had time to analyze the politics of her decision. All I know is that it probably means something that Kelsey and Cole aren't here, and that Brent and Murali treat their tickets like something golden they unwrapped from a Willy Wonka bar.

When we get to the BC stadium, I see why. We may as well have tickets to see the Beatles.

"Fifty bucks," a guy says to us as we push our way to the concourse.

"One hundred," I tell him.

"Anne! What the hell." Remy drags me away. "It's BC versus *Notre Dame*."

"Okay." I shrug.

Murali stares at me. "Have you ever been to a college football game?"

"I've never been to *a* football game," I say.

My uncle Jason has Giants season tickets. My dad goes with him all of the time, and they've asked me, but I never had an interest. I say as much.

"Don't talk to me." Murali covers his face. "Just don't talk to me."

I bump my shoulder into his as security scans our tickets.

"Ugh, I'm so thirsty," Remy says when we get to our seats. It's uncharacteristically hot for October. She and the guys have already taken off their hoodies.

"I saw a concession stand on the way in," I say.

"We'll miss part of the quarter," she says. I don't know if she really cares about the game that much, or if she's just being Remy. She hates missing out on things.

"I'll go," I say.

"Are you sure?"

"It's fine. I want to stretch my legs." And really, there's no polite way to say I couldn't give less of a shit about the game. I feel bad Remy wasted the ticket on me. But it is nice to get away from Wheatley. Even if it's not for long enough.

I don't know if it will ever be for long enough.

I walk in what feels like a circle until I see a sign for a food court. It's on Level 4. I double back to the stairs and climb up a level, pushing through a sea of gold and maroon, punctuated by the random person in Fightin' Irish gear. As far as I can tell, the Notre Dame fans aren't holding to their name. Or maybe they know they're outnumbered and don't want to get their asses kicked.

A man in a green hoodie leaning against the railing on the third level catches my eye. There's something sketchy about the way he seems to be looking for someone—if there's anything that sticks out to me these days, it's a sketchy person.

He turns, scanning the level, his eyes passing over me. My breath catches in my throat. I *know* him.

It's Spencer Vandenberg.

I duck behind the nearest corner, by the bathrooms. I can see him, but he can't see me. He checks his phone. Slips a hand in his pocket, as if he's checking to make sure something is there.

He picks his head up; I can tell the person he's waiting for is here.

"No way," I mutter under my breath.

Caroline Cormier-Frey stands next to Spencer at the railing, keeping about a foot of space between them.

Alexis was right: Spencer was lying when he said he didn't know Caroline.

A group of guys ambles by, blocking my view of Spencer and Caroline. "Move," I mutter. They stop, standing in the middle of the concourse, laughing and fist-bumping each other.

I hiss under my breath and move around them, careful to hang at least twenty feet back from Caroline and Spencer. Even if I can get closer, there's no way I'll be able to hear them over the sounds of the game.

And just like that, the meeting is over. Caroline turns and heads for the lower level, walking straight past me without noticing me. She's fuming.

I take off after Spencer before I lose him in the crowd. I don't know why I'm tailing him—whatever conversation he had with Caroline is clearly over.

I stop in my tracks when Spencer does. My feet are frozen to the ground as he turns, scans the crowd. His eyes lock on mine.

He gives me a wolfish smile that doesn't reach his eyes. He lifts two fingers and makes a gesture right at me.

Bang.

CHAPTER
TWENTY-FOUR

No cops or I kill her.

It dawns on me that Spencer could have been signaling that he would kill Natalie, not me. Or maybe both of us.

My knees feel weak as I make my way back upstairs. I could have just locked eyes with the person who sent me the text message.

I don't realize until I get back to the stands that I forgot our drinks. When I return with them, no one notices: BC is approaching the end zone.

No one except Brent.

"What happened to you?" he asks.

Apparently he's not that interested in the answer, because then BC scores a touchdown and our section goes wild.

"So the guys want to go to the pool tonight," Remy says to me when the noise dies down. "Diego's tennis coach gave him a key to the athletic complex so he can practice whenever he wants. The guys hid some beers in his locker."

My mind is still on Spencer, so only half of what Remy says

registers for me. "Swimming. I don't think I have a bathing suit here."

"You don't need one." Remy wiggles her eyebrows in a way that's probably supposed to be suggestive, but it just looks like a bug is flying at her face. I laugh in spite of myself—and notice that Brent is laughing next to me.

"Eavesdrop much?" I nudge my shoulder against his.

His ears get really red, and I open my mouth to ask what his problem is, then I remember what Remy said before we cracked up. No bathing suit. Skinny-dipping.

Oh.

Brent is uncharacteristically quiet for the rest of the game, even though BC wins. I don't want to believe he's *that* disturbed by the prospect of seeing me naked later, so I think back to my absence during the game. Brent definitely noticed.

And Spencer *definitely* noticed me.

I have to tell Alexis that I saw Caroline with him.

When we get back to our room, Remy wants to go to the library to study for Tuesday's quiz on *Heart of Darkness*.

"I'll meet you there," I say. "I have to call my mom quick."

She shrugs. "I can just wait for you."

"Nah, it's okay. It might not be so quick."

"Okay." Remy looks at me funny and slips out the door. I exhale and find Alexis's number in my recent calls. She picks up on the first ring.

"What?"

"Hello to you, too. Did you know Caroline was meeting Spencer at the BC game today?"

"No. You're sure it was them?"

"Of course I am."

There's a pause, with nothing but the sound of Alexis breathing heavily. "I knew it. She's on something, and she's buying from Spencer. Probably Zannies. Probably exhausting being such an uptight bitch all the time."

"Wait," I say. "You don't think they met to talk about Natalie?"

"At a *football* game?" Alexis is using her *are-you-too-stupid-to-live* voice. "They'd only meet in person if there was an exchange going down. College sporting events are like a prescription drug trade mecca."

"But it didn't look like a drug deal," I say. "Caroline looked *furious*. And when Spencer saw me—"

It's as if a bomb goes off on the other end of the phone. "They *saw you*?"

"Only Spencer," I say.

"And how long do you think it'll be before he and Caroline put the pieces together? We were *just* interrogating him at the country club."

"Trust me, if they had something to do with Natalie's disappearance, being caught spying on them is the least of our problems. Natalie's boyfriend is dead. Murdered."

"You don't understand. Caroline will *destroy* me if she gets wind that I'm involved," Alexis hisses.

Anger spasms in me. "This isn't about you, Alexis. I'm not in this to help you take down your cousin."

"You think Caroline is really what this is about?" she says. "I gave you Spencer. I helped you. Now *you* have to help *me*. Tell me what you know about my dad and Travis Shepherd."

I can't. I won't. *Your dad showed up at Shepherd's house with a gun and didn't plan on coming out alive. He dropped the gun when I told him to think about you.*

For once, it's not Anthony or me I'm trying to protect by holding onto the truth of what really went down that night.

"You don't know what it's like to lose everyone you love," Alexis shouts. "I just want my dad back—"

The door keypad lights up, which means someone just slipped a key in it. I snap my phone shut.

Remy stares back at me, her face saying she's been outside the door for a while.

"I forgot my book."

"Rem—"

"I really hope you know another Alexis."

I open my mouth, ready to say something stupid and cliché like *I can explain,* but I just *can't.*

"Were you, like, using me to get to her or something?" Remy's cheeks are splotched with red, like she's going to cry.

"Of course not—"

"You *were.* After Isabella died, you were always asking me about Alexis. She told me you were using me, and I should have believed her."

Now my throat is tight, blood rushing to my face. "Why did you even ask me if you already have your mind made up?"

"I can't believe you," Remy cries. "I stopped being friends with her *because of you.*"

"I never asked you to do that!" I feel myself unraveling. "You're the one who wanted to be friends with me. All of you guys. I never asked for anyone to latch on to me."

Remy's jaw sets. "Well if you wanted to be left alone so badly, you should have just said so."

I wince. Remy grabs *Heart of Darkness* from her desk and stalks off.

Remy never comes back to the room. I'm too humiliated to go to dinner, even though I know it'll look twice as bad if I don't show up at all.

I have no idea who to go to, or how to get myself out of this mess, so I call Chelsea, my best friend from home.

"Hey, babe!"

Someone in the background—a guy—makes a suggestive "ooooh" sound. Chelsea tells him to shut up. My loneliness guts me. That used to be the two of us: the girls at the party who blew off creepers and then stumbled home, laughing about it until we fell asleep at three in the morning.

Now, I just think being drunk on a Sunday night is sad, and I wish Chelsea would go outside so I could talk to her.

"Where are you?" I ask.

I can barely hear her response over the shouting and music coming from her end. "Just some pregaming before a freshman mixer. Fordham guys are lame."

"You're in the Bronx? Be careful, Chels."

"It's okay, Madison is with me," she shouts.

Madison Feldman was always our third wheel. The thought of her being bumped up to Chelsea's second-in-command makes me even more homesick.

"I miss you," I say.

"What?" The noise from the party is so loud I have to move the phone away from my ear.

"Nothing," I say, but the call's already been dropped.

I roll over and bury my face in my pillow. And I cry—not for Ms. C or for Dr. Muller but for myself, because I'm a selfish bitch. Falling apart isn't even an accurate way to describe my life—*imploding* is more like it.

I almost call home, just to hear my parents' voices. When I was a kid and thought I heard noises at night, I'd yell for my dad until he came into my room and checked under my bed and in my closet. But now the monsters are real.

A knock at the door startles me. At first I think it's Darlene, my RA, telling me it's lights out. But it's only nine, and curfew isn't until eleven since it's a holiday weekend.

Remy could have forgotten her key earlier. I wipe the smeared mascara from beneath my eyes and get up.

He knocks again as I'm looking through the peephole. Brent.

I shut my eyes and silently bang my forehead against the door. Fantastic.

"What's up?" I open the door and rub my nose, trying to play off the redness in my eyes as an allergy attack.

"Anne, have you been crying?"

I motion to shake my head, but find myself nodding. "If you're looking for Rem, she's super pissed at me and probably in April and Kels's room."

"I'm not," Brent says. "You weren't at dinner, so I was worried. What's going on with you and Remy?"

"It's stupid. And I really don't want to talk about it."

Brent puts a hand to his chest. "Did *I* do something? Because you've been weird around me, too."

I'm tired of holding back. Especially with him. "No. I've just screwed up every single good thing I had, and you being here right now reminds me of that and it sucks." A single tear catches on an eyelash. "So no. You didn't do anything."

He's quiet. "Do you want me to go?"

I shake my head and take a step back. Brent slips inside my room and shuts the door. He holds my face in his hands, using his thumb to wipe away the tear pooling in the corner of my eye.

I don't know who kisses who. It's one of those kisses where it doesn't matter. He kisses me so deeply that I can't tell where I end and he begins.

We wind up on my bed, my head on his chest. The spot where I rest it is warm, like it's been waiting for me. Brent wraps his arms around my body, as if he's trying to block out the rest of the world from getting to us.

"Everyone's probably at the athletic complex by now," I say.

"I don't want to go to the stupid pool," Brent murmurs, tracing kisses down my ear, my neck. They wind up on my lips.

"Brent," I say. He leans forward, stopping my words with another kiss.

"They're going to notice we're not there," I say.

"So what." He kisses the tip of my nose. My cupid's bow. Then finally, my lower lip. "I'd rather be with you. As long as you give me the choice, I'll always choose you."

I run my fingers through my hair, tugging at the roots, which I·know drives him crazy. Brent hooks a finger in the top of my pants and pulls me to him so our bodies are mashed together.

The words are on the tip of my tongue: *I'm sorry. I screwed up. Please say this kiss means it's not too late.*

"I go back to that night all the time," he whispers in my ear. "I think about where we'd be if I'd said no, that wasn't it for us. It wasn't the end."

So do I.

"Don't think about the bad stuff." I trace figure eights on the small of his throat. "Not now. I just need a break from all the bad stuff."

He flips me so he's on top. Our eyes meet, and he smiles. I prop myself up on my elbows so our lips meet, and we stay like that, kissing, until I know curfew must be approaching. But it doesn't feel like long enough.

"I don't want to go." He rests his forehead against mine. It's warm.

"Then don't," I say.

"I guess . . . that if someone left the window in the lounge open, I could sign out and come back." Brent tugs my V-neck down just enough to kiss below my collarbone. He smiles; I grin back and he takes my hand.

After I sneak into the lounge, open the window, and hurry back to my room, heart pounding, I'm alone with my thoughts again. I'm pretty sure I just blew up the hot mess scale by making out with my ex-boyfriend.

I'm not dumb enough to think that this changes anything—that Brent and I will magically forget all the horrible crap that happened between us, the ways we hurt each other. And I don't think that having him back by my side will make it okay that Remy hates me and my favorite teacher might be dead and if I'm not careful, I could be next.

But only for tonight, I don't care.

———

When I wake up, I'm alone. I roll over—Remy's bed is empty, too. I panic for a moment, worried that she never came back from the athletic complex last night. Then I remember that she's angry, and probably sleeping in Kelsey and April's room.

Especially if she came back here last night and saw that I was with Brent.

Brent. Who's gone.

I pull on a pair of jeans and a fleece and grab my ID card. Before I run downstairs, I text Kelsey.

Is Rem with you?

She responds instantly.

Yup. At breakfast. Where were u last night?

So Remy didn't tell anyone about our fight. That's good—I think. I reply to Kelsey.

Are the guys with you?
Nope.

I pocket my phone and head downstairs. As I power-walk over to Aldridge, I tell myself that Brent probably snuck back to his room early and didn't want to wake me.

When I get to the lobby, I call him. He doesn't pick up. I try again, hanging up when I see Phil emerge from the lobby elevator.

"Is Brent upstairs?" I ask.

Phil shrugs. "Didn't see him. Want me to sign you in?"

When I get upstairs, the guys' room door is open. I poke my head in. Cole is sitting on the couch, eating a bowl of cereal. He doesn't look surprised to see me.

"Hey," I say. "Brent here?"

"Said he was going for a run." Cole's face is funny.

"Did he say anything before he left?"

Cole looks over his shoulder at Murali, who's emerging from the bathroom. They share a look. Cole turns back to me. "He said to me, 'I swear all we did was make out,' then he said, 'shit,' and he ran out."

My stomach dips. "We did just make out. But I don't know why that's anyone's business but ours."

Murali sits on the couch next to Cole. "We wanted to talk to you about that. Here, sit."

I glare at him as he clears a stack of video-game boxes off the couch. "Is this an intervention?"

"More of a Brentervention," Murali says.

Cole puts down his spoon. "Seriously, man? Be quiet." He rounds on me. "Anne, you rock and everything, but we're just looking out for Brent. We don't want him to get all messed up again, if you're not, you know, serious about him."

I regret ever sitting down. "Messed up?"

"He's been looping his Bon Iver album," Murali says. "We'd like him to stop."

Cole tosses a soggy piece of cereal at his face and misses. "You sound like a selfish dick. He's our best friend, dude."

"And he's not my friend, too?" I glare at Cole, who blinks at me. Obviously, he and Murali didn't take the time to prepare their arguments before they double-teamed me. They should know better. My dad's a lawyer.

"Look, Brent's a big boy. He can kiss who he wants."

"Yeah, and there are a lot of girls who are into him," Cole says. "But he won't even look at them if he thinks there's a chance he can get back with you."

"That's what you're worried about?" My voices hitches up an octave. "That I'm *cock-blocking him*?"

"Anne—" Murali gets up, but I'm already at the door.

———

Brent isn't in the dining hall, but since I already swiped to get inside, I may as well eat breakfast. I head for the juice bar, keeping one eye on the entrance to see if he shows up. I balk, seeing the back of two familiar, tall, athletic bodies with perfect blond French braids.

"Are they back together?" Jill asks, a touch of disappointment in her voice.

"Probably just a hump and dump," Brooke says.

No doubt they're talking about Brent and me. I inch up the line behind them.

"You think they did it?" Jill's voice is hushed.

"Everyone saw his walk of shame," Brooke says. "She's unbelievable. I mean God, she almost got *expelled*. Keep your legs closed."

White-hot rage bubbles in me. "Excuse me," I say to the boy in front of me in line. I push my way around him and dump my glass of cranberry juice onto Brooke's tray. It splashes onto the front of her shirt. She shrieks and jumps back to avoid the red dripping from the counter onto the floor.

"Oops." I smile at her even though I'm trembling inside. Suddenly, I'm not very hungry. Before everyone starts catching on to the scene I just caused, I make a break for the exit, and smack right into Brent. He puts his arms on mine to steady me.

I yank away. "Why did you bail on me this morning?"

The area under his eyes is gray with lack of sleep. "I—I just needed to process. I freaked out."

I lower my voice. "Kissing me was that bad?"

"No. Of course not." He scratches his eyebrow. Runs his thumb alongside his mouth. Anything to avoid looking me in the eye. "But last night—I've been thinking about that happening since we broke up. I *wanted* that to happen."

"You didn't exactly have to twist my arm, remember?"

He runs his hands over his face. "Have you seen him? Since you've been back?"

Anthony. I should have known this was about Anthony. "What does that have to do with us?"

"Everything. And you know it." Brent's eyes flash. "Do you realize how much it killed me to see you with him that night? It was like you were waiting for us to break up so you could be with him."

"That is *not* true. I was never *with* him." I'm not exactly whispering. People are looking at us now. Brent casts a glance over his shoulder and lowers his voice.

"Don't lie. Did you have feelings for him when we were together?"

My stomach clenches. "Yes. But I never acted on them."

A muscle in Brent's jaw twitches. He shrinks away from me.

"Wait," I say. "The things I felt for him, are, like, *nothing* compared to what I feel for you."

I don't realize what I've said until his face softens a bit. *Feel*, not *felt*. Desperation claws at me. "You're the one who's always been there," I say.

His mouth forms a line. "Just not the one time it mattered."

I'm speechless.

"That text message," he whispers. "I know it's not a prank. Does *he* know what it's about?"

And just like that, I'm angry.

He has it so wrong. How am I supposed to convince Brent that I'm done punishing him for not believing me last year? How am I supposed to tell *anyone* what really happened at Shepherd's house—that Anthony followed me inside and Travis Shepherd would have shot him if Steven Westbrook didn't kill Shepherd first.

Anthony thinks I'm a monster who almost got him killed. If I tell Brent the truth, he'll think I'm a monster, too.

It's not just the truth about that night—but also the truth about Dr. Muller and Ms. C and the text messages. Brent won't let me do this alone. And not because he feels guilty he didn't believe me about his dad and his coach last year—it's who Brent is.

He said he'd always choose me if I gave him the choice. But I won't give him the choice if it means putting him in danger again.

"You are so, so wrong," I tell him.

He doesn't follow me as I walk away.

CHAPTER
TWENTY-FIVE

Someone shouts my name as I'm storming out of the dining hall. But it's not Brent—it's a girl's voice.

I turn around. Farrah jogs to catch up with me. Her crutches are gone.

"Hi," she says breathlessly. "I'm sorry it took forever, but I did it."

"Did what?" I blink away the tightness behind my eyes. The last thing I need is a freshman to catch me crying.

Farrah's deep brown eyes seem to twinkle. "You know. The thing you wanted."

The security feed. She cracked it.

A mix of adrenaline and unease floods through me. I never should have let Farrah hack the system in the first place. Dan was different; breaching Wheatley's network security settings was his specialty long before I arrived here. Farrah is a freshman, with everything to lose.

But I need to see the man's face. I have to figure out who he is, and if he's the same person who sent me the threatening messages.

"I have it on my computer," Farrah says. "Are you free now?"

"Yeah. Sure." I follow her across the quad, sneaking a glance at my phone. No texts.

The inside of the freshman dorm building is nearly identical to Amherst—except for the high-pitched laughing and shrieking of fourteen-year-olds and prominently displayed NO BOYS sign at the front desk. Farrah signs me in and we take the elevator up to the fourth floor.

"Are you okay?" she asks. "You're all red."

"I'm fine." It comes out snippier than I intended. It's not Farrah's fault she found me in the middle of my meltdown. "Thanks for this. You're amazing."

Farrah beams and lets me into her room. Right away, I pinpoint her side: a neatly made bed with a pink polka-dot comforter that her mother probably picked out. The roommate is a slob; Farrah has to kick aside blazers and dirty towels to make a path to her desk.

Farrah plops down in her chair and goes straight to a website called Secure Alert. I look over her shoulder as she enters information into a page entitled "Remote Log In."

"Wait." I put a hand on her shoulder. "Can this be traced back to you? I *really* don't want you to get in trouble."

"Don't worry, I made sure that there's no master log of who signs in. No one will even know we were on."

I relax a bit as the screen loads, revealing the view from four campus security cameras. One is outside Amherst—I spot Remy talking to Kelsey by the bench outside the building. They're whispering. My stomach is sick thinking of what Remy could be telling Kelsey.

"Okay," Farrah says. "How far back am I going?"

I gnaw the inside of my cheek. "Monday night. Around one thirty. Outside the admin building."

Farrah clicks on Playback Mode and drags the cursor positioned over the video feed time line. She isolates the screen to one camera, giving us a full view of the administration building.

"Night vision isn't very good," she says. "What are you looking for?"

I fast-forward the video fifteen minutes. That's about how long I was in the building before my "friend" joined me.

At 1:49, he shows up. He taps a card to sensor outside the front entrance.

"Can you freeze this frame?" I ask. Farrah hits a pause button.

I peer at the man's face. It's not the clearest picture, but I can tell I've definitely never seen him before. He has a heavy brown beard and hair combed over to the side. He's wearing a tweed jacket and a huge Rolex that's probably worth a year's tuition at Wheatley. The man leaves in a huff at 1:53. He wasn't even in there five minutes.

He's on the phone.

"Is there audio on this thing?"

Farrah raises the volume, but the camera is too far away to catch what the man is saying. He doesn't look happy. Within seconds, he's gone.

"Who is that man?" Farrah asks. Her voice isn't accusatory or worried. She's curious. That's worse.

"I don't know." I stand up. "Hey, do you think you could keep this between us?"

Farrah nods.

"Thanks. You rock."

Remy is in the room when I get back.

"Remy."

"Yeah?" She doesn't turn around. My jaw sets.

"I'm sorry."

"Sorry for what? The Alexis thing, or something else I don't know about?"

I feel myself deflating. She must take my silence as an admission of guilt. Remy finally turns around.

"I already had a best friend who used me and lied to me," she says. "I don't need another one."

Before I can respond, she grabs her towel and leaves. I bite my fist and scream. Then I do what I should have done yesterday: I send Alexis a text message.

I can't screw with Caroline anymore. You're on your own.

I stick my phone in my desk drawer as I sit down to start my history paper, even though I know I'll be glancing at it every thirty seconds.

I have my introductory paragraph written by the time my phone finally buzzes.

From: Alexis

I found out something huge about Natalie. Can't say over the phone. Front steps of Haverford Day in Brookline, tomorrow at four. Don't tell anyone you're coming.

Alexis could be bluffing. She could be trying to draw me out in order to confront me face-to-face and try to manipulate me into changing my mind about helping her.

Or she's telling the truth, and she really does know something—something so big she has to tell me in person. Something she found out from snooping through Caroline's phone.

I can't focus in any of my morning classes. Remy would never forgive me if she knew I was going to meet Alexis. But from the looks she throws my way during lunch, it doesn't look like she's going to forgive me anyway.

Remy is the slow freeze type when she's angry. In front of

everyone, she'll act like nothing is wrong. You'd have to be paying attention to even know she's pissed—the subtle way she sits in between Kelsey and April instead of next to me. The way she'll pull out her phone and become immersed in something on the screen when I'm talking.

The way she catches my eye and I mouth *I'm sorry*, only for her to look away.

"Where is everyone?" Kelsey asks Cole once he sits down with his tray. He's got his usual fare: a hamburger, fries, a salad with only lettuce and dressing. And that's just the first course.

Cole shrugs. "Murali's in Campbell's office, going over his Brown essay," he says.

"I saw Brent talking to Kaylee on the way in," Phil says, squirting ketchup over his fries.

"Who's Kaylee?" The words spill out of my mouth before I realize how pathetic I sound. Cole avoids my eyes.

"Hot junior," Phil says. April jabs him in the ribs; Phil looks up at me, as if he didn't even realize I was here. He probably didn't. Probably smoked a bowl before lunch.

I do a quick scan of the dining hall and spot Brent at a table by the salad bar. He's leaning in, laughing at something a cute brunette is saying. She has dark eyebrows and pin-straight hair that falls past her shoulders. My stomach feels like it's trying to swallow itself.

Everyone is watching me. I set my fork down. "Can we skip the awkwardness and eat our damn lunch? I'm fine."

"He's trying to make you jealous," Kelsey says under her breath. "What a jackass."

Cole clears his throat. "He's not a jackass. He told me she was cute, like, over a year ago."

My gaze meets Remy's, and the guilty look on her face says she knew about Kaylee, too. She picks up her spoon and swirls her lentil soup so she doesn't have to look at me anymore.

I mumble an excuse about forgetting dressing for my salad

and push my chair away from the table. I can't be pissed at Cole for being honest.

I remember Brent's face after I told him I had feelings for Anthony, and I start to think that this whole honesty thing is a scam.

I'm dreading my last class—history—because Brent and I sit next to each other. He doesn't say anything before Kazmarkis starts the lesson, but I catch him eyeing me as I check my phone to see if Alexis has texted me again.

So does Kazmarkis. She barks at me to put my phone away, and that's that.

Brent hangs back to walk with me when class is over, even though I purposely take my sweet-ass time packing up, hoping he'll leave.

"How'd you do on the quiz?" He leans against the table, unbuttoning the top button of his shirt. The first step in his end-of-classes ritual. Next is ditching the tie when we're out of Kazmarkis's sight.

"Eighty-five," I say. "Totally blew the extended response on federalism."

Brent nods, twice. Two slow bobs. "You seem weird."

"If you mean it was weird for me seeing you flirt with another girl when you told me you wanted to get back together a few nights ago, then yeah. I feel weird."

Brent is quiet as he trails behind me out of the room. "What do you want me to say? I told you how I feel."

I spin to face him when we reach the elevator. "You told me how you feel about Anthony and me. Which is that you can't get past it."

"I could. I mean, I would, if I really believed that you wanted me to." His voice is barely above a whisper, even though we're the only ones outside the elevator.

"I don't know what I want." It's a lie. Really, I can't have what I want, which is to have it both ways. To have Brent back, but to keep hiding what I'm up to.

I can't do that again. It already blew up in my face once.

"We were just talking," Brent says. It kills me he won't say her name, almost as if it confirms my suspicions. "I wasn't trying to make you jealous or anything."

I'm silent as I punch the down button, sick of waiting for the elevator.

"*Anne*. Give me a little more credit than that."

The elevator dings. I do give him enough credit to believe this isn't a ploy to make me jealous—and that's exactly what sucks.

Somewhere in between my conversation with Brent and realizing I don't want to go back to my room, I decide to head into the city and meet Alexis.

Haverford Day reminds me of St. Bernadette's, my old school. It's a series of brownstones tucked into the city street, red banners marking which buildings belong to the school. I shield my eyes from the afternoon glare, surveying the street. A bunch of girls in royal blue blazers and wool skirts filter out of a building across from me. They congregate on a set of sprawling concrete steps.

Alexis isn't among them. I check my phone, worrying I may have missed her. I texted her on the way here, letting her know I was on my way.

She responded. *On your way where??*

My breath catches in my throat. *Get out of here. Now.* I turn to head back in the direction of the T stop.

And I'm face-to-face with Caroline Cormier-Frey.

CHAPTER
TWENTY-SIX

I am so freaking stupid it makes me sick. Caroline smiles at me as if she knows what I'm thinking, and she agrees.

"I'm glad you made it," she says.

I drop my gaze to my phone.

"Don't even think about tipping her off," Caroline says. "If you do, this is going to be so much harder than it needs to be."

I don't want to know what *this* is. "You texted me from her phone?"

Caroline peers at me with those unblinking eyes. "I forgot how dumb high schoolers are. Lesson one: If you're going to screw with someone, don't leave your phone out where the person you're screwing with can see your messages."

I cringe. "What do you want?"

Caroline finally blinks. "You're afraid of me. What kind of lies did *she* plant in your head?"

"Do you mean Alexis, or Natalie?"

"I haven't. Seen. Natalie Barnes. *In twelve years*," Caroline snaps. A woman stopping to let her dog pee on the curb eyeballs us. Caroline lowers her voice. "Yet you and my cousin seem to think I'm involved in some sort of Natalie conspiracy. Why?"

I return Caroline's stare. "You attacked Natalie. *Why?*"

"Get this through your pretty little head," Caroline seethes. "I never *touched* Natalie."

"What about your friend? On the bike?"

Caroline's upper lip curls. "That was a *joke*. And the car was halfway down the street. Annabeth's mother made a huge deal out of it. I should have known Alexis would bring that up." Caroline takes a step toward me. "I don't know who screwed up Natalie's face, but it wasn't me."

"Then why did she say it was you?"

"Because she hated me, and she obviously didn't want whoever *did* hit her to get in trouble."

"Spencer?" I ask.

Caroline reddens at the mention of Spencer's name. "Didn't I just say I don't know? But yes, Spencer would be my first guess."

I tilt my head, holding her gaze so she knows I don't believe her. She reddens another shade. "And if it wasn't Spencer, it was her creep brother."

"Luke?"

"How should I remember his name?" Caroline scowls. "All I know is that Natalie told me she went to boarding school to get away from him."

The blood rushes to my head. That is *not* what Luke Barnes said when I asked about his sister. Caroline isn't the only one who played me.

"How was he a creep?" I ask.

"I don't waste my brain space on my high school roommate's problems." Caroline sniffs. "But I do remember she said he threatened this guy she was dating in middle school. In a jealous, overprotective way."

I feel sick at the possibility I've been completely wrong this whole time, thinking that Caroline and Spencer had gotten rid of Natalie together. Could it be that Natalie's own brother had done something so terrible to her she felt she had to change her name to get away from him?

I need to get back to school. Put as much distance between Caroline and me as possible before someone sees us together. She steps in front of me, blocking my path.

"I didn't get you out here to discuss Natalie," she says. "But think of what I just told you as my way of showing you how serious I am."

"Serious about what?"

Caroline gives me a thin-lipped smile. "Getting rid of Alexis. You're going to help me."

"No, thank you." I try to sidestep Caroline, but she puts a surprisingly toned arm out in front of me.

"You're going to help me, or I'm going to call Dean Tierney and let her know that one of her students has been harassing me and cavorting with a known drug dealer."

"Cavorting? You're the one actually buying drugs from him."

"No." Caroline gives me a wry smile. "*Alexis* is. Or at least that's what it'll look like when they find these in her locker."

Caroline shoves an orange prescription bottle into my hand and covers it with my fingers. "You two have put me in a really tough spot. Spencer won't do business with me anymore, and Alexis seems to think she can blackmail me."

"So you're trying to blackmail *me*," I say. "Are you sure you and Alexis aren't related by blood?"

Caroline makes a disapproving noise. "I'm not going to sit back and lose my job because of some silly little childhood vendetta Alexis has. I couldn't care less about you, but unfortunately, I need your help."

There's a thrumming sound in my ears. I try to make eye contact with the people zipping past us on the sidewalk. If I look terrified enough, will someone come to my rescue?

If Caroline tells on me, Tierney will expel my ass so fast I'll get whiplash. And this time, she'll want answers. As will my parents.

"Why do you need me?" I ask Caroline.

"You look like a Haverford Day student." Caroline extracts a blue blazer from her Kate Spade shoulder bag and hands it to me. "Put it on. You should be able to slip through the main doors without a problem. Alexis's locker is 1506, on the first floor. From what I hear, locks aren't a problem for you."

I look at the blazer in my hands. "Alexis will be expelled. Maybe even arrested."

"She'll never see the inside of a jail," Caroline scoffs. "I want her out of my house and off my back."

"Someone might believe that you set her up," I say.

"Really? Who? Because my mother caught Alexis snooping through my phone. She'll gladly go on the record saying that. And plenty of people saw *both* of you with Spencer at the country club."

My face feels damp with sweat. Everything is spiraling out of control—Caroline has me exactly where she wants me.

I put the blazer on, my arms trembling so hard I miss the sleeve hole.

"Don't be nervous," Caroline says. "It's the end of the day. No one will see you. Now give me your phone so I know you won't tip her off."

I motion to hand it over, because what choice do I have? Caroline can end me with one phone call. If I'm expelled again, my life is pretty much over. Never mind the fact that Ms. C— Natalie—is still missing, Dr. Muller's killer is still out there, and there's absolutely nothing I can do about it from New York.

Besides, Alexis *hates* me. If the situation were reversed, she'd save her own ass over mine.

I don't owe Alexis anything. She tried to get me expelled after Isabella's murder—she even started a rumor that *I* was the one who killed her.

"Give it to me." Caroline's gaze is on my fingers, which are curling protectively around my phone. The thrumming in my ears has reached a crescendo. I can't move or speak.

"Is something wrong with you?" Caroline barks.

"No." I shove the pill bottle back at Caroline and shake the blazer off of me as if it's diseased. "Something is wrong with *you*."

Caroline grabs my shoulder as I try to push past her. "Do you realize what you're doing?"

I shake her off of me and keep walking. For the first time, I realize *exactly* what I'm doing.

And it scares the hell out of me.

CHAPTER
TWENTY-SEVEN

My time is running out.

If Tierney is looking for a reason to kick my ass back to New York, allegations that I've been buying drugs is a pretty compelling one.

If she wasn't bluffing, Caroline could be calling the school right now. I could be expelled before I even get off the train or set foot back on campus.

I don't believe that Caroline is bluffing. She took the trouble to draw me out—was willing to get her own cousin in serious, deep shit—so why not go the extra step to try to screw me over?

But there was something in Caroline's eyes when she said that she didn't hurt Natalie: desperation for me to believe her. And Natalie had already kept her mouth shut to protect Spencer once—the night she was caught at the annex.

Or, if Caroline's story is true, Natalie may have lied to protect her own brother.

I think it's time to dig around and see if I can find any skeletons in the Barnes family's closet.

———————

When I get back to my room, I park myself at my desk and google Luke Barnes again. I skip over all of the White Pages and LinkedIn info and open an interview with him on a technology blog. It's dated ten months ago.

> Luke Barnes, 29, came up with the idea for Net Space during his senior year at MIT. But don't jump to label him the next Zuckerberg wunderkind—Barnes graduated in 2008, when the country was on the brink of financial collapse, and had to set aside his plans for Net Space in order to navigate a punishing job market. Five years later, Technology Today named Net Space one of "Ten Social Media Platforms to Keep an Eye On." I called Luke to hear about his journey, which has been anything but an overnight success story.

I skim the interview, which has a bunch of boring details about Net Space and Luke's "vision" for the site. I pause when I'm three-quarters of the way down the page.

> **TT:** Last January you relaunched Net Space to a warm reception from critics. Net Space already has two million users. How did you do it?

> **LB:** It was a situation where a very dark place in my life ended with me doing something positive. . . . My father died two years ago. It was unexpected, and I went through a really hard time. It turned out he had a life insurance policy I didn't know about. I really wanted to use the money in a way that would honor his memory. So I hired a couple of developers, went back to the drawing board, and that's how Net Space came back and really found its footing.

I sit back in the chair, letting everything sink in. A life insurance policy *Luke and his mom* didn't know about. No mention of a sister. Could it be that Luke had forgotten he even had a sister, until his father died and he inherited what sounds like quite a bit of money?

Maybe Luke really did notice Natalie that day she saw him in Boston—he could have panicked, thinking she'd learn about the inheritance and come after him for her cut. But what if Natalie's goal was always to get away from her family—to get away from Luke?

I'm pretty sure that 90 percent of murders happen over money or sex. It turns the contents of my stomach over, thinking that what's going on with Ms. C could be some sick combination of both. If Caroline's story is true, Luke may have felt a little too close to his adopted sister.

Had he gone further than threatening Natalie's boyfriend? Is that why she fell apart when she was sent home after being expelled—she couldn't take his advances anymore?

I exhaust every available resource cyber-stalking Luke Barnes. The most I can gather is that he's a super-private guy. The kind who has the maximum privacy settings on his Facebook account. There's a generic Net Space Twitter account, but it tells me nothing about Luke the person, and as far as I can tell, he doesn't even run it.

I minimize the screen when I hear the door lock begin to stir. Remy slips in, quiet as a cat.

"Hey," I say.

"Hi." She sits on my bed—I'm too shocked to come up with a response to that, but she speaks first anyway. "I didn't say nothing about Kaylee on purpose. It just . . . never came up."

"I know," I say. "I know you would never keep something important from me."

She averts her eyes to my comforter, no doubt thinking of last year, when I found out that Remy and Brent hooked up before I even came to Wheatley. Nausea rolls through me.

"Nothing happened between them," she says.

"It doesn't matter," I say. "But thanks."

Remy gives me a smile. It could almost be real. She's definitely trying.

It kills me that I may not be around to see her actually forgive me.

After class lets out the next afternoon, I'm on the train to the city to do a little surveillance on Luke Barnes.

I have to spot Luke Barnes on his way out of the Net Space office. To make sure it's a one-way viewing, I have my hair tucked in a low bun that gives the illusion of a pixie cut. That, combined with a swipe of lipstick and sunglasses, is enough that he shouldn't recognize me.

I park myself at a café across the street with outdoor seating and order a rooibos tea and a croissant. We're reading *Candide* in World Literature, so I crack it open and get a head start on the chapters Knight assigned for this weekend.

The book is good in a wacky way, so I almost forget to pick my head up and periodically glance across the street at the Net Space building. I sip my tea and admire the ring of lipstick on the mug—MAC, in Lady Danger, a coral-red shade I'm rarely gutsy enough to wear.

I amuse myself by pretending I'm a French intelligence agent and Lady Danger is my cover. Lady Danger has short hair and no problems with men, because she has no time for them. Maybe she has a cat. One of those hairless ones; I'm allergic.

The longer I sit here, the harder it is to let the thought of her go. The idea of trading my life for someone else's is tempting. It's impossible.

I want it so much right now it hurts.

Is this how Ms. C felt? Like she had nothing left, except becoming Jessica Cross?

The dregs of tea in my mug are cold and I'm fielding dirty looks from the waiter by the time I've finished the book. I check my phone—it's after five. I've been here almost two hours. I'm scoping out the other businesses nearby, looking for a backup stakeout spot, when I see motion behind the Net Space building door.

The man who steps outside is not Luke Barnes—but the man behind him is. They hang out outside the building, chatting, and I hide my face with my book. I peek around it to see Luke shaking the guy's hand. They split up, each heading in a different direction.

I leave an obscenely large tip on the table since I don't have time to wait for change. I stay on my side of the street, about half a block behind Luke.

Luke passes the T station, to my relief. There's no quicker way for me to lose him than on a train car during rush hour. He makes a right onto a side street, taking us deeper into the Back Bay area.

About ten minutes later he stops outside a brownstone apartment building. I slip into the space between two buildings a few hundred feet away. I count to twenty and poke my head around the corner.

Luke is gone, inside the building.

It's a five-story building with a gated door, buzzer, and an entry keypad. I scan the windows, spying potted plants, a decal for a sorority, and even a row of glass beer bottles arranged by color. Looks like mostly college students live here.

A light goes on in one of the third-floor windows. A man's silhouette passes by. It's him. He lowers the blinds, and moments later, what little light is leaking through the slits goes out.

And a cab pulls up outside the building.

Is Luke leaving already? I panic, scanning the street for an escape route where I won't run into him if he comes downstairs. I spot a narrow side street in the opposite direction from which we came.

I'm about to dart across the street when the front door to Luke's building opens. He hurries out, slowed down only by the bags he's carrying: A suitcase and a duffel bag. I press myself against the corner I'm hiding behind, but Luke doesn't stop to look across the street before he gets into the cab.

My breath is staggered, unable to keep up with my heartbeat.

It looks like Luke Barnes is leaving town.

CHAPTER
TWENTY-EIGHT

Leaving town with two large bags isn't proof that Luke is running from something. It's entirely possible he was leaving for a trip, and he was worried he was going to miss his flight.

If he hadn't made the trip out to Wheatley just to follow me, I'd be more inclined to believe that.

The cold works its way into my fingers. I stick my hands in my pockets and leave in the opposite direction from which I came, just in case anyone saw me.

That could pose a problem if Luke comes home and figures out that I was in his apartment.

Somewhere between the Starbucks on Boylston and the walk back to Luke's street, I almost change my mind and head back to Wheatley. If I'm going to do this—break into his apartment—I have to do it while I'm here. Before I lose my nerve.

The sun goes down and I return to my spot across the street from Luke's building. I wonder when I passed the point of no return. Was it when I agreed with my dad that I needed to come back to Wheatley? Or am I deluding myself, and it was the moment I decided to find Isabella's killer on my own?

Two girls in Mass Art sweatshirts come out of the building, reusable grocery bags draped over their arms. They laugh all the way to the corner, moving apart so a man walking a golden retriever can walk through them.

Is that what my life would have looked like next year if I hadn't gotten myself into so much trouble? Those girls could be Remy and me in Harvard sweatshirts.

If Tierney believes Caroline, I'll be gone by the end of the week. Expelled for real this time, from the second prep school in less than a year.

I'm not going to have the life my parents always wanted for me.

And the worst part is that I'm realizing I never wanted it for myself.

I don't know what's left for me, or where I go from here. And I'd be lying if I said I'm not terrified of finding out.

An older woman rounds the corner the college girls disappeared around. She's lugging a wire cart behind her, filled with grocery bags. She's got one of those weird plastic hoods over her head, I guess in case it rains or whatever. She stops in front of Luke's building.

I cross the street.

"Need a hand?"

The woman looks up and blinks at me.

"With the groceries," I say.

"Oh. Yes, yes, thank you." She lets go of her cart. I lift it up the steps while she enters the building access code: 0-0-7-9. I file it away in my head for future reference.

The woman leads me into the lobby. It's cramped. On one side, there's a bulletin board of notices and flyers advertising guitar lessons from someone named Shana. And there are about twenty mailboxes.

"They finally fixed the dang elevator," the woman wheezes.

"A whole week to fix it. I says to the super, I never heard of it taking a week to fix an elevator."

I glance over her shoulder, scanning the mailboxes. Dunton, 412, Feldman, 203, Barnes, 310.

"Well, thanks, doll," the woman says as the elevator door opens. My cue to leave. I have about .05 seconds to get on that elevator with her without looking like a psychopath.

"I'm actually headed upstairs," I say. "Visiting my dad this weekend."

I help her lift her cart over the elevator threshold.

"Oh, that's lovely," she says. I can't tell if the blank look that crosses her face is suspicion. She motions to push the button for her floor. *Please not 3, please not 3.*

She hits 5. A small sigh of relief escapes me as I hit 3.

"Do I know him?" she asks.

My toes curl in my shoes. "He . . . just moved in. My parents are separated."

"I'm sorry to hear that." The woman gives me a sympathetic look. The doors open for the third floor.

"Take care, doll," she says, before they close on her. I nod, even though she's already gone.

I turn and head down the hall, panic cornering me. The sound of a TV blasts from Apartment 306.

The building is old and the doors have handle locks, almost like rooms in a house. With trembling hands, I get out my nail file. The seven P.M. news continues to blare across the hall.

I pause with the file wedged in the lock and press my ear to the door. I can't hear anything. I don't know what I expected—Natalie's cries for help? Luke isn't stupid. He wouldn't leave her here, let alone hide her here in the first place. If he's got her.

The door clicks open and I slip inside the apartment. It's narrow, with an exposed brick wall covered in artsy prints and photographs. There's a kitchenette attached to the dining room/living room. The door off the living room is closed.

I search inside my bag for my pepper spray, just in case, as I approach it. I swallow and turn the knob, opening the door an inch.

Luke's bedroom is empty, save for a crisply made double bed, a nightstand, and a dresser. The room leads into a pristine master bath. I reach for the nightstand handle; as an afterthought, I use a tissue to open it.

Inside are two rows of neurotically folded socks and a moleskin journal. I pick up the latter and flip through scattered sketches of what look like website interfaces.

It's useless. And there's a chance everything I find in this apartment will be useless. But I can't leave if there's a chance something here holds a clue to where she is.

I sit at Luke's desk, in the living room. He has a desktop computer with a huge monitor and CD towers: one of those build-it-yourself types. I turn the computer on and almost immediately get a password prompt.

Damn it. I'm no Dan Crowley, and I know next to nothing about Luke Barnes. There's no way I'm getting on this computer. I shut it down, noticing a paper-clipped set of papers next to the keyboard.

It's a photocopied itinerary for a trip to Austin. The flight leaves in an hour. I browse the papers, also finding hotel information, airport transportation arrangements, and a schedule of events for the fifth annual Innovations in Internet Technology and Social Media Convention.

I resist the urge to bang my head on the desk. Luke Barnes is on his way to Texas for a stupid geek conference. He'll be back in a week, according to the flight info.

I sigh, reminding myself that if Luke were really leaving town for good, he wouldn't be dumb enough to leave incriminating evidence behind anyway. I turn my attention to the filing cabinet. Maybe his computer password is hidden inside.

The folders are arranged alphabetically by category. I flip through the tabs, hoping to see one that's labeled PASSWORDS, but no such luck.

But there is a folder labeled PHONE.

Inside it is every Verizon bill Luke Barnes has received in his life. Or, since 2005. I wonder if Luke will notice if I make a pot of coffee in his kitchen, because it's going to take me *hours* to go through these bills to see if he's been in touch with Natalie.

I sit back on my heels, trying to think like someone on the run. The first thing I would do is get one of those disposable cell phones: nothing with a contract or wireless tracking device. Natalie's too smart not to do the same—so there's no way she'd use the same cell phone for very long.

I pull Luke's bill from last spring; I know which cell phone number she was using then, because she gave it to me in class in case I needed to text her. That way we'd have no excuse for not understanding the homework, she said. She was always there to help.

I wonder if she really meant it, or if she only did it because it was something the real Jessica would have done.

As I browse through the phone records for March, April, and May, the real Luke Barnes couldn't be any clearer.

He's a liar. There are three phone calls from Natalie's number in April alone. According to the bill, each call lasted around nine minutes.

So much for Luke not hearing from his sister for years.

Something grazes my legs.

"Jesus." I cover my mouth, even though the only one who heard me is the gray-and-white cat sitting at my feet. It looks up at me and head-butts my ankles. I rub its neck and shuffle the phone records back into order. I have to get out of here; there's a neatly stacked tower of cat food cans on the kitchen counter.

Luke must have appointed a human to come open them while he's away, and there's no telling when he or she will show up.

As I look for *P* to replace the phone records, my fingers graze over *N*. There's only one folder. It's not labeled.

I open it. There are two check stubs inside, dated from February and April last year. Both are made out to cash. Each is for $2,500.

N for Natalie? If so, it looks like Luke Barnes tried to pay his sister to go away.

As I'm getting up, I see a piece of paper sticking off the edge of Luke's desk. It's smushed between two books, as if he was trying to get it out of view.

I recognize the school crest on the paper. But it's not Wheatley's: It's Plymouth's.

CHAPTER
TWENTY-NINE

I swore I wouldn't steal anything from Luke's apartment, so I snapped a photo of the paper with the Plymouth crest on it.

It was a map of the reform school. A building was circled in red pen. I tried to pull up a similar image on Google, but I couldn't find a map of the school. Luke must have had access to a primary source—or at least an old book.

Even though I've read up on it what feels like thousands of times, I do an Internet search on Plymouth again. I have to be missing something—some reason why Natalie and her brother would be so interested in it.

Wikipedia Entry: Plymouth Reform School

The Plymouth School, also known as the Massachusetts State School for Boys, was a reform school in Surrey, Massachusetts, a town in Suffolk County. The school was founded in 1870 by notable writer and behaviorist Radcliffe H. Sullivan. While Sullivan intended for Plymouth to be a secondary school for orphaned or previously incarcerated boys, the institution was

criticized in the 1900s for becoming little more than a juvenile
detention center. In 1961, the state officially closed the Plymouth
School, citing a lack of funding and years of poor performance
evaluations, including allegations of squalid living conditions and
abuse of students at the hands of staff.

The entry is pages and pages long, and I've read most of it,
anyway. I search for mentions of "Wheatley School." I get a hit at
the bottom of the page, under the section entitled "1961–present."

After its closure in 1961, local residents complained about
trespassing and vandalism at the site of the abandoned school.
The state ordered the school to be bulldozed in 1965. The
question of how to handle the 1,000-acre land was fraught with
contention for years. Many argued the land was a historic site
that should be preserved by the state; however, taxpayers
favored the private sale of the land, which would have been
expensive for the state to maintain. In 1985, the nearby Wheatley
School expressed interest in purchasing the land for an
extension of the Wheatley campus. It wasn't until 2000 that the
state court approved the sale of the land for $15 million; attorney
Nathan Roe represented the Wheatley School in the transation.
Headmaster Benjamin Goddard announced the school's plans to
move forward with his legacy project, the Wheatley annex, in
2001. In 2006, the $5 million project was completed.
        The Wheatley annex is used by the school for biannual
leadership outings, as well as private events such as corporate
outings, birthday parties, and weddings, which generate an
estimated $1.5 million in revenue a year for the school.

Fifteen million dollars, plus another $5 million, for a glori-
fied obstacle course and picnic area. Damn. Goddard sure takes
the term *legacy* pretty seriously.

It's a link to Natalie Barnes, at least. I'm just not sure it's
the one I'm looking for.

Natalie was caught trespassing on the land Goddard wanted to develop for his precious annex. Then he expelled her and made sure no headmaster in the area would accept her into his or her school.

What had she really done—or seen—at the annex that night?

Everyone is busy discussing plans for Halloween weekend when I get to dinner. Remy is trying to convince the group to go to a costume party at a BC frat, but the guys want to stay in the dorms and watch *The Blair Witch Project*.

"Apparently I missed you all turning a hundred," Remy snipes.

"We're guys," Murali says. "We're not going to get into a frat party."

"Speak for yourself," Brent says. "You haven't seen my sexy nurse costume."

"They don't care as long as you pay," Remy says.

"It's kind of true," Cole says. "I'm still not going, though."

"Whatever. Saves us from being embarrassed by your lazy-assed costumes." Remy shares a triumphant smile with me. I smile back; does this mean I'm on some sort of probationary friendship? I'm afraid to ask.

My head isn't in the Halloween debate. I can't stop thinking about the new, bizarre pieces to the puzzle.

Luke gave Natalie money and lied about not hearing from her in years. I definitely don't trust him, but if Natalie's alive, he's my best chance of figuring out where she is.

And then there's Spencer. Natalie had spent nearly three years of her life researching Plymouth Reform School—the same place she'd been with Spencer the night she was expelled.

I have to find out what really happened that night.

But Natalie's not here to explain, and Spencer definitely isn't telling. And if I even try to approach him again, best-case scenario is that it'll end with me being legally required to stay fifty feet away from him. *Best* case.

"Anne?" Remy is tapping my shoulder. I think it's because

I've spaced out again, and someone is trying to talk to me, but when I look up, the whole table is quiet.

Because Dean Tierney is standing behind me.

"Would you like to start or should I?"

We're back in Tierney's office. She folds her hands on the desk in front of her and waits for my response.

I hesitate. "I'm not sure what you're referring to."

"I received an anonymous message that you were seen purchasing drugs at the BC-Notre Dame football game this weekend."

I resist my urge to put a fist through Tierney's desk. "It wasn't anonymous. And it's not true."

Tierney leans back in her seat. She drums her nails—long, unpolished—on the armrests. "True or not, this is a serious accusation, Anne. I'd be remiss if I didn't look into it."

My jaw sets. "I know it's serious. That's why someone with a grudge against me would make it."

Something flashes in Tierney's eyes—hesitation. "Do you know who would do such a thing?"

I dig my nails into my kneecaps. Caroline wanted to screw me over, but she wanted to protect her own identity more. Just in case I could turn around and prove that she was the one buying from Spencer. I can't tell Tierney the truth without raising suspicions about what I've done to piss off the other side of Alexis's family.

I shrug. "I dumped a glass of cranberry juice on Brooke Dempsey's tray the other morning."

Tierney blinks at me. "And why did you do that?"

"She pretty much called me a whore. Sorry for my language."

Tierney sucks in her breath.

"Am I expelled?" I blurt.

She's quiet for a beat. "No. But you'll report to Amherst when you leave my office and undergo a *voluntary* room check."

I let a small sigh of relief escape. Having a bunch of RAs go through my room in the middle of the day isn't exactly good PR for me, but they won't find any drugs in there. It could be that I dodged a bullet. For now.

As I get up from my chair, Tierney holds up a finger.

"You'll understand that I need to check your bag, too."

My stomach feels like it's sinking to my toes. I hand my bag over to Tierney, willing my kneecaps not to tremble. *Please don't go through my phone.*

She sets my bag on her desk and uses a pen to open it up, as if she's a damn airport security agent or something. She pokes around, her brow furrowing when she sees the stack of papers held together with a butterfly clip.

The ones from the library. Pages and pages of information on Plymouth Reform School.

Tierney frowns at the stack and replaces it in my bag. She hands it back to me, a troubled look in her eyes. "Thank you for your cooperation."

I nod, slinging my bag back over my shoulder. It's not until I'm in the elevator that I realize what's bugging me: After Tierney saw the papers on Plymouth, she didn't even bother checking the pockets of my purse.

There's no debating what just happened: Tierney was completely freaked by my interest in Plymouth.

She had Natalie Barnes's file on her desk.

I'm nearly certain that Tierney knows the truth about Ms. C's identity.

Is Tierney also the person who got rid of her?

I lay low the rest of the week, almost positive that Tierney has every pair of available eyes on me. I even spot Mr. Buckley at breakfast on Wednesday morning. He gives me a wave as he grabs a to-go cup of coffee and passes by our table.

Watching me.

I'm so busy watching my back that I have no energy to care about the rumors swirling about me and my room search. Luckily it becomes old news by the time Friday rolls around.

I desperately want to stay on campus while everyone goes to the costume party so I can come back here and see what else I can dredge up on Plymouth. But it seems that Remy has me on some sort of probationary friendship, and I can't screw that up.

When I get back to the dorm after class, she's lecturing April, who's sitting on her bed. Kelsey is sitting on mine.

"Zombie prom queen is going to make you look like you're in high school," Remy says. April rolls her eyes.

"We *are* in high school."

"Oh, whatever." Remy glares at her. "If you're wearing that nasty makeup all over your face, no one will want to hook up with you."

April looks disturbed by this. She looks down at the costume laid out on Remy's bed—a red sequined dress, a string of pearls, and a feathery headpiece. She's going as a flapper.

It dawns on me that I have nothing to wear.

"What are you being?" I ask Kelsey, panicked.

She pulls her knees up to her chest. "Lady Gaga. She has short hair now, too."

"Be a prom queen with me," April says. "Oh! We can be *vampire* prom queens."

Remy's quiet. She approves.

"I . . . don't even know if I brought a dress," I say.

April is already going through my closet. "You did."

She holds up a long-sleeved silver dress with a super low back. I feel as if the air's gone out of the room. It figures that dress got caught up with my other clothes: It's the one I wore to the spring formal last year. It's the dress I was wearing when Brent and I broke up.

"That dress has some seriously bad juju," I say. April holds it up to herself. The silver looks amazing against her chestnut hair and warm-tone skin, which still has a hint of a summer tan. "But someone should wear it."

"Really?" April grins.

"We're the same size," Remy says to me. "Take one of my dresses."

I give her an appreciative smile. She returns it, and I think maybe this night won't be that bad. I haven't seen Brent with Kaylee all week, and as far as I know, he's coming tonight.

April and I come up with a battle plan for authentic makeup. Because I don't half-ass anything.

Except maybe homework.

I have baby powder and fake blood on my face and I'm wearing a sequined black dress that I practically had to stuff myself into because Remy's a size two and I'm a four. My cardigan and pantyhose are doing nothing but reminding me that it's too goddamn cold for this.

We're waiting at the T station for Brent and Phil. They're fifteen minutes late, and Remy is freaking out that we're going to miss most of the party. I remind her that it's only a quarter to ten—the party probably hasn't even started yet. In any case, we have to take a cab back around midnight, because senior weekend curfew is twelve thirty.

Remy checks her texts and grunts. "What the hell are they doing? There's no way it's taking them this long to get ready."

It took Remy roughly two and a half hours to get ready. Her pin curls and red lips do look amazing, though. I almost wish I'd put as much thought into my costume.

April and I made sashes out of an old top sheet she didn't want. We wrote PROM QUEEN on them with Remy's fabric markers—because fabric markers are the types of things Remy has just lying around in her dorm room. My hair is in a knot at the top of my head, and April's is flat-ironed. We both have red dripping from the corners of our mouths.

We look hot. When we signed out, the security guard at the gate told us we were dressed to "get in trouble." I wanted to tell the bastard that I've had a gun pointed at me twice, so a sexy Halloween costume is the last thing I'm worried about.

"They're meeting us at the party," Remy announces as another train rolls in. "We're not freezing our asses off for them."

A couple people whistle at our costumes as we get on the train. A few of them are in costumes themselves—college-aged kids, mostly, plus the occasional Wheatley student. I spot Jill Wexler and the rest of the blondetourage, dressed as packages of Taco Bell hot sauce. Jill is fire, Brooke is hot, and Lizzie is mild. I wonder if they picked who got to be what based on their levels of attractiveness, because it's eerily accurate.

"Ugh, I hope they're not going to the same party as us," Kelsey whispers in my ear as the train lurches forward. Remy hears her.

"Of course they're not. There's no way they're getting in," she hisses.

"And how exactly are we getting in?" I ask.

"I met this guy Leo during a tour this summer," Remy says. "He's a sophomore. It's his frat."

When we get there, I figure out that *his frat* is Alpha Beta Phi, and suppress a groan. I've encountered Alpha Beta Phi before, at NYU parties during the first half of my junior year.

Alpha Beta Phi is like the chess club of fraternities. But I guess that's sort of the point, because Remy's older brother Mike wouldn't be caught dead at the party.

Remy texts Leo, and he meets us outside the town house with peeling paint. I know automatically that Leo went to Wheatley—he's got the side-swept hair and grass-fed cow look that all the Wheatley guys have. He's dressed as a banana.

"Glad you could make it." He beams at Remy and extends his hand to each of the rest of us, saying "Hi, I'm Leo" with each shake. All manners, this guy.

I need a drink.

The house is so crowded we almost take out a couple costumes on our way to the kitchen. A bass-heavy remix of a pop-
ular song is pounding. Three guys—Mario, Luigi, and someone
in a blue skin suit—are working the keg. The sour smell meets
my nose, and just like that, I officially don't want to be here.

Leo gets us beers and Remy drags us out to where there's
beer pong and flip cup games going. Kelsey and I opt for flip cup.

A few games later, I check my phone. No missed calls or
texts from Brent. I don't see him in the crowd. Kelsey is flirting
with blue suit guy, whose costume is still pulled over his face.
He could have, like, serious buck teeth going on, but maybe she
likes the mystery.

That's when I see Remy, using a guy in a BC T-shirt as a
standing device. He's leading her somewhere. She smiles when
I approach them.

"Hey! I've got to pee," she says. "This fella here was going
to help me to the bathroom."

"Fella? You're taking your costume pretty seriously." I level
with the guy. "What are you supposed to be?"

He gives me a lazy smile. "College student?"

"Nice try." I drag Remy away from him. I don't trust any
dude who shows up to a costume party not wearing a costume.
Remy giggles in my ear as I try to steer her to a bathroom.

"The guys here . . . are so not cute," she says.

"And you are so not sober," I say. "Remember, we have to
convince the RA we're not drunk in like, two hours."

"That's not good. 'Cause I'm boozy. Is that a word? It should
be. Hey, the guys are here."

I look up as much as I can with Remy hanging around my
neck like an infant. Phil is pushing his way through the crowd,
wearing a top hat, a green suit jacket, and a fake red beard that's
several shades away from matching his hair.

"What the hell are you?" Remy blurts.

"A leprechaun." Phil frowns, touching his beard. I look
around him, searching for Brent. It's almost impossible to miss

him, since he's wearing his Wheatley uniform and big black glasses. There's a lightning bolt drawn on his forehead with eyeliner.

He's carrying a broken branch piece.

"Nice wand, Harry Potter." I can't help but grin at him. "Did you find that outside five minutes ago?"

"Yup. Just like the rest of my costume." He laughs a horribly awkward laugh, and I'm about to ask what the hell is wrong with him. But I don't get that far. The reason is standing behind him.

She pokes her head around, then moves so she's standing next to Brent, like a kid awaiting her parents' permission for something. Kaylee, the junior girl. Now Kaylee the adorable flapper.

Remy scowls, looking down at her own flapper costume.

"Uh, this is Kaylee," Brent says.

"Hi." It comes out tightly, almost bitchy. Not because I wanted it to. Because if I open my mouth all the way, I'll either cry, or throw up, or do something equally mortifying. "I need to get Remy to the bathroom."

"Oh, shit," Remy says, as I drag her to the stairs, where people are waiting for a door the size of a Harry Potter closet. I squeeze my eyes as we lean against the wall, not saying anything. *Oh, shit* pretty much sums it up.

"Hey, I had no idea he was—"

"I know you didn't." I fan my eyes. I won't cry and create a fake eyelash glue disaster. "I know you'd never not tell me something like that, even though you're pissed at me, so you don't have to explain yourself."

I don't know what I expect her to say or do. It's definitely not taking my hand and squeezing it. I squeeze back. And that's when the tears come.

"Rem, I'm the shittiest person ever."

"Nonono." She pulls me to her, hiding my face in her shoulder. "I know there's a lot of messed-up stuff you won't talk

about. I hear you in your sleep. I know you're scared of something."

"Everything is just so messed up." I sniff. "I never wanted
to hurt you."

"I didn't want to hurt you either." Now she's crying, and
we're making a scene. "God, Anne, *I'm* the shittiest person
ever. Kels hates me, and she should. I knew what I was doing
with Cole . . . flirting and like, talking about the stuff we used
to do."

She lets out an unattractive, snot-filled snort. "I told Cole I
was sorry, and that I really don't feel that way about him, and
it's never going to happen. I'm not going to be that girl who's
with the guy just because she doesn't want someone else to
have him."

I think of Brent, and Kaylee, off doing whatever right now,
and I expect guilt to ripple through me—did I only want Brent
back because I couldn't stand the thought of seeing him with
someone else? But all I feel is the lump at the back of my throat.

This is how I made Brent feel. All because I couldn't let Anthony go.

Anthony's not the only one who wishes he knew back then
that it wasn't fucking worth it.

I squeeze Remy, wishing I didn't have to let go of her, even
though it's borderline creepy. Because right now, it feels like
she's all I have. And I'm starting to think the more we care
about people, the more stupid and selfish we act around them.

My phone begins to buzz in my pocket, and a super pathetic
part of me hopes it's Brent, even though he would just come
find me if he had something to say.

Instead, it's the only person who could possibly make me
feel worse right now.

Anthony.

CHAPTER
THIRTY

I swallow and answer, taking a deep breath so it doesn't sound like I've been drinking and hysterically crying—although I'm starting to think I'd qualify if drinking and hysterically crying were an Olympic sport.

Turns out I should have saved my breath, because Anthony is clearly obliterated.

"Where are you?" he slurs.

"I'm . . . out," I say. "What do you want?"

There's silence on his end. "I just . . . really need someone right now. I need you."

I stick a finger in my other ear, trying to drown out the sounds of the party. I think I hear a car horn in the background. "Anthony, where are you?"

"I . . . I was on my way to you, but I turned around." Another horn blaring.

On his way to me. On his way to the school. *Shit.* I think I know where he is. "You're not on the overpass, are you?"

He says nothing. My heartbeat comes to a full stop. "What are you *doing* there?"

"Nothing. I shouldn't have called." His voice is scratchier than usual. As if he's been crying. "I'm sorry."

He hangs up. Remy's watching me. She's sliding down the wall like a limp piece of spaghetti. I prop her back up, my throat beginning to tighten.

"Are you okay?" she asks, glassy-eyed.

"I'm . . . I think I need to go," I say.

The corners of her mouth are turned down. She heard the phone call. "Don't go by yourself."

"I can take a cab." My voice is trembling. "Let me find Kels first—"

"Anne, I'm fine." Remy touches her nose, as if taking a sobriety test. "Go, okay?"

So I do. I don't stop on the way out, even though I know Brent is watching me from his spot at the beer pong table.

I've worked myself up to believing that Anthony's gone already, so I almost gasp when I see the dark figure leaning against the overpass guardrail.

"Right here is fine," I tell the cab driver. He gives me a funny look, but doesn't question it. Probably because campus is less than half a mile away. It's visible from here: a brick and ivory village set atop a hill, bathed in a soft yellow glow.

I climb over the guardrail to get to Anthony, my stomach dipping when I see what he sees: a fifty-foot drop into the rocks below. Just beyond the rocks is the lake that flows all the way to the quarry.

When he looks over at me, I'm struck by how different his face looks from my memory of it. His eyes are less of a brilliant gray—now they just remind me of the color of the clouds before a storm.

I'm trembling. "You scared the shit out of me."

"I couldn't sleep," he says.

I'm suddenly aware of how little I'm wearing, and the ridiculous makeup on my face. I motion to rub some of the fake blood away from my lips. Anthony stops me. Touches my chin, tilts me so I'm facing him full on.

He laughs. It's brief and quiet, but it still looks wrong on him. His eyelids are shiny and heavy, and he hasn't shaved in at least a few days.

"Thanks," he says. "For coming. You didn't have to."

"Are you kidding?" Anger creeps into my voice. And I realize that yes, I am angry. "You're on a *bridge* in the middle of the night."

"I wasn't gonna do anything." He takes his hand back. Buries his face in his palms. "I just needed to get out of there. Away from everything. I just want it all to stop."

"You're not exactly pleading a convincing case," I say.

"Look, I know I messed up." He looks up at me. "After what happened, I thought everything would just go back to normal. But you were *gone*, and I just got to thinking that I'd be better off without you at all."

I bite the inside of my cheek. "Thanks for letting me know."

"I don't expect you to get it." He gets up and paces, angrily, to the edge of the overlook and back to the guardrail. "I saw Shepherd, holding a gun, and I ran *toward* him. For you."

"You didn't have to," I say. "You hate me for almost getting you killed, but you didn't have to do anything we did."

Anthony blinks. "You think that's why I've been avoiding you? That I blame you for what happened?"

"You can barely even look at me," I choke out.

"Hey." Anthony takes my hand. His is ice cold. "We both decided to go to the house, and neither of us would have gone if we'd known he was there. I don't blame you."

It's not what I expected him to say, but there's still a weight pressing down on me. Maybe the problem is that I can't stop blaming myself.

"I was ready to die for you, and afterwards I realized I don't even know your middle name. Or your favorite color." Anthony's upper lip quivers. "I thought it was because of somethin' crazy, like maybe I was in love with you—but I've been replaying that moment, and even though I was trying to protect you, I think it just felt like my life meant nothing to me."

Neither of us says anything, the occasional car speeding beneath us punctuating the silence. Anthony is the one to speak finally.

"When I said I'm not in love with you—I meant that I'm pretty damn close." He looks over at me. I avert my gaze to my feet, which are throbbing in my heels. If it weren't so rocky up here, I'd take them off.

"Anne. Say something."

"I don't know what *to* say."

I changed this summer, along with my feelings for Anthony. I know now that when you love someone, you can't pick and choose which of his demons you can live with. You can't pretend there's still that shiny layer on the surface once it's stripped away and all you can see is the person underneath. The real one.

Anthony chose to follow me into the dark that night because he was already living in it.

And now that it's my turn to decide, I can't follow him.

"I'm calling Dennis," I say. "You're drunk."

Dennis doesn't question it when I call him from Anthony's phone, saying he needs a ride home. Anthony doesn't fight me. Much.

"I'm fine to drive. My bike is at the Seven-Eleven."

"Did you leave it there before or after you had a couple beers?"

"After. I walked here."

"Still stupid."

Headlights approach us on the overpass. A gray Honda Accord pulls up. Dennis gets out of the car, wearing a flannel shirt and jeans. I feel awful that I called him on his night off. I wonder what he even does on his nights off.

"It's all good, jefe." Anthony's voice has sobered up. He walks an imaginary line, like, *See?*

Dennis is the type of guy that keeps most of his thoughts to himself, but judging by his face, I can tell exactly what they are right now. He shakes his head at Anthony. "Get in the car."

I try to ignore the fact that I just called a *cop* to pick up a drunken teenager. "Thanks, Dennis."

He nods to me. "Let me take you back to school."

I wanted to walk, to air out the smell of beer on me, but I'm too tired and cold to argue. "Thanks."

I get into the front seat next to Dennis. Anthony is already in the back, staring out the window. Dennis drops him off at a house I don't recognize.

"Sleep it off on the couch," he commands. "I'll bring you home later."

Anthony doesn't argue. Instead, he quietly thanks Dennis and gets out of the car. He stumbles to my side and taps on the window. I sigh and open it a crack. Dennis turns his head the other way.

"I want to do better than this," Anthony says.

"I can't show you how," I say. "I'm trying to figure the same thing out myself."

Anthony reaches for my hand. Kisses the knuckles. "Just stay safe, 'kay?"

I nod. I wonder if I'm doing the right thing, and whether I should have said something more.

But talk is cheap. And I'm tired of should-haves.

Dennis and I spend the ride back to school in silence. For the most part.

"In high school, there was this girl—"

"Dennis, come on." I roll my eyes.

"Anyway. I was a lot like Anthony as a kid. Thought I was the angriest guy in the world, that no one would ever understand the shit I was going through." Dennis shrugs. "This girl, I really liked her, but one day, she just got tired of trying to fix me."

I'm quiet. Dennis looks over at me.

"I didn't even go through half the stuff Anthony's been through," he says. "Someday he'll figure out how to deal. But you're a smart chick for not sticking around and waiting."

His scanner crackles when we get to the curb.

"FD still has Founder's Path closed off."

Dennis frowns and mutes the scanner. I don't miss the sideways glance he gives me first. I nod at the scanner.

"What was that about?"

"Car fire earlier this afternoon," he says. He's holding something back.

I gnaw the inside of my cheek. *Founder's Path.*

The Wheatley annex is on Founder's Path.

"What's really going on?" I ask.

"You're going to find out anyway." He sighs. "We found an abandoned vehicle this afternoon. Torched. The car is registered to someone named Lucas Barnes. He reported the car stolen over a week ago."

My old headmistress said you should never ask a question you don't want to hear the answer to. I swallow. "What was inside?"

Dennis rubs the area below his eyebrow. Wipes his hand down his face. "A body."

CHAPTER
THIRTY-ONE

"Whose body?" I demand.

"There wasn't much left," Dennis says. "It'll take us weeks to find out."

We're idled at the curb. I can see the security guard in the booth, reading a newspaper.

My throat is tight, like someone's tried to choke me. "Do you think it's her?"

"I don't know." He pauses. "But it does appear to be female, yes."

"Oh, my God." I lean back and press my fingers to my eyes. I'm tired of keeping my cool in front of people. She's really dead, and the worst part is I've known it all along and refused to let myself accept it. I cry, like a little kid, whimpering *Oh my God* over and over.

"Anne. Anne. Hey." Dennis pries a hand away from my eyes. "It could be anyone in there."

"Do you really believe that?"

There's a loaded silence. "I know you really cared about this woman, but she lied to you. She lied to a lot of people, from the looks of it. If it's her, we'll find out who did this."

I wipe the tears from my lash line. My fingertips come away black. I don't have it in me to point out that the detectives told me the same thing after Isabella was murdered. I'm not going to call Dennis out on empty promises when he's been so nice to me tonight.

"Luke Barnes is in Texas until tomorrow," I say. "He couldn't have done it."

Dennis gapes at me. "And you know that because . . ."

"I . . . talked to him. I'm sorry."

No cops or I kill her. What does it matter, if she's already dead?

"It's okay." Dennis sighs. "You've gotta promise me you won't do anything drastic until we find out more, okay?"

Now I nod. "Promise."

At least I'm not the only one making promises I can't keep.

I have two missed calls from Remy when I get back to the dorm. I wash the tear-smeared makeup off my face in the bathroom and collapse into bed, ready to text her back, when my door swings open. Remy's headpiece is askew and her curls are falling flat.

"Oh, thank God. I was so worried about you," she says.

"I'm okay. You're back early." It's only a little past midnight.

"April puked right after you left. We had to take a cab to the Quick Mart and get her coffee." Remy flops onto her bed. "Ugh, I have the spins. Night, lady."

"Night."

She turns the light out, and she's snoring lightly within minutes.

I grab my laptop and sit up in bed. I can't go to sleep. Not when there's a charred body in the morgue that may be Natalie. I log into the campus security feed with the passcode Farrah gave me.

Like they say, if you're looking for Gretel, find the first breadcrumb. Or something like that.

I can't forget the last date that Ms. C was on campus—May 15—because it's the same day I was unofficially expelled. I enter the date into the search box and get an alert.

The date you have entered is more than six weeks old.
Retrieving the footage could take an hour or more.
Continue?

Fantastic. Well, I doubt I was going to fall asleep tonight anyway.

Finally, there's movement on my computer screen. The frame has defaulted to the camera by the security gate at midnight the day that Ms. C disappeared.

An eerie feeling settles over me. In this moment, I'm asleep, with no idea what the day ahead is going to bring. Travis Shepherd is still alive.

I toggle the screen so it's displaying the cameras outside the administration building, the humanities building, and the parking garage. I figure Ms. C had to have taken one of these paths at some point in the morning. It'll take a while, but I can use the pieces of footage to reconstruct her day.

I fast forward through frame after frame of the empty campus. There probably won't be any movement on-screen until around five, when the athletes start their morning runs.

I pause around three thirty, my heart hammering in my chest. There's a dark figure heading for the parking garage. She keeps her head down and avoids the floodlight at the entrance, but the light reaches far enough to illuminate her red hair.

It's her.

She's carrying a briefcase: that's the detail I absorb about her before she disappears into the garage. What the hell is she doing in there at the ass-crack of dawn?

I wait for her to come out, but there's no movement on the screen. I fast forward—nothing. By the time the sun rises past the garage and teachers start driving through the gate, Ms. C still hasn't emerged.

I switch my view to the full screen of the humanities building, where Ms. C's office is. Teachers trickle in, balancing their coffees with stacks of papers. At 7:22, Ms. C leaves the building. I blink a couple times—she never *entered* the building.

At least according to the camera. But I know better. Cameras lie. Especially at Wheatley.

I freeze the frame on Ms. C holding the door open for another teacher. Her hair is falling out of her bun and her scarf is lopsided, but she was always kind of disheveled like that. I can't get a good enough view of her face to tell whether or not she looks worried.

My gaze moves to her briefcase. Something is different about it. I zoom in; it looks like she's stuffed the case with manila folders and couldn't close it properly.

I switch cameras and rewind just to be sure: Her briefcase didn't have those folders before she went into the parking garage.

Either she took the folders from the office, or from a room in the underground tunnel when she used it to get from the parking garage to the humanities building.

I fast forward to the end of the day, trying to track her final movements on campus. She leaves the humanities building and heads for the garage, briefcase in tow.

Two minutes later she drives out of the garage in a black car. I pause it, trying to get a clear picture of the license plate, but it's too fuzzy.

I rub the area below my eyes. What if May 15 wasn't Ms. C's last day on campus? After all, it was the next morning that the teacher in the office across from hers told me she was gone.

My fingers move faster than my brain can direct them. I pull up the feed outside of the main campus circle for the morning of May 16—the morning I was sent home. I start with when I was called down to Tierney's office—around eight A.M.—and work backwards.

At 7:38 A.M., Ms. C walks into the administration building.

Ten minutes later, she comes out. She's upset—her fingers are pressed to her mouth. Her strides are long as she bypasses the humanities building, where her office is. She heads for the garage.

To a casual observer, it looks like Ms. C just got fired.

But who was it—Tierney? Goddard?

Or the man who followed me into the administration building—the third horseman?

At breakfast the next morning, April sets her tray down and surveys everyone, as if she's about to make an announcement.

"So I heard something about Headmaster Goddard," she says.

I nearly choke on my bite of apple. The acid stings my nasal cavity as I cough up a piece of skin. But no one seems to notice.

"I know what you heard, and I don't know if you should be sharing that info," Murali says to April.

"Well if both of *you* know, you probably found out from your parents," Remy says. "So spill."

April's father is on the board of Massachusetts General Hospital. And Murali's mother is a surgeon there. "Is Goddard sick?" I blurt.

"Stage three lung cancer," April says quietly. "Murali's mom did his surgery."

"Okay, you just broke like three different HIPAA laws," Murali says.

"Relax." We all turn our heads toward Brent, who's putting milk in his coffee. "I already knew. I thought everyone did."

Kelsey frowns. "That's so sad. Is he going to die?"

"Stage three lung cancer?" Cole shakes his head. "I'll be shocked if he makes it six months."

Quiet settles over the table. Either everyone is trying to be respectful, or no one has anything left to say. I, on the other hand, have thousands of questions. About the annex, Plymouth, and how everything ties back to Natalie.

There's nothing I can do about the body in the burned car for now. But I can head back to the library and see if there's anything else on Plymouth that might point back to Natalie.

Goddard may have the answers, but time is running out before he takes them to the grave.

The library is as empty as you'd expect it to be on a Saturday morning at nine thirty. Read: The only other person there is Peepers. I find him replacing books in the main stacks as I head for the archives.

"Hey, Artie."

He looks up at me, pushing his glasses up his nose. "What are you doing here?"

"Just a little side project." I nod to the books in his hands. "What about you?"

"I . . . uh, I work here." Artie shrugs.

So that's how he knew about the secret library passage to the tunnels. "Oh. That's neat. Like a work-study thing?"

"No. I just wanted to. So they let me."

Color seeps into his cheeks, and I feel awful for embarrassing him. "That's cool. Really."

"Thanks." He replaces another book. "If you're looking for something, I could help you."

I consider the offer; with Artie's help, I can track down the articles in half the time. And if he comes with me, the reference librarian probably won't follow me and breathe down my neck.

"Sure," I say. "That would be great."

Five minutes later, we're in the periodicals section, combing through old editions of *The Boston Globe*. I catch Artie reading the headlines on one of the papers he pulled.

"Are you researching Plymouth Reform School?" he asks.

"Yeah. I think it's kind of fascinating."

"It's *way* fascinating," Artie says. "Especially the settlement with all the former students."

"Settlement?"

"One sec." Artie types something into the reference computer. He murmurs to himself and wanders over to the drawer of papers from the 80s. "Here."

He produces a paper with a headline about an oil spill in the gulf. "Not that," he says. I take a closer look—the right column is entitled FORMER PLYMOUTH STUDENTS SEEK UN-DISCLOSED DAMAGES FOR ALLEGED ABUSE.

"Students sued the school?" I ask.

"The state. The students came forward and said the guards beat them," Artie says. "And not 1950-style beatings with paddles. One said he was burned with a cigarette for not finishing his lunch."

"That's horrible."

"Yeah." Artie looks at me, curious. "I thought maybe that was why you were researching Plymouth."

"It is. I think." I take the newspaper from Artie, rereading the headline. This paper is from 1989. "What happened with the lawsuit?"

"They settled, not that long ago," Artie says. "The state just wanted the whole thing to go away and paid the accusers a buttload of money."

I feel Artie's eyes on me as I scan the article. "Thanks. For helping."

"No problem." He looks around, awkwardly. "Okay. I'll be in the stacks, if you need me."

When he's gone, I gather all the papers and sit at the table in the center of the room. I start with the 1989 article. There's a photo of the old Plymouth School: a sparse white building with a barbed-wire fence around the perimeter. It looks like a prison.

Nearly three decades after its closure, Plymouth Reform School is back under public scrutiny amid allegations of physical and psychological torture from two former students.

Raymond Nesbitt, of Worcester, is the first plaintiff named in the suit against the State of Massachusetts. Mr. Nesbitt, who attended Plymouth from 1954–1958, claims that the school staff "engaged in regular beatings that far surpassed levels of acceptable punishment." In the twenty-page lawsuit, Mr. Nesbitt and another unnamed plaintiff outline the alleged horrors that took place at Plymouth, including being strapped to their beds and whipped.

According to Mr. Nesbitt, the most extreme offenders were relegated to the "jail," where they were chained to a wall and deprived of food and sleep, sometimes for days. In the lawsuit, Mr. Nesbitt claims he was sent to the cabin for fighting with another boy in the school's cafeteria. "There was no light in the room," he recalled during a phone interview with the Globe. "Except for when they come in [sic] to whip us more."

The state conducted several investigations at the school since allegations of mistreatment surfaced in 1951, when a student was reportedly transferred from the Plymouth infirmary to a nearby hospital with several broken bones. The school was placed on

probationary status pending the results of the
investigation; ultimately, investigators released a
report detailing "poor living conditions and low staff
morale," but "no concrete signs of institutional abuse."
Upon the administration's failure to improve the
conditions at Plymouth, the state shut the school's
doors in 1961.

Now, surviving students such as Nesbitt are calling
for a formal investigation. However, most of the
school's records were damaged in an administration
building fire a year prior to Plymouth's closing. The
remaining records, investigators say, are incomplete,
illegible, and riddled with errors. The state estimates
as many as twenty Plymouth students—apparent
runaways—are unaccounted for.

When asked why he is coming forward now, Nesbitt
says, "They abused their power and got away with it
for too long. Now they want to bulldoze the place for
good."

I flip through the papers until I find the next mention of the
lawsuit. Apparently it wasn't settled until nearly ten years
later. I find the story tucked in the front cover of a 1999 edition
of the *Globe*.

There's a photo of a man in this one—an elderly black man
with an oxygen tube feeding into his nose. He sits on a porch,
frowning at the camera. According to the caption, this is Raymond Nesbitt.

The state attorney's office confirmed Tuesday morning
that it agreed to settle a civil case involving alleged
abuse at Plymouth Reform School. The undisclosed
settlement amount is said to be in the mid–six figure
range, to be paid out to two plaintiffs, former Plymouth
students.

Alan Greenburg, the attorney for Raymond Nesbitt, the first plaintiff in the suit, released a statement in the wake of the agreement:

"The decision to settle was a difficult one for my client, who experienced years of trauma at the hands of Plymouth Reform School Staff, most of which are not alive today to answer for their crimes. The settlement money is small compensation for the years of my client's life that were taken away. We are disappointed that justice was not done for him, and countless other boys."

Nesbitt was sent to Plymouth in 1959 by a judge after assaulting his stepfather with a bat. At 55, Mr. Nesbitt is once again under the care of the state. After several hospital stays due to severe emphysema and a mini-stroke, Nesbitt was transferred to the Worcester Nursing Home. When asked why he and a now deceased, unnamed plaintiff were the only students to come forward, Nesbitt commented, "We was [sic] the only ones left."

The state attorney's office declined to comment on the settlement.

I have to stop reading. Students tied to beds. Whipping. Starvation. And I thought Wheatley was bad.

Plymouth Reform School sounds like hell on earth.

One phrase from the first article sticks in my brain.

The jail.

The jail.

I hurry back to my room and tear through the bag I was using the day I went down into the tunnels. It's still there—the note I found on the floor.

I'm afraid if I go to the jail again I won't come back.

According to the online library catalog, the Boston Public Library has the case documents from the Plymouth settlement on file. I also need to find more information on the jail, and figure out if the journal entry I found was really written by an abused Plymouth inmate.

And how it—or he—wound up at the Wheatley School.

There are remnants of toilet paper and shaving cream on the walk to the T station. Someone's adorned the overpass railing with silly string. I can't remember if it was there last night.

I hear it before it pulls up next to me: a red Camaro. I'm trying to get a look inside the driver's window when the door swings open. I take a step back, but he has me by my arm. And he's a hundred times stronger than I'll ever be.

He throws me into the passenger side and locks the door. I beat my fist on the window and scream for help, but he's already driving away.

I fumble in my bag for my phone, but Spencer smacks it out of my hand. He pulls over; we're about a mile from campus, at the scenic overlook. If I can just get out, I might be able to run fast enough to get us out in the open.

"Relax, sweetheart," he says. "I just want to talk."

"You came all the way to Wheatley to talk?"

"I like to slum it sometimes." Spencer smiles.

"What do you want from me?" I ask.

"I wanna know why you've been up my ass. I saw you at the Notre Dame game." His smile fades. "You a narc?"

"I don't care about your business."

"Interesting."

I massage the spot on my shoulder where he grabbed me. "You as rough with everyone that you find interesting?"

"Depends on which of my sides they find themselves on."

"That what Natalie did to deserve two black eyes? Got on your bad side?"

"The fuck you talking about?" Spencer growls.

"Her sophomore year. Someone messed up Natalie's face," I say. "Caroline thinks it was you."

"Caroline was probably high as a kite when she said that." Spencer snorts. "And it *wasn't* me. I don't beat up girls."

No. He just shoves them into his car against their will. "When was the last time you saw Natalie?"

Spencer looks bored. "I told you. The night before she got expelled."

"I don't think you told me everything about that night. I think Natalie saw something at the annex."

There's the slightest crack in Spencer's poker face.

"Tell me," I say. "Tell me and you'll never see me again."

"She didn't see anything," Spencer says. "She made a bunch of shit up to try to get out of trouble. Nat would never tell that I was dealing. Not if she thought it would screw up her chances with me."

"What did Natalie say she saw?"

Spencer laughs. "Two men with shovels. Arguing, digging up shit."

A chill runs through me. "Why would she make that up?"

"Because," Spencer says, "she said one of them was Goddard."

CHAPTER
THIRTY-TWO

"What if it's true?" I say.

"Yeah, and there was a chupacabra running around the annex, too," Spencer says. "Natalie lied. And it wouldn't have been the first time."

"That's a pretty huge lie."

"She was about to be expelled," Spencer says. "She had nothing to lose."

"What do you mean, 'it wouldn't have been the first time'?"

"What do you think? Someone messed up her face, and it wasn't me or Caroline."

Luke's face springs into my mind. Natalie could have been protecting her brother by claiming that Caroline attacked her.

"What are you going to do with me?" I ask Spencer.

Spencer unlocks the door. As I reach for the handle, the lock clicks again. I slump back in my seat. He grabs my chin and forces me to look in his eyes.

"I'm gonna let you go back to school like a good girl," he says. "And we're not going to meet again. At least until you turn eighteen."

He winks and unlocks the door. I scramble out of the car, my legs threatening to give out beneath me. I don't stop running until I'm back at the campus gate.

Shovels. Goddard.

I'm bursting to tell someone. If I keep this to myself one second longer, I'm afraid it will eat away at me from the inside. Problem is, I have no one left to tell. Anthony is definitely out of the equation, and Brent . . . I don't know what Brent is.

If Ms. C were here, she's exactly the person I would tell. But she's not, and it's finally hitting me why I can't let that fact go.

The good people never seem to get out of here.

I need to get out of this room. I need to *do* something. But leaving campus is out of the question—especially after my run-in with Spencer.

The first-floor lounge is still empty. I park myself there with an empty notebook. It was supposed to be for World Literature, but Professor Knight prefers that we don't take notes during class discussions. We can't engage that way, she says.

I scribble a list on the page.

1999: SETTLEMENT IN NESBITT'S CIVIL SUIT
1998: ANNEX ACQUIRED BY WHEATLEY
2002: NATALIE EXPELLED
2006: ANNEX CONSTRUCTION COMPLETED

I let my pen hover back over 1999—the same year the state paid off Nesbitt to stop telling his Plymouth horror story, Goddard was finally able to get his paws on the land.

The paper had said Nesbitt's settlement was worth somewhere in the mid-six figures. Like Artie said, it's not exactly a buttload of money. Especially if he was initially seeking somewhere in the millions.

I comb over all the articles about the settlement. There's no mention about the terms—nothing that indicates Nesbitt would have to keep quiet, stop the stories about the abuse and missing boys in exchange for the money.

"You look . . . focused."

Brent slides into the seat across from me.

I slam my notebook closed. "How did you get in?"

His face says that's not the reaction he was expecting. "Not everyone in this dorm is pissed at me."

"I'm not pissed. I didn't leave last night because of you."

"What happened?"

"I don't want to talk about it," I say. "And please stop looking at me like that."

Brent blinks. "Like what?"

"Like I'm a fragile bird."

He meets my eyes. "Fragile is the last thing I think you are."

He doesn't say what he *does* think I am. Hurt, maybe, that he didn't tell me he was bringing Kaylee to the party? It must have somehow slipped his mind while he was telling me how glad he was that I was going, too.

Of course it hurt, seeing him with her. Even if he's not mine and I have no right to be hurt by him moving on when I was ready to do the same thing so quickly, it sucks. She's not me, and it freaking sucks.

Brent's gaze drops to a newspaper on the story about the annex. There's a photo of Goddard, Harrow, and another man at the annex opening ceremony and festival. His smile fades as he slides the paper away from me.

I try to grab it back.

"Anne." His eyes lock on mine. "What—"

"I don't know," I murmur. Because Brent's thumb is next to the third man's face.

The face of the man who followed me into the administration building.

CHAPTER
THIRTY-THREE

Nathan Roe. The attorney who represented the Wheatley School in the acquisition of the former Plymouth land.

"Anne." Brent's voice drags me back to reality. "What's going on?"

"You wouldn't believe me if I told you," I say.

"I wish you'd let me decide that for myself." His eyes are pleading.

So I tell Brent everything: About Ms. C, Natalie Barnes, the annex. Spencer and Goddard, and Luke Barnes. He sits, silent, absorbing everything. By the time I'm done, people are pouring out of the dorm in droves, heading for lunch.

"Dr. Muller told you all this? In New York?" Brent sounds troubled.

"Not all of it. Only the part about Natalie Barnes." I chew the inside of my cheek. "Everything else I found out on my own."

Brent stretches, and I realize how long we've been sitting here. I fish around in my purse and show him the journal entry I found in the tunnels.

"I think one of the boys at Plymouth wrote this," I say. "What if Goddard and the attorney never turned the records they found over to the state once the school was bulldozed?"

Brent frowns. "Why would they do that? It's illegal."

"Because." My mind is racing. I point to the article about the annex. "*Five million dollars* of the school's money was tied up in the contract with the construction company to level the school and build the annex. Not to mention what they spent on the land. If the state reopened an investigation based on documents like *these*"—I point to the journal entry—"then Goddard would have fallen on his sword."

"His legacy project would be a multimillion-dollar embarrassment," Brent says. "Anne, this is crazy. I mean, you're not crazy. This makes sense. But it's crazy."

"Natalie must have heard them say something that night on the annex," I say. "Whatever it was, it was enough for her to risk everything to come back and try to prove that Goddard was covering up the truth about Plymouth. Except I think she got caught, snooping around in the tunnels."

I tell Brent about the security feed the night before Ms. C left. How she went into the tunnels. "Let's say Goddard or Tierney pulled up the feed. They saw she was sticking her nose where she wasn't supposed to, so they gave her the axe."

"But Goddard was gone that morning," Brent says. "It must have been Tierney who fired her. And why would Tierney know to pull the security feed and look for Ms. Cross on it that morning?"

"She didn't," I mutter. "She was looking for me. And Coach Tretter."

Brent is quiet. "You think Tierney is involved with whatever happened to Ms. C next?"

"I don't know." My mind is racing. "She had Natalie's file on her desk. So maybe she busts Ms. C for snooping, fires her. Then does some snooping of her own. Discovers Jessica Cross is a lie. She tips off Goddard—they put two and two together, and he realizes who she really is."

"But then what?" Brent asks. "Goddard is a lot of things, but a killer?"

"It could have been Roe," I say. "He had just as much to lose if they were covering something up. Goddard could have told him to find her, talk to her—maybe things got out of hand. She wouldn't agree to shut up."

Brent drums his fingers against the table. His leg jiggles. He believes me.

"So what do we do now?" he asks.

"You have your car here, right?"

Once Brent and I arrive at the Worcester nursing home, I offer to pay for the gas it took to get here.

"Knock it off," he says as we pass through the automatic doors at the front entrance.

"I'm serious," I say. "You probably have a thousand better things to be doing."

"Maybe," he says. "But nothing I'd rather be doing."

We make our way to the visitor's center and ask to see Mr. Nesbitt.

"He's on his way to lunch," the woman at the desk says. "And he's not feeling real friendly today."

"It'll only take a minute," I say.

She narrows her eyes at me. "Are you a reporter?"

"No," I say. "I'm a friend."

"Hmph. Now that's a new one. I'll call his room."

The woman rolls away on her chair and makes a call. She covers her mouth so Brent and I can't hear what she's saying.

"Have a seat," she says. "He's on his way down."

Brent and I sit on the couch across from the circulation desk, watching an ABC Family movie with a few elderly people in wheelchairs who eyeball us. Brent's knee bounces up and down as we wait.

"What's the matter?" I ask.

"Nursing homes freak me out."

"They're not so bad," I say. I tell Brent how I had to visit my grandpa Harold in the nursing home for three years. My dad says my grandfather was like *Law & Order.* He held on for five seasons longer than he should have.

"Is that them?" a throaty voice booms. It's followed by a phlegmy cough.

Brent and I turn to see a man in a wheelchair rolling toward us. There's an oxygen tube running into his nose. In the photo, Raymond Nesbitt looked like a sick young man. Now he looks like a sick old one: paper-thin skin, gaunt body hunched over his chair.

"Hi, Mr. Nesbitt." I extend a hand. "My name is Anne."

"This about Plymouth?" he asks automatically.

I'm taken aback. "How did you know?"

"Don't got any family. I'm all settled up with the IRS. And Dolores here says you're not a reporter." Another cough. "Unless you lied about that bit."

"I didn't," I say softly. "I'm a student. At the Wheatley School. It's not far from the old Plymouth site."

Mr. Nesbitt contemplates me. Jerks his head toward Brent. "Who's he?"

"My ride."

Brent jabs my ribs. Mr. Nesbitt coughs again. "Let's go somewhere more private."

"I read about you," I say, as he leads us into the empty dining room. It smells like slimy hot dogs and coffee. "About the things they did to you."

Mr. Nesbitt is quiet as he watches Brent and me sit. "What's it you want?"

"Those twenty boys—the missing ones," I say. "Do you know what really happened to them?"

"Not supposed to talk about that." Mr. Nesbitt's tone has changed. There's a protective edge to it now.

"Why not? Was it part of the settlement terms that you couldn't talk anymore about what they did?"

"I just can't girl, all right? What's it matter when they're all dead anyway? All them men who beat me are dead, and there ain't nothing more to do about it."

"Please," I say. "I'm trying to find my friend. She disappeared, and I think she was trying to find the truth about Plymouth—"

"You want the truth?" Mr. Nesbitt gives another hacking cough. "That place is a goddamned graveyard, and you'd best stay away from it."

Graveyard. Shovels. Goddard.

"You think those boys . . . are buried on the land?" I ask.

Mr. Nesbitt is silent.

"We found something that might change your mind," Brent says. "About nothing being left to do. I'm sure some of those boys have family who are alive. Sisters, brothers. They deserve to know what happened."

Mr. Nesbitt is still silent. Brent nudges me. I put the journal entry on the table and push it toward Mr. Nesbitt. He grunts and looks away. I read it aloud to him.

His face contorts at the mention of "the jail." He puts a waxy, wrinkled hand on the paper and pulls it toward him.

"Charlie," he says. "Charlie kept a journal. One of the only boys who could read 'n write. Said the police caught him with a gal in a car and sent him to Plymouth. His drunk old daddy never come looking for him. That's what they did: rounded up all the troublemakers and sent 'em to Plymouth to get the piss beat outta them."

"What happened to Charlie?" I say quietly.

"One day he didn't show up for breakfast. Rumor was he got transferred to another block, but we knew better than to ask questions or we'd get sent to the jail ourselves. Then I saw two of 'em head for the grounds with shovels."

"Mr. Nesbitt." Brent leans forward, sets his hands palms-down on the table. "Did someone threaten you, or pay you, to stay quiet about the things you saw at Plymouth?"

Nesbitt is quiet, and I realize it's his way of telling us *yes*. I take out the news article about the annex with the photo of Goddard and Roe.

"Was it any of these men?" I ask him.

Nesbitt's eyes widen. He lifts a shaky finger, and taps Dr. Harrow's face.

CHAPTER
THIRTY-FOUR

We're quiet as we exit to the parking lot. Brent starts his car and grips the steering wheel. "This is so fucked."

"Goddard obviously sent Harrow to do the dirty work for him," I say. "He was Goddard's right-hand man at the time of the settlement."

"It couldn't have been Harrow with Goddard at the annex that night, though," Brent says. "Harrow only taught at Wheatley for five years."

"I think it was Roe, the attorney, with Goddard," I say. "They obviously found the records together and decided to hide them at Wheatley instead of turning them over."

"Until someone found them in the tunnels," Brent says. Natalie.

I call Dennis when I get back to the dorm and tell him I need to speak to Dr. Harrow. I think he's going to hang up on me.

"Anne," he finally says. "When I told you not to do anything drastic, this was exactly what I had in mind."

"Well that's silly," I say. "It's not like I went ahead and did it."

That's why I need Dennis's help: As a minor, I need to be

accompanied by a parent if I'm going to visit an inmate at the prison Dr. Harrow was transferred to once he pled guilty and got eighty years in prison.

I need to be accompanied by a parent—or a law enforcement officer.

"I know," Dennis sighs when I remind him of this. "I just don't think this is a good idea. At all."

I'm not afraid of James Harrow. I know it sounds crazy, because he tried to kill me, but you'd have to have seen the look in his eyes when he pointed the gun at me. He didn't want to do it. That's why I believe that he didn't mean to kill Isabella. He's greedy, arrogant, and pathetic, but he's not a sociopath.

I know because I remember the way Travis Shepherd looked at me. He was going to kill me, and he was going to enjoy every second of it. He was going to kill me to shut me up, just like he did to Sonia Russo, Matt Weaver, and Alexis's mother. If there was one thing Travis Shepherd wanted more than anything else, it was to control the narrative of his own life. He didn't just want control—he enjoyed taking control. Even if it meant taking people's lives.

All Dr. Harrow wanted was money.

Travis Shepherd may be dead, but he still scares me more than Dr. Harrow ever will.

Dennis isn't happy with me. He doesn't even say hi when we meet outside the station on Sunday morning—just sighs and checks over his shoulder to make sure he doesn't have an audience.

"Thanks for doing this," I say once we're in his car.

"Not sure I had a choice."

What is he talking about? Does he think I'll try to blackmail him over how he helped Anthony and me without his boss's permission last year?

I think back to our conversation at his desk a couple weeks ago, when I told him he owed me, and that his boss wouldn't be happy about Dennis helping us off the record.

Okay, so technically I may have hinted about the *possibility* of blackmailing him. But I would never actually do it. I'm not Alexis.

Dennis flashes his badge, and I have to show my ID and a copy of my birth certificate, and sign an affidavit. Dennis coughs—I look up to see the guard glaring at me from the other side of the glass. No doubt she noticed I didn't actually read the affidavit. I sigh and look it over while Dennis checks his phone.

I slide the paper beneath the glass. The guard eyeballs it and presses a button. The gate gives an earth-shaking buzz, and Dennis motions for me to follow him through the metal detector.

By the time we're in the holding room, I have to put a hand on my wrist to steady my pulse. Dennis's voice is in my ear.

"You don't have to do this."

And that's what makes me realize that I don't want to do this. Dr. Harrow will be behind glass, and I'll talk to him through a phone, but what if I have to pass by other inmates on the way in? What if they look at me and say things?

There's another buzzing noise, and a guard opens the door. "Harrow?"

I'm frozen. Dennis nods. The guard eyes me. "This way."

My stomach dips when I see Dr. Harrow behind the glass.

He has a patchy beard. The area beneath his eyes is swollen and gray. I wonder if it's because he can't sleep in here—if it's because he has a roommate and he has to stay up every night to watch his back.

It's what he deserves.

Harrow nods to Dennis. "Who's he?"

"Adult supervision," Dennis says. He taps my shoulder, telling me to sit. I do, and he hands me the phone. I clear my throat.

"Anne." Dr. Harrow's voice is breathy, and I notice all the extra weight in his face. "I'm so sorry for what I tried to—what I did to you."

I will myself to stare straight into his eyes. "Don't be. I'm the one who's still here."

Dr. Harrow's knuckles whiten as he grips the phone. Dennis shoots me a warning look.

I take a breath. "I know about the tape recorder in Goddard's office. You were monitoring him."

Harrow's eyes flick to Dennis. "I was."

I set my free hand on the table. "Why?"

"I wanted to know if he suspected me. . . ." Harrow's voice trails off, but he doesn't need to complete the thought. He wanted to know if Goddard suspected that he had something to do with Isabella's murder.

"On the tape," I say, "did he mention anything about Plymouth Reform School?"

Harrow leans forward on his elbows. "What if I told you that you're not the first to come here and ask me that?"

She was here. "A young woman with red hair?" Harrow nods.

"When?" I ask.

"The spring."

I have to speak around the lump in my throat. "And she wanted the tape?"

Harrow nods. "She didn't say why. But when I said I couldn't get her the tape, she asked if Goddard had said anything about Plymouth and the school records."

"What records?"

"The ones he hid instead of turning over to the state."

Dr. Harrow's wolfish smile returns: the smile of a man who collects secrets and waits for their value to grow, like stocks in a portfolio.

"You already knew about the records," I say. "Did Goddard tell you about them?"

"No. I found out like I did with everything else." Harrow smiles. "Talk less. Listen more. You'd be surprised what you overhear."

"That's not all, though." I lean forward and lower my voice. "I spoke to Raymond Nesbitt."

Harrow's expression darkens. "Did you, now."

"I did. And I know that you had no reason to pay him to stay quiet about Plymouth unless Goddard asked you to do it."

"I'd appreciate your discretion," Harrow snaps. "They can use anything in this conversation against me."

"No offense, but you're serving seventy-five years. The only way you're getting out of here is in a body bag."

Harrow's hand curls into a fist. Dennis leans forward and whispers in my ear. "Don't antagonize him or he won't give you what you want."

"Sorry," I say into the phone. "You have really great genetics, obviously, so maybe you'll get out."

I can practically feel Dennis cringe behind me. Harrow's lips slide into a smile.

"So maybe the headmaster did ask me to make a generous monetary gift to Raymond Nesbitt."

"But if you knew where the records were this whole time, why didn't you use them to *your* benefit?" I ask.

"Why would I risk it all for an apple when I already had an entire tree?" Harrow says.

He's talking about Senator Westbrook, who has five times Goddard's money and half his brains. Point taken.

"Goddard's not your boss anymore," I point out. "Why not expose his crimes?"

"Attempting to extort that old bastard from prison isn't worth losing my outside time."

"But you told Natalie where to find the records," I say. "Why?"

"Goddard screwed me. I figured I'd let her screw him. And she just had this quality about her. You can't help but like the girl. We had similar interests."

Money. So that's what Natalie wanted from Goddard and Roe. The whole time, she wanted to extort them.

"Is that all, Miss Dowling?" Dr. Harrow asks.

"Would Goddard have Natalie killed to cover up the truth about the annex?" I ask.

Harrow gives me a wry smile. "I think you know the answer to that."

I hang up on him.

CHAPTER
THIRTY-FIVE

"Anne," Dennis says when he drops me off in front of the school, "I think it's time to let me take it from here."

"So *you're* going to send a cavalry to interrogate Benjamin Goddard in his hospital room?" I ask.

Dennis's face says everything. Of course the Wheatley Police Department would never dream of doing such a thing. "*Anne.* Definitely do not do that."

"Okay."

An hour later, I'm on the T with a potted Gerber daisy, en route to Massachusetts General Hospital to accuse a dying old man of murder.

If there's a hell, I'm most certainly going there.

I sign in at the front desk with a fake name and head up to the fifth floor with my visitor's pass.

Private suite or not, there's no masking the smell of hospital—bleach, urine, and mashed potatoes.

I don't know what I expect Goddard to be doing when I get to his room, but it's not sitting in an armchair by the window, watching the news.

He looks up at me, recognition flitting across his face. "Miss Dowling. How unexpected." He mutes the television. "What a lovely daisy."

I set the pot down on the table but don't let it go—I don't want him to see how badly my hands are shaking. "I'm sorry to hear you're not well."

"You don't have to pretend that's why you're here." Goddard's voice has changed. "Sit. Please."

I eye my options—there's a free armchair close to Goddard. Too close to Goddard. I sit on the edge of his bed.

"So this is why you resigned," I say quietly.

"No. I wasn't diagnosed until August." He eyes me carefully. "I didn't resign. I was asked to step down as headmaster."

This is news to me. "By who?"

Goddard laughs—or at least he tries to. It comes out as a silent guffaw. He puts a hand to his chest. "Your surprise is charming. But naturally, you'd think the headmaster is the most powerful person at Wheatley. Are you aware of how you wound up back at Wheatley?"

A chill slices through me. "No. I'm not."

"I believe you're acquainted with Lee Andersen." Goddard coughs. "Michael Andersen's son."

Lee Andersen, Isabella's stalker. "Yes."

"Mr. Andersen voted against your expulsion," Goddard says. "Coincidentally, it was after Dean Tierney called a private meeting with him to discuss his son's unsettling behavior toward female students."

The chill is back. Or maybe it's just that cold in here. *Tierney* was the one behind my expulsion being overturned? She actually *blackmailed* Michael Andersen into voting in my favor?

"The headmaster is the puppet, and the board of trustees pulls the strings." Goddard's IV drip beeps. "The headmaster is simply the figurehead. Or in my case, a scapegoat. Never mind that I wasn't headmaster when Matthew Weaver was murdered.

I employed Lawrence Tretter for seventeen years without knowing the truth. And that's what they blame me for—not seeing
what was in front of me. But as I say, sometimes we only see
what we want to see."

A chill passes through me. Is that why I see Goddard as
Natalie's killer—because I want to?

"My attorney was not happy I woke him in the middle of the
night to get you out of the administration building," Goddard
says.

"How did you know I was there?"

"You tripped the silent alarm I set on the back door," he
says. "I had to leave behind sensitive information, in case I was
served a subpoena in Dr. Harrow's case. I couldn't risk it getting into the wrong hands."

"The records. But they already had gotten into the wrong
hands." I level with him. "Tell me about Natalie Barnes."

I expect him to reach for his call button. Get a nurse to drag
me out of here. But instead, he folds his hands in front of him,
and says, "What would you like to know?"

"How did she get hired?"

"Diana Upton's resignation was unexpected. I instructed
Dean Tierney to hire the first candidate with a BA who could
string two thoughts together." Goddard meets my eyes.
"Jessica—Natalie—slipped through the cracks when our institution was weakened."

"You didn't recognize her."

"Of course not. I've had hundreds of students over the years."
His expression darkens. "But none that ever regarded me so
vehemently they tried to *extort* me."

"She was going to go public with the truth," I say.

"No. She wanted fifty thousand dollars to destroy the records she stole from me," Goddard says. "I understand you were
quite fond of Ms. Cross. But you have to understand that the
woman you knew was a lie. She came back to Wheatley solely
with the intention of extorting me and disappearing again.

And she did a very poor job of it. But I suppose greed makes people stupid."

Dr. Harrow in the woods with the knife.

"Isn't that why you covered up the truth about Plymouth?" I ask. "Your own greed?"

Goddard's eyes flash. "The opposite. I had no use for money. I have plenty of money. There will come a time in your life, Miss Dowling, when you are too old to care about riches and too young to accept fading into oblivion. That's when you'll care about your reputation. Your name. What people will say about you when you're gone."

Goddard pauses, tracing the armrest of his chair. "The annex was for my father. Did you know that my father went to Wheatley, too? He was the first in his family to finish high school." He looks out the window. "My father built a life for me from the bottom up. The annex was about *his* legacy, not mine."

"Touching story," I say. "What about the part where you caused the families of the missing Plymouth boys pain and suffering?"

Goddard snaps his head toward me. "Families? Those boys had no *families.* No one was looking for them, and that's a tragedy which falls outside the realm of my responsibility."

"You knew they were there," I say. "You just didn't care about the truth."

"Ms. *Barnes* didn't care about the truth either," Goddard says. "She only wanted to profit from it."

"What did she do with the records?"

"I don't know."

"Where is she?"

"I don't know," he says. "You'll have to speak to my attorney."

Because he's the one who killed her.

I fly down the stairs because I don't want to wait for the elevator. I call Dennis's cell.

"Nathan Roe," I say into the phone, wheezing. "Goddard's attorney. He represented Wheatley in the Plymouth land sale. They hid the school's records together, and they killed Natalie to stop her from telling everyone."

Dennis is silent. "Forensics pulled apart the car with the body."

I stop in my tracks. "Is it her?"

"We still don't know. The body . . . was in bad shape. Before it was burned."

My stomach lurches. "I'm telling you. *Goddard* did it, with Roe. I know it."

"Anne." Dennis's voice is sharp. "We're awaiting confirmation on the car, and then the cops are going to Lucas Barnes's house later to question him. I need you to stay away from Goddard until then, okay? He's old, and he's sick, and if you go around accusing him of murder, it's not going to end well for you."

I hang up on Dennis and start heading in the other direction. I'm not going back to Wheatley.

I'm going to Luke Barnes's.

CHAPTER
THIRTY-SIX

Luke is the last thread. If I pull at it, everything will unravel.

I need him out in the open, so I enter 310 on the buzzer outside the apartment. There's silence for a moment. Then Luke's voice. "Yo."

"We need to talk."

A pause. "Who is this?"

"I'm a little offended you don't remember me. I thought we connected."

More silence. I picture Luke, leaning against the wall next to his intercom. Debating whether or not he should ignore me or call the cops.

I hit the intercom button again. "I know why Natalie came back to Wheatley. And I think you do, too."

Luke doesn't respond. A full minute of silence goes by. This is not going well.

Then the door opens. I take a step back as Luke gets in my face.

"What do you want?"

"To talk. But we can't do it here."

"What? Is this about Natalie? Because I told you I don't know where she is," he says.

"You're lying. And you lied when you said you haven't talked to her in years. I know about the phone calls. And the money. And Plymouth."

Luke's lips part. "How—"

"That's neither here nor there."

Luke's eyes flash. "Are you stalking me or something?"

"It's not you I care about," I say. "You may not give a crap what happens to your sister—"

"You don't know her, okay?" Luke looks around the sidewalk. Lowers his voice. "You don't know what she's capable of. And I have to go."

"Where?" I step in front of him.

He sighs. "The police station. My car was stolen. There's an issue with it."

I look Luke Barnes straight in the eye. "Did you threaten your sister's boyfriend in middle school?"

"What?" Luke's eyes flash. "Where did you hear that bullshit?"

"Her old roommate," I say.

Luke lets out a sharp laugh. "Of course Natalie would say I did something like that."

"What do you mean?"

"Because my sister is a pathological liar."

My head hurts. I don't know what—or who—to believe, but I know that Luke and I need to get the hell out of here before the police show up inquiring about his missing car. I convince him that we have to put distance between his apartment and us so I can explain everything before the cops show up to ask about his car.

Luke says he has something to show me anyway.

"She called me about six years ago," he says as we cross the street. He's leading the way. "She said there were dangerous people after her. That's why she fled to Georgia. She also needed five grand, to disappear."

"Did you give it to her?" I ask.

"No." There's the faintest trace of guilt in his voice. "You don't get it. It was exactly the thing Natalie would do—lie to get something she wanted. It's the whole reason my parents sent her to boarding school."

"What do you mean?"

"When she was in the seventh grade, my parents got called to the school. Nat had bruises on her arms. It started happening every month. And the bruises got worse. On her thighs and stuff." We're waiting at another crosswalk. "She wouldn't say who did it, so the school sent a social worker to our house. My parents had her see this child psychologist, who said Nat was probably hurting herself. For attention."

There's a sour taste in my mouth as I think of the description of Natalie's injuries in the discipline report.

"My parents thought the smaller classes at boarding school would help," Luke says. "But when she got expelled, and moved home, the lying got worse. It turned into stealing, then drugs. So I wasn't too quick to believe her evil henchmen story."

Wait, wait, the crosswalk voice tells us. This light is taking forever to change.

"She showed up at my place three years ago," Luke says. "I swear I had no idea about the stolen identity thing. All she told me is that she was back. And she needed money again. She'd heard that Dad died, and she wanted her share of the inheritance."

The light changes, but Luke doesn't motion to cross the street. His jaw is set. "Our goddamn father died, and she didn't come to the funeral. But she showed up at my door, asking for his *money.*"

"I'm assuming that you didn't give it to her," I say as we cross the street.

"I'd already put most of the money into the company," Luke says. "I gave her a few thousand dollars and told her I never wanted to see her again."

"Did she mention anything about Wheatley, or the school?"

"Not until last year," Luke says. "She called and said she was in Wheatley. She was about to come into a lot of money. She sent me all this weird shit in the mail, like a map of the old reform school.

"She said what she found was huge. And that she had to get out of town afterwards. Fast. And she needed my help. I told her she was nuts."

"She came back to Wheatley so she could extort Headmaster Goddard from right under his nose," I say. "She had dirt on him."

"She said if I didn't help her, she'd take me to court over the inheritance, Luke says. "My father had never cut her out of the will. She would have won, and I couldn't afford it. My company is already in trouble. . . ."

Luke's voice trails off. He's pale, as if the reality of his situation is finally hitting him. I'm afraid he'll faint right here in the street.

"She called back a few months ago and said it all went wrong," he says. "Said I had to get her a ticket to Moscow and a passport under the name Jessica Cross. If she stayed here, she'd be killed, or worse. I didn't believe her—I just wanted her gone."

"So you gave it to her," I say.

We're at South Station.

"The lockers," Luke says. "One is hers. She gave me the combo and told me to leave the ticket and passport here. She said she'd leave the cash. But I haven't picked it up. I swear that I wanted no part in whatever she was doing. You'll see that."

I follow Luke down the steps to where the lockers are. He leads me to 52A and enters the combination. He opens the locker; inside is a black pouch. Luke's face falls.

"What's the matter?" I ask.

Without a word, he opens the bag and shows me the contents. A plane ticket and a passport.

"When was she supposed to pick them up?" I ask.

Luke pales. "Two months ago."

CHAPTER
THIRTY-SEVEN

There's genuine worry etched on Luke's face now, and I know when he said he wanted Natalie gone, he hadn't meant that he wanted her dead.

"I swear I thought she was lying," he says. "If I'd thought there were actually people after her—"

I hold a hand up to him. "Shh. You're stressing me out. I can't think."

"What is there to think about?" he demands. His tone of voice and expression make him look thirteen, not thirty. "I have to call the cops. Tell them the truth."

"The truth is that Natalie's burned body might be in your car right now." The words tumble out of me. "I'm sorry."

"Are you kidding me?" Luke covers his face. "I have to call a lawyer."

"*Don't* do that," I say. "Not yet. It'll make you look guilty."

"Guilty? Of what?"

"Just tell the police the truth," I say. "Everything. Start from the beginning, when she left for Georgia."

Luke pales. I think of one more thing. One more piece to the puzzle that doesn't quite fit.

"Are you *sure* she didn't say anything else about being in trouble?" I say. "Who she was running from before she turned up in Georgia?"

"I don't know," Luke sputters. "She—I don't know. Like I told you, she was living in Brockton for a while, getting into some bad stuff—"

"Brockton? You didn't tell me that."

"Why *would* I tell you that? It has nothing to do with any-thing."

Luke looks at me funny. My head is spinning.

Brockton is where someone shot Tyler and Ryan Becker to death.

Execution style.

When I'm back on campus, I call Brent and tell him to meet me outside his dorm. He's already waiting on the bench when I get there. He stands up, taking in my face.

"Are you okay?"

"Fine." I'm out of breath. I practically ran here from the T station. "You have your car here, right?"

"Yeah. What's going on?"

"I think Natalie hid the Plymouth records on the annex before Goddard had her killed. Brent, we have to get to them before Roe does. They're going to get away with it."

Brent runs his hands down my arms. "How can you be sure she hid the records there?"

"She sent her brother this." I show Brent the map of Plym-outh on my phone. "See that building that's circled? That's where the jail was. Why else would she send Luke a cryptic clue like this? She wanted someone to be able to make the records public if she couldn't."

"Okay," Brent sighs. "Let's go."

We make it to the highway before Dennis calls me.

"Shit." I pick it up, against my better judgment.

"Do you want to explain why you were at Luke Barnes's place when I specifically *told you not to do anything*?"

"He didn't kill Natalie, Dennis. Goddard and Nathan Roe did."

Dennis pauses. "Are you on the *highway*?"

"Anne," Brent hisses. "You have to hang up. He can be tracing the call."

"Dennis, I've got to go—"

"Anne, turn around and go back to school *right now*. If you don't, I'll have to call this in."

I squeeze my eyes shut. "I'm sorry, Dennis."

And I hang up.

CHAPTER
THIRTY-EIGHT

We're silent as Brent gets off the highway and makes the turn for the annex. He's looking peaked, and I hate myself for the position I've put him in.

"You know I can't go back after this," I finally say. "You have to leave me, and come up with a story about how I made you do all this."

"I'm not doing that."

"I just ignored directions from a cop."

Brent grips the wheel. "I'll say whatever you need me to say for you."

I wipe my palms on my knees. "No. Tierney will expel you for helping me."

"I don't give a flying fuck about Tierney, or some meathead cop. We're in this together."

I don't know what else to say, so I grab his hand. He squeezes it.

Brent stops speeding when we get to the annex. He parks just outside the lot.

My mind races. "Circle the annex, and bolt if you see the

police or Dennis. If I'm not back in fifteen minutes, just leave. I'll call you and tell you where to pick me up."

I jump out of the car before he can protest. Fifteen minutes, no doubt, before Dennis figures out where I am and sends a cavalry to retrieve me. Ten minutes to find where the jail once stood, and figure out where Natalie hid the records before Goddard had her killed.

Fifteen minutes. It's nearly impossible.

She's not the person I thought she was. She lied, she blackmailed, and she let me believe she was someone she wasn't.

But Ms. C believed in me. I owe her the same thing—I owe those lost boys the same thing.

She didn't deserve to die. Neither did they. Not like that.

I make it to the lodge before Brent calls me.

"Anne, get as far away from here as you can," he barks.

"What?"

Brent screams. I take off running for the parking lot.

Brent is staring straight ahead when I emerge over the guardrail. He mouths something at me. I run toward him, stopping in my tracks when I see Natalie Barnes pressing a knife to his throat.

CHAPTER
THIRTY-NINE

Natalie Barnes.

Ms. C.

Alive.

Natalie rolls the back window down. "Give me your bag."

"What are you doing?" I blurt, stepping forward.

She presses the knife closer to Brent's neck. "Easy, Anne. Don't make me slip."

I glance at Brent helplessly. He mouths *run.* But I won't. I'm not going to run and leave him here with this psychopath. Even if she wasn't holding a knife to his throat.

I hand my bag to Natalie through the window.

"You're alive," I say. "I thought Goddard had Roe kill you. Why are you doing this?"

Natalie's expression darkens. "Trust me. You were the last person I wanted to get hurt. You should have backed off when I gave you the chance."

"You followed me," I choke out. "You're *alive.*"

"Anne." Brent swallows. He moves his eyes to meet mine. Silently telling me to run. Natalie notices.

"I don't want to cut your throat, but I will if I have to," she tells him.

"Oh, my God." My legs shake beneath me. "You killed Dr. Muller. It was *you*."

"I had no choice." Natalie's voice is pleading. "I left him for his own good. I told him never to contact me again. Then he found my mother in Rhode Island. *He* told you about Natalie. He was going to ruin *everything*."

"He loved you," I choke out. "He couldn't let you go."

"He should have gotten on his plane," Natalie snaps. "This never had to happen. Get in the car, Anne."

Natalie keeps her knife trained on Brent as I climb into the front seat. She commands him to drive away from the annex.

"What about those guys in Brockton?" I ask, stalling for time. "The Becker brothers. You killed them, too, didn't you?"

A slow smile spreads across her face. She grabs the hem of her shirt. I flinch, but she lifts it up to show me a crescent-shaped scar on her hip.

"Tyler gave me this. And a nasty heroin addiction," she says.

"I don't believe you. I know about the bruises. I know you hurt yourself."

"You know nothing!" Natalie slams her free hand against the back window. Brent twitches. I move my hand to his knee.

"Tyler passed me around to his brother, and all his druggie friends while I was too strung out to fight back. So yeah, I put fucking bullets in their heads," she says. "And every single second I've had to spend on the run has been worth hearing them beg for their lives."

My veins turn to ice.

"You're not going to get away with this," I say.

"Really? Because everyone short of you two thinks I'm dead." Natalie jerks her head back toward the way we came. "And when they find your bodies, they'll also find a note in Brent's handwriting saying you wanted to go Romeo and Juliet style."

"I'm not writing shit." Brent's voice trembles.

"You will, unless you want to watch me cut her into a million pieces." Natalie presses the knife to my cheek. Brent steps on the gas. She rounds on him with the knife. "Not so fast. Get on the freeway."

Brent obeys.

"Good boy." Natalie pats him on the head. "Why didn't I date a boy like you instead of a dick like Spencer in high school? Then none of us would be here right now."

I swallow. "I know why you were expelled and Spencer wasn't. You saw Goddard that night. He must have said something about the records."

"Try *collusion*," Natalie says. "The construction workers found them when they knocked down the cabin. The lawyer told Goddard it was a felony to destroy the records. So they buried them. And that's when they saw me.

"I don't think he really believed I knew what they were doing. I was just some simple townie girl. Disposable. I'll bet he never thought of me again after he expelled me."

"But you thought of Goddard," I say. "Every day, didn't you?"

"I thought about killing him." Natalie leans in toward me. "When I was strung out of my mind. Thought about going up to him and *bam*." I jolt in my seat. She smiles. "But I didn't want to spend the rest of my life in jail. I've been there. The women are horrible."

I meet Brent's eyes in the mirror.

"When I became Jessica, I realized I didn't want the headmaster dead like I wanted Tyler dead." Natalie's eyes are frightening. "I liked being Jessica. She was smart. People *loved* Jessica. No one ever loved Natalie. People used Natalie. My mother left me in an orphanage when I was ten days old. My parents adopted me to fill a void in their pathetic little lives, then sent me away when I couldn't.

"It was so easy to come and go, to be someone else. I thought

Natalie, and everything that happened with Tyler and Ryan back in Brockton, was gone for good."

"You could have disappeared," I say. "You didn't have to come back to Wheatley."

"It takes money to disappear," she snaps. "And Rowan made me see that I could never stop running. If I was going to live the lie, I was going to have to do it alone. He figured out I wasn't really Jessica. I needed to get out of the country, and I needed a golden ticket. The records.

"Do you know how long it took me to find the map to the records? Months. And *you* almost ruined it, by doing your own snooping down there." Natalie nods to me. "I thought the photo in the drawer would get you to back off."

"You—" I resist the urge to lunge at her. "You left that picture—of Isabella's *dead body*—" I freeze. "You sent me all those texts. *You* threatened me."

I wait for her to deny it, but her face says I'm right. Her betrayal hits me all over again.

"Quit looking at me like I'm some *monster*," Natalie says. "I'm not the bad guy, Anne. *Goddard* is. You told me yourself. He protects people who don't need protecting. Like that creep who stalked your roommate. Who do you think cares about those dead Plymouth boys? Goddard was going to let their corpses rot here forever. To protect his *legacy*."

Natalie laughs, almost as if it's a private joke. "When Tierney introduced me to him, he didn't even look me in the eye. He just said, 'It's lovely to meet you, Jessica.' Maybe if he looked me in the damn eye, he would have known it was me."

"We all dig our own graves, Anne," she says.

"Except for you, right? Shouldn't you be on a plane to Moscow by now?"

"Nicaragua." Natalie smiles. "Moscow was a decoy, because I knew Luke would sell me out. They'll never find me. Tyler and Ryan are nothing but maggots in the ground by now, and they *still* haven't found me."

Brent is eyeing me. *Get ready*, he mouths. I swallow.

"Where are you taking us?" Brent asks Natalie. He's doing a solid sixty, and cars are whizzing past us in the left lane.

In the split second Natalie turns to look at the signs on the freeway, I punch her in the eye.

She recoils, but doesn't drop the knife. I leap into the back-seat while she's holding her face. I try to wrap my hands around her throat, but she recovers and holds up the knife.

"Put it down," Brent shouts. "Put it down or I'll drive into oncoming traffic, and we're all dead."

Panic corners me—I know he must be bluffing, but his voice is shaky. Serious. As if he's willing to do it, since Natalie is planning on killing us anyway.

"Go ahead," she says to Brent. Her eyes on are me. "Natalie's been dead for eight years."

"I don't believe that," I say. "This isn't about revenge. If it was, you wouldn't have extorted Goddard so you could leave the country and escape murder charges. It was never about him, was it? It was about Ryan and Tyler. You made a mess and realized you'd have to spend your whole life running from it."

Natalie's upper lip twitches. She holds the knife, daring me not to come closer.

"All you want is to get away," I say. "It's all you've ever wanted. So go. Go away, and no one else has to get hurt. Brent will pull over, and you can leave."

"Oh, Anne," Natalie says. "Do I look like a dumb bitch?"

And she swipes my face with the knife.

Brent screams my name, before veering into the car in the next lane. We spin and hit the guardrail, the airbags exploding.

Then he goes quiet.

CHAPTER
FORTY

I have a split second to decide whether to reach for my phone or go after Natalie. She's kicked the busted door open, knife in hand.

Screw it. I won't be able to accomplish much in my state. I'm bleeding, and the numbness in my hands says I'm about to go into shock. I dig my phone out of my bag and call 911. Then I climb into the front seat while I'm on hold.

Brent is massaging his head.

"Oh, thank God." I pull his chin into my hands and examine his face. "Where are you hurt?"

"I think I'm okay." He holds my hands to his face. "I'm okay now."

"I thought—when we crashed . . ." A sob escapes me. "She got away."

Brent pulls me to him. "She can't get away. It's not going to happen."

When he pulls me to him, I know it's true. Natalie Barnes has spent most of her life running, but she won't get away. Not this time.

And this time I kiss him first. It's not about letting him choose me.

This time, I choose us.

I'm crying so hard that Brent has to take the phone from me and explain our emergency to the operator himself.

There are police officers waiting for us at the hospital. I don't recognize any of them. I wonder how far away from Wheatley we are. The EMTs hold me down and pluck glass from the windshield out of the cut on my face.

"This is deep," one of the EMTs says.

"It's from a knife."

They hold gauze to my face while someone runs off to get what the doctor needs to stitch me up. I yell for Brent.

"He's got a concussion," a doctor tells me, shouldering his way past the EMTs. "But he's okay."

They wheel my stretcher into the emergency room. People fret over my face, but for once in my life, I don't give a crap how I look.

"Where are they?"

I don't think I've ever been relieved to hear Tierney's voice, but there she is, standing in the sliding doors to the ER.

Half the Wheatley Police Department trails behind her.

"Anne," Tierney barks, coming up beside me. "You don't have to talk to them until your parents get here."

"No." I wince. "I want to."

"Why don't you start at the beginning," one of the cops says.

"Yeah," I begin. "About that. . . ."

SIX MONTHS LATER

If I'd waited for Dennis instead of going to the annex myself, I may have gotten away with everything. It turns out that Goddard and Roe didn't know Natalie hid the records. They never would have gotten to them first.

But Natalie would have gotten away. I don't know how far she would have gotten, but she'd done a "bang-up job" (the DA's words, not mine) of planting enough lies and evidence to make it look like Goddard and Roe had had her killed. Not enough to get a jury to convict them, maybe, since it was all circumstantial evidence. But I think making them look guilty in the eyes of the world was enough for her.

I was nothing but a pawn in her plan. She planted the burner phones she texted me from in a dumpster a few blocks away from Nathan Roe's office. She knew I'd suspect Goddard's involvement the closer I got to the truth.

I wonder when she figured out that she'd rather use me than get rid of me. Was it when I wouldn't back off, like Dr. Muller? Or was it even earlier—when I confided in her about Isabella, Lee Andersen, and Goddard's cover-up?

The body in the burned car was a woman Natalie had car-jacked at a truck stop. The coroner determined a single gun-shot wound was the cause of death. Execution style. It took months to identify the body—Natalie figured that by the time the police figured out it wasn't her in the car, she'd be hidden away safely in Central America.

Natalie Barnes played me. She played everyone.

But she didn't get away. And that's why they sent me to Stonehill Creek School for Girls and not jail, I think.

I wound up in reform school. The irony is so ridiculous I could probably write a killer memoir. But I won't profit off the stories of the Plymouth boys. I'm not like Natalie Barnes.

She had told Dr. Muller that I reminded her of a younger version of herself. She was wrong.

After I told Tierney and my parents what happened the night Travis Shepherd was killed, they called the DA's office and said I was willing to testify at Steven Westbrook's trial.

But it didn't matter. Steven Westbrook already accepted a second-degree murder plea.

The state is in the middle of a brand-new investigation to determine Goddard's involvement in concealing the Plymouth records. His cancer is in remission. He's not going to die. Not yet, at least. I almost think that his real punishment—living the rest of his life with the knowledge of his sins—is worse.

As for me, I'm two months away from finishing high school. Stonehill isn't so bad. I have to go to group therapy three times a week and do a lot of stupid macaroni crafts. The other girls here have a higher school expulsion count than me, for the most part.

Most of them are cool. A lot of the younger girls look up to me, come to me for boy advice and stuff, which is silly because we're not allowed off campus, and we're only allowed one visit a week. I don't know what's waiting for me when I get out of here, but sometimes I think I might not be terrible at this stuff. Talking to people. Helping them.

Brent is eyeing Columbia for the fall. He says he won't pick a school in New York to be closer to me. But I guess he could do a lot worse than Columbia.

He says he could do a lot worse than me. My new goal is to convince us both that it's true.

I want to be better. Not just for him—for me. For my parents.

Most of my other Wheatley friends write and call, too. Remy is already planning a release party for me. There was a lot of petitioning to get Wheatley to overturn my expulsion, especially once all of the details about Natalie's scheme emerged.

Then I told the truth.

The whole truth—Matt Weaver, Travis Shepherd, everything.

I always knew I would lose everything if I told the truth, but it turns out, starting from scratch isn't so bad.

Today I have a meeting with my social worker about discussing reintegration plans once I get out. College is obviously out of the question. My father wants me to come work in his office, but I don't think I have a promising future in terms of a legal career.

Besides, I'm kind of tired of my parents digging me out of my holes.

Danica, my social worker, gives me a funny look when she grabs me from the cafeteria.

"You have a visitor," she says, clinging to her folder like it's a life raft.

"It's not the weekend," I say.

She frowns, and makes a "follow me" gesture with her finger.

We walk down the corridor, and Danica deposits me in a room with a table and four chairs around it. We're not alone: There's a woman at the table. She has one of those faces where she could be anywhere from thirty to fifty. Her chin is prominent and she's in a black suit. She nods to Danica, who scurries out of the room.

"Anne Dowling," the woman says. "I've heard a lot about you."

She's not smiling. I can't tell if she means it as a compliment. In this place, probably not.

"Okay," is the best response I can come up with.

She folds her hands in front of her. "I spoke with Jacqueline Tierney. It's quite a story, how the Wheatley PD found Matthew Weaver's body after all these years."

So that's what this is about. "Are you a cop?"

For some reason, that gets a smile out of her. "You're not in trouble, Anne. Not with me, at least."

I level with her. She has small brown eyes that could benefit from a swipe or two of mascara. "So what do you want with me?" I ask.

"I want to offer you an opportunity."

Opportunity. I would laugh if it weren't so damn rude. I've burned every bridge I have in this world. Who the hell is this lady?

I lick my lips. Rosebud salve is one of many luxuries I've had to get used to being without in here. "Not too many opportunities for a screw-up like me."

"You're eighteen now, correct?" The woman's expression unsettles me. She's serious.

"Who . . . are you?" I ask.

"I recruit young people to work for my agency," she says. "People with the right combinations of skill set and personality. Most of the time it's out of college, but we have a training program for . . . exceptionally bright candidates that show extraordinary potential."

I feel as if the floor is falling away. "How could you—how could anyone want me after the things I've done?" I ask. "The FBI *hates* me. I screwed up their investigation of Eugene Andreev."

"Good thing I'm not FBI."

I'm silent as she pushes a folder toward me. The top half of a circular logo peeks out: Central Intelligence Agency. "Yevgeny Andreev was only the tip of the iceberg, Anne."

Her tongue rolls over the syllables of Andreev's Russian name perfectly. I wonder if she looked at my transcript and noticed how many different languages I've taken. A chill rolls through me, making me feel even more exposed. Almost as if this woman might know things about me that I don't even know myself.

For once in my life, I'm completely speechless.

"This is not a glamorous opportunity." The woman's eyes are serious now. "If you complete the very rigorous program, and your training, your family and closest friends won't be allowed to know what you do. Life as you know it will be over."

I don't say it, but that life has been over for a while. I reach for the folder.

Because some bridges have to be burned down before they can be built again.